A tall man, all lean physique and long stride, prowled along the quay, his coat flying open.

He walked as if the ground owed him homage, his by right. Images of the pirate who haunted her dreams with his strong, clever fingers and wicked mouth danced across her mind.

Shocked, she squeezed her eyes shut against the flutter of desire low in her belly. Embarrassed, she ignored the salacious sensations.

The last passenger was level with her now. A scarf swathed about his head covered all but his eyes beneath a hat pulled down low. He wore a fashionable greatcoat—a thing with many capes. Too short. Perhaps that was why he'd left it undone. The boots on his feet were scuffed and worn. A man who, for all his appearance of pride, wore second-hand clothes.

'Mrs MacDonald?'

The man's voice had the lilt of the Highlands and a raspy disused quality. And he had spoken her name. Her heart followed her stomach to the floor.

'I am Mrs MacDonald,' she said, unable to keep the edge from her voice.

He bowed, hand to heart. 'Andrew Gilvry, at your service.'

AUTHOR NOTE

I am so sad that I have reached the end of my *The Gilvrys of Dunross* series. I have enjoyed writing the stories of these brothers so much, and I hope you have enjoyed making the journey with me. I was very glad that Drew finally came home. In the beginning I wasn't sure he could.

Scotland has always held a special place in my heart as I lived in the wilds of the Outer Hebrides as a pre-teen and loved the wildness and the lonely spaces, so I was delighted to be able to set this Regency series in the Highlands. For all that the Prince Regent, later King George IV, was unpopular with his English subjects, he did make Scotland *the fashion*—with the help of Sir Walter Scott. And during his reign there were at least some changes that made life for Highlanders a little easier. The change to the distilling laws addressed in these books was one of them.

If you want to know more about my books, find out what is coming next, or simply drop by and say hello, you can find me at www.annlethbridge.com

RETURN OF THE PRODIGAL GILVRY

Ann Lethbridge

MAGNA   26.9.14

First published in Great Britain 2014
by Mills & Boon, an imprint of Harlequin (UK) Limited,
Large Print edition 2014
Harlequin (UK) Limited, Eton House, 18-24 Paradise Road,
Richmond, Surrey TW9 1SR

© 2014 Michèle Ann Young

ISBN: 978-0-263-23985-0

Harlequin (UK) Limited's policy is to use papers that are natural, renewable and recyclable products and made from wood grown in sustainable forests. The logging and manufacturing processes conform to the legal environmental regulations of the country of origin.

Printed and bound in Great Britain
by CPI Antony Rowe, Chippenham, Wiltshire

Ann Lethbridge has been reading Regency novels for as long as she can remember. She always imagined herself as Lizzie Bennet, or one of Georgette Heyer's heroines, and would often recreate the stories in her head with different outcomes or scenes. When she sat down to write her own novel it was no wonder that she returned to her first love: the Regency.

Ann grew up roaming Britain with her military father. Her family lived in many towns and villages across the country, from the Outer Hebrides to Hampshire. She spent memorable family holidays in the West Country and in Dover, where her father was born. She now lives in Canada, with her husband, two beautiful daughters, and a Maltese terrier named Teaser, who spends his days on a chair beside the computer, making sure she doesn't slack off.

Ann visits Britain every year, to undertake research and also to visit family members who are very understanding about her need to poke around old buildings and visit every antiquity within a hundred miles. If you would like to know more about Ann and her research, or to contact her, visit her website at www.annlethbridge.com. She loves to hear from readers.

Previous novels by this author:

THE RAKE'S INHERITED COURTESAN†
WICKED RAKE, DEFIANT MISTRESS
CAPTURED FOR THE CAPTAIN'S PLEASURE
THE GOVERNESS AND THE EARL
  (part of *Mills & Boon New Voices…* anthology)
THE GAMEKEEPER'S LADY*
MORE THAN A MISTRESS*
LADY ROSABELLA'S RUSE†
THE LAIRD'S FORBIDDEN LADY**
HAUNTED BY THE EARL'S TOUCH
HER HIGHLAND PROTECTOR**
FALLING FOR THE HIGHLAND ROGUE**

And in Mills & Boon® Historical *Undone!* eBooks:

THE RAKE'S INTIMATE ENCOUNTER
THE LAIRD AND THE WANTON WIDOW
ONE NIGHT AS A COURTESAN
UNMASKING LADY INNOCENT
DELICIOUSLY DEBAUCHED BY THE RAKE
A RAKE FOR CHRISTMAS
IN BED WITH THE HIGHLANDER
ONE NIGHT WITH THE HIGHLANDER **

And in Mills & Boon® Historical eBooks:

PRINCESS CHARLOTTE'S CHOICE
  (part of *Royal Weddings Through the Ages* anthology)

And in M&B:

LADY OF SHAME
(part of *Castonbury Park* Regency mini-series)

*linked by character
†linked by character
**The Gilvrys of Dunross*

DEDICATION

This book is dedicated to my dad, without whom I would never have had the wonderful adventure of visiting Scotland and thus the desire to return.

My thanks go out to all involved in making this a better book, in particular Joanne Grant, my editor.

Chapter One

Dundee, November 1822

How dare he? The anger inside Rowena Mac-
Donald increased with each oar stroke of the
longboat crossing the grey waves between the
ship and the quay where she stood. She wrapped
her threadbare cloak tighter against the November wind screaming in from the North Sea.

The dark afternoon suited her mood. After two
years of absence and no word, how dare her husband demand she welcome him back to Scotland?
The rage she had worked so hard at suppressing
these past two years lashed her the same way the
wind whipped the wave tops into foam.

The letter, forwarded on from her last address,
had scarcely arrived at her place of employment
in time for her to meet the ship. She'd toyed with

the idea of refusing his summons. But he was her husband and had the power to further ruin her life. And now, after she had been sure she was free of him, how easily he'd found her and brought her to heel.

Or so he thought, no doubt. As to that, he was going to hear a few home truths. If nothing else, she would make sure he knew she would never ever forgive him for his lies. Or the heartbreak of realising how pathetic she'd been in thinking that he had actually married her for more than her fortune. That he had some tender feelings towards her.

Not love. She had known it wasn't love, but she had thought he cared, at least a little.

She fought the stab of pain as she recalled his betrayal. She would not show how deeply she'd been hurt. Or how greatly she dreaded their re-union. Calm reason must be the order of the day. She took a deep breath of icy-cold air and steeled herself against any sign of weakness. The mois-ture trickling from the corner of her eyes was caused by the sting of the salt-laden sea. Noth-ing else.

The boat drew closer. Close enough to make

out its occupants. Six sailors at the oars. Three passengers, all men, muffled in coats and hats and scarves against the wind, arriving on the last merchant ship from America before winter made the Atlantic crossing impossible. And oddly, upright in the stern, a barrel.

An uncomfortable feeling curled in her stomach. None of the passengers looked in the slightest like her husband. Admittedly, she had only been married two months before Samuel had fled like the proverbial thief in the night, but surely she would recognise him from this distance, despite the other people crowded around her at this end of the jetty making it difficult to see, tall though she was? On her side of the barrier, there were longshoremen waiting to unload the ship's cargo. A small family consisting of a mother and two children stirred with excitement at the approach of the boat, no doubt meeting a loved one.

All those waiting were held back by the formalities of landing. The visit to the harbour master, the presenting of passports, paperwork for Customs. And still Rowena could not pick out

Samuel amid those mounting the jetty steps to dry land.

Could he have lied to her again? Changed his mind?

Her stomach dipped all the way to the cold stones beneath her feet. Her hand tightened around the strings of her reticule containing his letter. His command to be waiting at Dundee dock.

How could she ever have trusted herself to such a feckless man? Sadly, she knew exactly why. Because she had wanted to believe in him, instead of trusting what she had always known. Handsome gentlemen did not fall in love with her type of female. They just didn't. As he'd made quite clear after the wedding, it was a marriage of convenience, colluded in by a cousin, who ought to have had her interests at heart. But didn't.

Two of the passengers left the quay, one disappearing into the arms of the little family squealing their glee and quickly led off. The second signalled to a waiting carriage and was whisked away.

Finally, the third, a tall man with the carriage of a man in his prime, all lean physique and long stride, prowled along the quay, his coat flying open. He walked as if the ground owed him homage, his by right. Images of the pirate who haunted her dreams with his strong clever fingers and wicked mouth danced across her mind.

Shocked, she squeezed her eyes shut against the flutter of desire low in her belly. Embarrassed, she ignored the salacious sensations. If anyone ever guessed the wicked thoughts that went on in her head in the long reaches of the night, they would never let her near their children.

She forced her attention back to reality. To a sailor pushing a handcart containing the barrel she had noticed on the longboat.

And the fact that there was still no sign of Samuel.

She wasn't sure if the feeling in her chest was more anger or relief. Or was it false hope? She turned her gaze back to the ship standing off from the shore. Could there be a second boat? Had he been delayed on board for some reason?

The last passenger was level with her now, a scarf, so swathed about his head it covered all but his eyes beneath a hat pulled down low. He wore a fashionable greatcoat, a thing with many capes, much like the one Samuel had worn during their whirlwind courtship. It looked too tight. Too short. Perhaps that was why he left it undone. The boots on his feet were scuffed and worn. A man who, for all his appearance of pride, wore second-hand clothes.

'Mrs MacDonald?' The man's voice had the lilt of the Highlands and a raspy disused quality. And he had spoken her name. Her heart followed her stomach to the floor. Samuel had fooled her again.

All she could see of the man's face was a pair of wary green eyes. They reminded her of dark ocean depths and fierce forest creatures. 'I am Mrs MacDonald,' she said, unable to keep the edge from her voice.

He bowed, hand to heart. 'Andrew Gilvry, at your service.'

She'd been right. Samuel had brought her here for nothing. 'And where, might I ask, is my husband?'

He recoiled slightly at her haughtily delivered question. 'I am sorry...'

She drew herself up to her full height, the way she did with her students. It was the reason they called her the dragon, out of her hearing. Not the younger ones. Or the girls. They didn't need such demonstrations of strength. The two older boys were a different matter. They, she'd learned quickly, would take advantage of any sign she did not have the upper hand.

'So he is not on the ship after all.' The anger she'd been so carefully keeping under control began to bubble hot in her breast.

The man hesitated. 'I gather you didna' get my letter, then?'

What, did he have some excuse to offer for Samuel's absence? 'The only letter I received was from my husband, requesting me to meet him at this ship. And he is not on board after all.'

'He was on board, in a manner of speaking,' the man said gently, the way people did when delivering bad news. He gestured to the sailor with the barrel. 'He charged me with seeing his remains home to his family.'

The air rushed from her lungs. Her heart seemed to stop for a second as if all the blood had drained from her body. The ground beneath her feet felt as if it was spinning. 'His remains?' she whispered.

'Aye.' He reached out and took her by the elbow, clearly fearing she would faint. His coat streamed out behind him, flapping wildly. He wasn't wearing any gloves, she noticed, and the warmth of his hand sent tingles running up beneath her flesh, all the way to her shoulder. Across her breasts. Female awareness. How could that be? Was the pirate now springing forth to plague her days?

She forced her thoughts into proper order. 'Are you saying he is dead?'

He nodded tersely. 'My condolences, ma'am. He was killed by Indians in the mountains of North Carolina. I was with him when he died.'

She stared at the barrel. 'He's in…?' She couldn't finish her question, but received another terse nod.

Staring at the barrel, she took a deep breath. And another. And then a third. 'But why? Why bring him here?'

While she couldn't see his face, she had the feeling he wished he was anywhere else but here. And that he disapproved of her question.

'He wanted to be buried in Scotland.' He released her elbow and stepped back. 'I gave him my word to see him home.' He gestured to the cart. 'And so I have. Or at least I will have, when I have handed him over to an agent of the Duke of Mere.'

'The Duke of Mere? Why on earth would you want to do that?'

The fair brows, just visible beneath his hat brim, lowered in a frown. 'He is executor to your husband's will.'

In the face of her distress, guilt squirmed in Drew's gut like a live thing. But for him, Samuel MacDonald might have been standing on this quay greeting his wife, instead of him. Mrs MacDonald looked ready to faint, but touching her again was out of the question. She was nothing like the antidote he'd been led to expect. *A veritable harridan of a female.*

He could see why the doughy Samuel MacDonald might have found her physically daunting. She was imposingly tall for a woman, though the top of her head barely reached Drew's eye level, and as lean as a racehorse to the point of boniness.

She was not a pretty woman. The features in her face were too strong and aesthetic for prettiness. Her jaw a little too square for womanly softness, the nose a little too Roman. Her best feature was her dove-grey eyes, clear and bright, and far too intelligent for a man to be comfortable. And yet for some odd reason he found her attractive. Perhaps even alluring.

He fought the stirring of attraction. The effect of too many weeks of male-only company on board ship when he'd been used to— Damn. Why think of that now? A shudder of disgust ran through him. Not only had the woman just discovered she was a widow, but there wasn't a woman alive who would welcome his attentions. Not unless he was paying. Not when they took a look at his face.

The old anger rose in his chest. The desire to wreak vengeance for what had been done to him was always with him, deep inside and like a carefully banked fire. Once brought back to mind, it blazed like a beacon that would never be doused. Not until he had exacted justice from his brother.

Getting a grip on his anger, he glanced up at the sky. It was three in the afternoon, the sun was already looking to set and no sign of the lawyer who should take charge of the matter at hand. Damnation upon the head of all lawyers.

He glanced along the quay with a frown. 'Where is your carriage, Mrs MacDonald?'

'Carriage?' she asked, looking nonplussed.

No carriage, then. A hackney? Or had she walked the mile from the town to the quay carrying the large bag sitting at her feet? The worn cloak, the practical shoes, the modest undecorated bonnet, things in the old days he would have taken in with one glance, now came into focus. Aye, she would have walked. For a man who bragged of his high connections and incipient wealth, MacDonald had not taken such good care of his wife.

So Drew would have to fill the breach. At least for a day or so.

He gestured for her to walk in the direction of the road at the end of the jetty. 'Do you have a room booked for the night in town?'

She eyed him with a frown. 'Of course not, Mr Gilvry. I must return to my place of employment. I spent last night here, but must leave today.'

Her strength of will in the face of adversity surprised him. A woman who would not sub-

mit easily to anyone's command. A burst of heat
low in his belly shocked him. He could not be attracted to this domineering woman, as her husband had described her in the most unflattering
terms. But there was no denying the surge of lust
in his blood. Had his last years among the Indians made him less of a man? His throat dried at
the thought. But he knew it wasn't possible.

Unnatural bastard. He'd heard the accusation
more than once from the women he'd brought to
his bed. But this would not be one of them.

The sooner he delivered her to her husband's
family and got on with the business of settling
his score with Ian, the better. 'I promised to see
you safe in the hands of your husband's family.
No doubt the lawyer will be here in the morning. Or I will send him another message. Let us
find a carriage to transport us and...' He glanced
back at the sailor with the cart, who was shifting
from foot to foot with impatience.

She followed his gaze and a small shiver passed
through her body. Clearly she was not as unaf-
fected as she made out.

'Very well,' she said. 'I will hear what this lawyer of yours has to say, if he arrives tomorrow.

The stage let me down at the Crown. We will go there and I will change my ticket to tomorrow night. I cannot stay a day longer.'

Drew swallowed a sigh of relief at her practical manner. Despite MacDonald's words, he'd expected to suffer through a bout of feminine hysterics. No doubt that would come later, when she got a good look at his face.

'Ye'll find a carriage for hire at the end of the jetty,' the sailor said, who had clearly been listening in to their conversation. The man trundled off with his burden, leaving Drew to escort Mrs MacDonald and carry her bag.

Her spine was so straight, her face so calm, he resisted the temptation to offer his arm for support. She clearly didn't need it or welcome it. So why did he have the feeling that, despite her outward appearance, she might collapse? She didn't look fragile. Anything but. She could have outmarched a general with that straight back of hers. Yet he could not get past the idea that, beneath the outward reserve, she was terrified. The woman was a puzzle and no mistake. But not one he intended to solve.

As the sailor had said, they found a hire carriage at a stand at the end of the quay and reached an agreement on terms to take them into the town centre. Drew helped the widow into the carriage, saw to the disposal of the luggage, then climbed up beside the driver. It would give her time to come to terms with her new circumstance. And allow him to avoid her questions, he admitted grimly.

The Crown Hotel was located in the centre of Dundee, about a mile from the quayside, and when the carriage halted, Drew climbed down and saw to the unloading of the barrel. The driver put his battered valise beside it on the cobbles.

Mrs MacDonald stared at the leather bag for a long moment. She raised her gaze to meet his and his stomach dipped. She must recognise it as her husband's. He had no choice but to answer her silent query.

'You are right. It is your husband's valise,' he said. 'I have made use of his clothes, since I had to leave mine behind.'

Not that he'd had much to leave, unless you counted a breechclout and a pair of moccasins.

She stiffened slightly. 'And you travelled on his ticket?'

He had not been mistaken in the quick wits behind that high forehead. 'Since he was making the journey in the hold, I saw no reason to purchase another.' He winced at the cold sound of his words. 'And I used what money he had for necessary expenses.' Like the makeshift coffin. And a pair of boots. He could hardly travel barefoot and MacDonald's boots had been far too small. He had bought the cheapest he could find, however.

'How very convenient,' she said.

She suspected him of doing away with her husband and stealing his property. And he had in a manner of speaking. He met her gaze without flinching. 'I gave my word to your husband that he would board that ship, Mrs MacDonald. I kept my promise.' Out of guilt. MacDonald had not really expected to die on the journey back to civilisation. He had been full of talk of a glorious future in his fevered ravings. And of riches beyond any man's dreams. Riches that would no doubt remain untapped now he was dead.

Guilt stabbed Drew anew. But it would not change what had happened, nor his intentions to follow through with his self-imposed duty. He would see MacDonald's remains and his wife delivered safely to the lawyer and that was all he would do.

He picked up the valise and strode into the inn.

'Off the ship, are ye, then?' the innkeeper asked, meeting him just inside the door.

'Yes. The lady needs a room with a private parlour,' Gilvry said. 'I'll bed down in the stables.'

The innkeeper looked him up and down as if trying to decide if he was trying to gull him.

'A chamber is all I require,' Mrs MacDonald said from behind Drew, her reticule clutched at her breast as if she feared its contents would not be enough to pay for her night's lodgings.

He pulled out MacDonald's purse and jingled the few remaining coins. 'The lady's husband charged me with her travel arrangements. A room with a private parlour, if you please, and the use of a maid. Mrs MacDonald will take dinner in her room.'

The innkeeper bowed. 'This way, please, madam.'

'Don't worry about the rest of the luggage, Mrs MacDonald,' Drew said as, stiff-backed with indignation, she followed the host up the stairs. 'I will keep it safe.'

She cast him a look of dislike over her shoulder. 'Then I hope you have a good night's rest, Mr Gilvry.'

Ah, irony. He'd missed its edge all these many years. No doubt she was hoping her husband would haunt him. Which he would, because, in a manner of speaking, he had been, ever since he died.

Drew turned and stomped out to the yard.

It was only when Rowena had removed her coat and hat inside her room that she fully absorbed the news. Samuel MacDonald was dead.

She squeezed her eyes closed against the sudden pain at her temples as her thoughts spiralled out of control. She had to think about this logically.

She was a widow.

A destitute widow, she amended. She had very little hope that anything remained of the money Samuel had realised from the sale of her half of her father's linen factory. Creditors had assailed her from all sides after his sudden departure for

America, leaving her no choice but to find work and support herself. Her anger at her foolishness bubbled up all over again. How could she have been so taken in after fending off so many fortune hunters over the years?

But she knew why. After her father died when she was eighteen, she had lived with his partner and cousin. She'd hated it. Not that these family members had been particularly unkind, but whereas her father had respected her mind and listened to her advice, her cousin had insisted she leave all business matters to him. He had not valued her opinions at all.

As far as he was concerned, women were brainless. Only good to decorate a man's arm and attend to his house.

And then she'd proved him right. She'd fallen for the blandishments of an out-and-out scoundrel who had fled almost as soon as he had his hands on her money, leaving her to face the creditors he'd apparently forgotten to pay. Her cousin, who had encouraged the marriage, had washed his hands of her, as well he might, once he owned everything.

She stripped off her thin leather gloves and sat

down on the chair beside the hearth, holding her hands out to the flames, revelling in the heat on her frozen fingers. It was a long time since she'd had such a warm fire at her disposal. But creature comforts could not hold her thoughts for long.

Was it possible her cousin had insisted Samuel settle some money on her future when he acted on her behalf in the matter of the marriage?

If so, it was a relief to know that her only family hadn't totally taken advantage of her lapse of good sense in accepting Samuel as a husband. When she'd learned her cousin had bought her half of the family business for a sum vastly below its true worth right after the wedding, she'd suspected her cousin of underhanded dealings.

It seemed she might have been wrong about her cousin. And about Samuel. Partly wrong at any rate, if arrangements had been made for her future.

Samuel was dead.

At least that was what Mr Gilvry had said. But how did she know for certain? She'd be a fool to take any man's word at face value. And she hadn't even seen Mr Gilvry's face. He had raised his hat when he bowed, but not removed his muffler. Nor had he removed it when he entered the inn.

All she had to go on was what she had seen in a pair of piercing green eyes and heard in a deep voice with a lovely Highland lilt. And felt in the flutter deep in her stomach. Attraction. Something she should know better than to trust.

He really hadn't told her what had happened to Samuel. Was there some reason behind his reticence she couldn't fathom?

She got up and rang the bell. It wasn't long before the maid the innkeeper's wife had assigned arrived to do her bidding. 'Be so good as to tell Mr Gilvry I wish to see him at once.' She glanced at the clock. 'Please tell the kitchen I would like dinner for two delivered at half past seven.'

The maid bobbed a curtsy and left.

Now to see if he answered the summons. And if he did not? Then she would know that she definitely should not trust him.

And if he did? Did that mean she should? Likely not. But it would help put an end to the strange feelings she had in his presence. He was just a man, not an enigma she needed to solve. She simply wanted the facts about her husband's death.

She opened her door to the passageway. He was a man who had done her a service, no matter how unpleasant. He should not have to scratch at the door like a servant. She shook her head at this odd sense of the man's pride as she took the chair beside the hearth facing the door.

A few minutes later, he appeared before her, his broad shoulders filling the doorway. How odd that she hadn't heard his footsteps, though she had listened for them. Nor had she realised quite how tall a man he was when they were out on the quay.

She frowned. He was still wearing his scarf, wrapped around his head and draped across his face in the manner of a Turk.

His dark coat, like the greatcoat he'd worn off the ship, fitted him ill, the fabric straining across his shoulders, yet loose at the waist, and the sleeves leaving more cuff visible than was desirable. His pantaloons were tight, too, outlining the musculature of his impressive calves, his long lean thighs and his— She forced her gaze back up to meet his eyes. 'Please come in, Mr Gilvry. Leave the door open, if you please.'

She didn't want the inn servants to gossip about

her entertaining a man alone in her room. People were quick to judge and she didn't need a scandal destroying her reputation with her employer.

The man did not so much as walk into the room as he prowled across the space to take her outstretched hand. His steps were silent, light as air, but incredibly manly.

The same walk she'd first noticed on the quay. The walk of a hunter intent on stalking his prey. Or a marauding pirate, or a maiden-stealing sheikh. All man. All danger. A betraying little shiver ran down her spine.

Trying to hide her response to his presence, she gestured coldly to the seat on the other side of the hearth, the way she would direct a recalcitrant student. 'Pray be seated.'

He sat down, folding his long body into the large wing chair with an easy grace. But why hide his face? She'd thought nothing of the muffler out on the quay. She'd tucked her chin into her own scarf in the bitter November wind.

'Please, make yourself comfortable.' She looked pointedly as his headgear.

The wide chest rose and fell on a deep indrawn breath. He straightened his shoulders. 'It is an in-

vitation you might regret.' There was bitter humour in his voice, and something else she could
not define. Defiance, perhaps? Bravado?

Turning partly away he unwound the muffler.
At first all she could see was the left side of his
face and hair of a dark reddish-blonde, thick and
surprisingly long. His skin was a warm golden
bronze. Side on he looked like an alabaster plaque
of a Greek god in profile, only warm and living.
Never had she seen a man so handsome.

He turned and faced her full on.

She recoiled with a gasp at the sight of the trib-
utary of scars running down the right side of his
face. A jagged, badly healed puckering of skin
that sliced a diagonal from cheekbone to chin,
pulling the corner of his mouth into a mocking
smile. A dreadful mutilation of pure male beauty.
She wanted to weep.

'I warned that you'd prefer it covered.' Clearly
resigned, he reached for the scarf.

How many people must have turned away in
horror at the sight? From a man who would have
once drawn eyes because of his unusual beauty.

'Of course not,' she said firmly, deeply regretting her surprised response. 'Would you like a dram of whisky?' She made to rise.

Looking relieved, he rose to his feet. 'I'll help myself.'

He crossed to the table beside the window and poured whisky from the decanter, the good side of his face turned towards her. It made her heart ache to see him so careful. He lifted the glass and tossed off half in one go. He frowned at the remainder. 'I didna' expect to find you alone. Did they no' give you the maid I requested?'

'She has duties in the kitchen, preparing the evening meal.'

He lifted his head, his narrowed gaze meeting hers, the muscles in his jaw jumping, pulling at the scars, making them gleam bone white. Her stomach curled up tight. She could only imagine the pain such an injury must have caused, along with the anguish at the loss of such perfection.

Anger flared in his eyes as if he somehow read her thoughts and resented them.

He did not want her sympathy.

She looked down at her hands and gripped them together in her lap. She had asked him here to answer her questions. She might as well get straight to the point.

'Mr Gilvry, I would like to know exactly what happened to my husband, if you wouldn't mind?' Did she sound too blunt? Too suspicious?

She glanced up to test his reaction to her words. He was gazing out into the darkness, his face partly hidden by his hair. 'Aye. I'll tell you what I can.'

She frowned at the strange choice of words. 'Were you travelling with Samuel, when... when—?'

'No. I found him some time after the Indians had attacked his party. He had managed to crawl away from the camp and hide, but he was badly injured.'

'Why? Why were they attacked?'

He turned his head slightly, watching her from the corner of his eye. 'I don't know.'

Why did she have the sense he was not telling her the truth? What reason would he have to lie? 'So you just happened upon him? Afterwards.'

'I heard shots, but arrived too late to be of help.' His head lowered slightly. 'I'm sorry.'

He sounded sorry. More regretful than she

would have expected under the circumstances he described. 'He was alive when you found him?'

He took a deep breath. 'He was. I hoped—' He shook his head. 'I carried him down from the mountains. For a while I thought he would live. The fever took him a few nights later.'

'And he requested that you bring his remains back to me?' She could not help the incredulity in her voice.

He shifted, half turning towards her. 'To Scotland. To his family. That is you, is it not?'

'I doubt he thought of me as family.' She spoke the words without thinking and winced at how bitter she sounded.

'He had regrets, your husband, I think. At the last.' His voice was low and deep and full of sympathy.

An odd lump rose in her throat. The thought that Samuel had cared. Even if it was out of guilt. It had been a long time since anyone had truly cared. She fought the softening emotion. It was too late for her to feel pain. How would it help her now? 'And his executor is to meet us here? In Dundee.'

'Aye. Or at least his lawyer. A Mr Jones. I wrote

to him from Wilmington. But if you didna' get my letter...'

'The address you used, it came from Samuel? Naturally it did,' she amended quickly at his frown.

'Aye.'

'I moved. I had no way of letting Samuel know.' She'd also changed her name. She could scarcely have Samuel's creditors coming to her place of employment. 'An old friend forwarded Samuel's note, because I asked him to do so.' Her cousin's butler, once her father's man, would not have forwarded a letter unless he knew the name of the sender. There had been too many odd requests for money and not all of them from tradesmen. 'I doubt your other letter was similarly impeded. Let us hope Mr Jones will arrive tomorrow.'

The sound of footsteps carried along the passageway outside. He turned to look, his fair brows raised in question.

'Our dinner,' she said with a little jolt of her heart, as if she was afraid he would leave.

'Ours?' He looked surprised.

'I thought we could talk while we ate. That is, if you have not already dined?'

'No, I havena',' he said warily. He turned his back on the room, once more looking out into the night as two maids entered, followed by the innkeeper's wife who directed the setting up of the table and the serving of dinner. The plump woman curtsied deeply. 'Will there be anything else, madam?'

'No, thank you,' Rowena said. 'I think we can manage to serve ourselves.'

The woman's gaze rested on Mr Gilvry's back for a moment, her eyes hard. 'Would you like our Emmie to serve you, madam?'

Rowena could see the woman's thoughts about single ladies entertaining a gentleman in her rooms.

She stared at the woman down the nose that had been her plague as a girl, but now had its uses. An arrogant nose, it put people in their place. Her father had used his own bigger version to great effect in his business. 'No, thank you, Mrs Robertson. That will be all.'

The woman huffed out a breath, but stomped out of the room, defeated.

Mr Gilvry turned around as the door closed behind their hostess, his expression dark. 'The woman is right. You should ask the maid to attend you. Or dine alone. You must think of your reputation.' He took an urgent step towards the door.

The vehemence in his voice surprised her. Was he was afraid for her reputation or his? Did he fear she might put him in a compromising position? It hardly seemed likely. 'You honour me with your concern, Mr Gilvry, however, I am not accountable to the wife of an innkeeper.' She lifted her chin as another thought occurred to her. 'Or are you seeing it as an excuse to avoid my questions?'

He glared. 'I have answered all of your questions.'

Had he? Then why did she have the sense he was keeping something back? 'You have,' she said. It would do no good to insult the man. 'But I have more. You must excuse my curiosity. I know little of my husband's activities in America.'

His mouth tightened. His gaze shuttered, hiding his thoughts. 'There is little I can tell you on that score, I am afraid. Perhaps this Mr Jones can tell you more.'

Avoidance. It was as plain as the nose on her

face. Her exceedingly plain nose on her exceedingly plain face, as Samuel had made no bones to tell her, once he had control of her money. But it wasn't because she cared whether this man found her attractive or otherwise that she wanted him to stay; she simply wanted to know if she dared trust him. That was all.

For one thing, she had never before heard of this Mr Jones. And she was hoping Mr Gilvry could shed some light on how he fitted into the scheme of things before she faced the man.

She offered a smile. 'I am sorry if I sound over forward, but I find I do not wish to eat alone tonight. My thoughts about the news give me no rest.' And nor did her suspicions.

His shoulders relaxed. 'Aye, I understand it has come as a shock.'

And a welcome relief. Guilt assailed her at the uncharitable thought. He would think her dreadful if he guessed at the direction of her thoughts.

She gestured to the table. 'The food is here. It would be a shame for it to go to waste.'

He swept a red-gold lock back from his forehead. 'To tell the truth, the smell of the food is hard to resist and I doubt they'll feed me in the kitchen, if yon mistress has aught to say in it.'

He glanced at the table with longing and it was only then that she realised how very gaunt was his face. His cheekbones stood out beneath his skin as if he had not eaten well in months. At first one only noticed the scars. And the terrible dichotomy they made of his face.

'Then you will keep me company?' she asked. She wasn't the sort of woman men fell over themselves to be with, but he was not a man who would have much choice in women. Not now. She stilled at the thought. Was that hope she felt? Surely not. Hope where men were concerned had been stamped out beneath Samuel's careless boots. What man would want her? Especially now, when she was poor.

He shook his head with a rueful expression. 'Aye. It seems I will.'

The gladness she felt at his acceptance was out of all proportion with the circumstances and her reasons for inviting him. A gladness she must not let him see. With a cool nod, she let him seat her at the dining table.

He took the chair opposite. 'May I pour you

some wine and carve you a portion of what looks to be an excellent fowl?'

'You may, indeed.'

While she had little appetite herself after the day's events, it was a pleasure to see him eat with obvious enjoyment. And his manners were impeccable. He was a gentleman, no matter his poor clothing.

She cut her slice of chicken into small pieces and tasted a morsel. It was moist and the white sauce was excellent. And she could not help watching him from beneath her lowered lashes as she tasted her food. He might not be handsome any longer, but his youth, his physical strength and powerful male presence were undeniable. Big hands. Wide shoulders. White, even teeth. A formidable man with an energy she could feel from across the table.

She wanted to ask him what it was that drove him. What he cared about. What he planned. It was none of her business. She would do well to remember that.

She held her questions while he satisfied his appetite. It was her experience, both at home and in the two positions she'd held as a governess, that men became more amenable with a full stomach. She waited until he had cut himself a piece of apple pie before opening a conversation that did not include passing gravy or salt, or the last of the roast pork.

'The locals say that it is likely to be a hard winter,' she said, lifting her wine glass.

'I heard the same,' he replied.

She waited for him to say more, but was not surprised when he did not. He said little unless it was to the point. Idle conversation had a tendency to lead to the baring of souls. He was not that sort of man.

She took a sip of wine and considered her next words. Shock him, perhaps? Get beneath his guard, as her father would have said? Her heart raced a little. 'The coat you are wearing is Samuel's, is it not?'

Eyes wary, he put down his forkful of pie. 'He had no more use for it. My own clothes were ruined on the journey to the coast.'

Defensive. But why? What he said made perfect sense. Perhaps he feared she'd be overcome by her emotions at the thought of him wearing Samuel's clothes? Another woman might be, she supposed.

She kept her voice light and even. 'It must have been a terrible journey?'

'I've had worse.'

She stared, surprised by the edge in his voice. He looked up and caught her gaze. His skin coloured, just a little, as if he realised he'd been brusque.

'But, yes,' he said, his voice a little more gentle, 'it was no' so easy.' His voice dropped. 'Your husband bore it verra well at the end, if it is of comfort to you.'

It did not sound like the Samuel she had known. He'd been a man who liked an easy life. The reason he had married her money. Could there be some sort of mistake? Her stomach clenched at the idea, but she asked the question anyway. 'You are sure that he is…I mean, he was Samuel MacDonald? My husband?'

Misplaced pity filled his gaze. 'There is no doubt in my mind the man was your husband, Mrs MacDonald. We talked. Of you. Of other things. How else would I know about the lawyer?' He frowned and looked grim. 'But you are right. Someone should identify his remains. To make things legal. I didna' think you…'

Her stomach lurched. She pushed her plate away, stood and moved from the table to the hearth. 'No. You are right. This Mr Jones should do it.'

'If he knew him personally.'

She whirled around. 'You think he did not?'

'Your husband was not always lucid, Mrs Mac-Donald. He suffered greatly. But he was most insistent on my contacting those in charge of Mere's estate.'

The Duke of Mere. Why did that name sound so familiar? She had heard it spoken of recently, surely? She didn't care for gossip, but now she remembered her employer's remark. She turned to face him. 'The Duke of Mere is dead.'

His jaw dropped. 'But...' He shook his head, got up and took a step towards her. 'One duke dies. Another follows right behind. Like the king.'

He was right. She swallowed. 'Of course.'

He drew closer. Very close, until she could feel the warmth from his body, the sense of male strength held in check, though why that should be she could not imagine. 'Mrs MacDonald,' he said softly, 'dinna fash yourself. Jones will come tomorrow and your husband's family will do their duty by you.'

What family? According to Samuel he was as alone in the world as she was. It was one of the things that had drawn her to him. His need for family. Not that he had needed her, once he had her money. It would be nice to be needed. To be able to lean on a man and have him take care of her in return. She felt herself leaning towards Mr Gilvry, as if his strength could sustain her.

Shocked, she straightened. She moved away, turning to face him with a hard-won smile against the melting sensation in her limbs. 'You are right. It seems that Mr Jones holds the key to everything.' She put a hand to her temple. It was throbbing again. Too much thinking. Too much worrying. Too much hope that she had not been entirely abandoned after all.

'Mr Gilvry, my husband asked much of you.' She looked at his poor ruined face and saw nothing but sympathy in his gaze. She hesitated, her mouth dry, the words stuck fast in her throat. She took a breath. 'Could I trouble you some more? May I request your presence at the interview with Mr Jones?'

If he was surprised, he hid it well. 'If that is your wish,' he said, his voice a little gruff.

Instinctively, she swayed towards all that beautiful male strength, her eyes closing in relief. 'Thank you.'

She felt his hand on her arm, warm and strong and infinitely gentle. Once more, strange tingles ran up her arm at the strength of his touch. Did he feel them, too? Was that why he released her so quickly?

'Sit down, Mrs MacDonald,' he said in a rasping voice. 'By the hearth. I'll ask our hostess to send up tea. And the maid. It is a good night's sleep you need. Things will be clearer in the morning.'

When she looked up, he was gone. So silently for such a tall man. A man whose absence left a very empty hole in the room. But he had said he would stand by her on the morrow. She clung to that thought as if her life depended on it and wondered at her sudden sensation of weakness.

Chapter Two

Drew paced up and down between the stalls, cursing under his breath. Frustration scoured through his blood. Desire. He struck out at a post and accepted the pain in his knuckles as his just reward.

What the hell did he think he was doing? The woman had just learned of her husband's death and instead of offering platitudes and help, he'd almost pulled her into his arms and kissed her.

He wasn't drawn to respectable women. Ever. He was depraved. And he knew where to find what he wanted. What the hell had he been thinking up there?

How could he possibly consider wanting her, let alone begin envisaging her naked and open and…? He hit the post again, then sucked the copper-tasting blood from his knuckles and re-membered her soft, wide mouth.

Damn him. Hadn't his experience with Alice Fulton been lesson enough? If his family hadn't been desperate, he would never have taken her in order to force a wedding. The moment he did it, he'd known it would never work. Not for him. He'd have spent his life in purgatory.

He'd never been so relieved as when she had backed out of their engagement. So why had he almost kissed Rowena MacDonald?

Because he felt sorry for her? Or because he was grateful that, after her first horrified look at his face, she'd acted as if he was normal. As if his appearance didn't make her stomach turn.

Jones had better turn up tomorrow and take charge of this woman, because if he didn't, Drew was just going to walk away. He squeezed his eyes shut. He couldn't. He'd sworn to himself that he would see her safe and secure. He didn't have a choice, not when it was his fault her hus-band was dead.

A man staggered down the steps from the loft. The old groom in charge of the stables. He glared at Drew, then recoiled as he saw his face in the light from the lantern hanging from a beam.

'Isn't it bad enough that your pounding and cursing knocked me out of my bed,' the old man railed, shaking his fist. 'Do you have to ruin my dreams with that devil's face?'

Drew laughed. He couldn't help it. The old man's reaction was exactly the same as everyone else's, but at least he had the courage to say it.

He bowed. 'I beg your pardon.'

'Aye, well ye might. If ye're wanting to bed down, you best get up that ladder now, because when I'm back from tending to nature I'm bolting the trapdoor from the inside. To keep out Old Nick, you understand.' He staggered to the door at the far end, still muttering under his breath.

Drew wished he had something to keep out the devil he carried around inside him. But he didn't. And while the devil wanted a woman, Drew wanted his revenge on Ian more. And so he would keep the devil caged. He'd done it for the past few years; he would continue.

He had to get Mrs MacDonald off his hands and his conscience. Then he would send Ian to hell, where he belonged.

* * *

'A gentleman to see you, Mrs Macdonald,' the maid announced from the doorway to her private parlour the next morning.

She looked up from her struggle to compose a suitable letter to Mrs Preston, her employer, asking for a few more days' absence. For a moment she thought it might be Mr Gilvry and her heart lifted a fraction. But at the same moment she knew it was not. He would not have asked the maid to announce him. 'Did the gentleman give his name?'

Emmie held out a square of white paper. 'His card, ma'am.'

Mr Brian Jones, solicitor, the card stated in bold black letters. On the reverse, a rather crabbed script added cryptically, man of business to the Duke of Mere.

'Show him in, please. And ask Mr Gilvry to come up, if you will.' The girl raised questioning brows, but hurried off without a word.

Rowena moved from the writing desk to the sofa and sat facing the door.

The man who stepped across the threshold a few moments later was surprisingly young for such a responsible position. In his mid-thirties, she thought, and reasonably fair of face, if one ignored the tendency of his long nose to sharpness and the slight weakness of his chin. But his pale blue eyes were sharp and his smile positively charming. He was dressed quite as soberly as one would expect for a lawyer, though his cravat was perhaps a shade flamboyant in its intricacy.

'Mrs MacDonald,' he said with a deeper bow than someone of her station warranted. An odd little slip for such a man.

'Mr Jones. Please, be seated.'

He settled himself into the armchair opposite without a sign of any nervousness. Indeed, if anything, he looked confidently in control. A small smile hovered on his lips as he waited for her to speak. She could wait him out. Her father had taught her the game of negotiation almost before she had learned how to sew a fine seam. But with her future in the balance, she wasn't in the mood.

'You received the message about my husband's death from Mr Gilvry, I assume?'

He arranged his face into an expression of sympathy. 'I did. May I offer you my condolences on your loss,' he said, inclining his head. 'Indians, I understand.'

She nodded. 'So I gather.'

'Most unfortunate.' A touch of colour tinged his cheeks. 'Did you—' He coughed delicately. 'Are you certain he did not survive the attack?'

His eyes were fixed intently on her face. A strange feeling rippled across her shoulders. Her scalp tightened at the shock of it. It was something like the sensation described as a ghost walking over one's grave, only more unpleasant. A premonition of danger. Clearly, she wasn't the only one who had wondered about the truth of Samuel's death. 'If you require confirmation, Mr Jones, you must inspect his remains. They have been returned to Scotland at his wish.'

Distaste twisted his mouth. 'Not me. I never met Mr MacDonald in person.' He coughed behind his hand. 'I have arranged for someone in the duke's household to confirm his identity.'

The duke's household? 'My husband never mentioned the Duke of Mere once to me during our marriage.'

'Ah, dear lady, it is a distant connection. Your husband's branch of the family has long been estranged from its senior branch. He visited Mere shortly before his departure for America. It was Mere's wish that relationships that were broken be mended. The identification is mere formality, you understand, but a necessary one.'

His smile felt just a little too forced. But then it was likely difficult to know what to do with one's face in the presence of a supposedly grieving widow. He drew a notebook from his pocket and a small silver pen. He turned the pages as if looking for something. 'It was a Mr Gilvry who discovered his body. It was his letter we received.'

'Yes. He accompanied my husband's remains from America.' His voice made her wonder if he harboured doubts about Mr Gilvry. She pursed her lips. Where was he? He had promised to attend this meeting. 'He will join us shortly.'

He looked around somewhat disapprovingly as if he expected Mr Gilvry to pop out of her bedroom.

'Nothing can move forward until the circumstances of your husband's death are fully documented and sworn to,' he continued. 'It is this—' he glanced down at his notebook '—Gilvry I need to speak to. As well as verifying the death of your husband and...' He frowned. 'And the validity of your marriage.'

'I beg your pardon?'

'None of the MacDonalds were aware that Mr Samuel MacDonald had taken a wife.'

'You will find it in the records of my parish church.'

Again that delicate cough. 'Or if there are offspring? Our contact with Mr MacDonald was most perfunctory.'

'No.' She raised her chin. 'No offspring.' And she'd been glad of it, too, given how he'd left her in the lurch.

'And Mr Gilvry?'

She glanced towards the door. Where on earth was he?

The call to attend Rowena and Mr Jones came at eleven. Damn it, not Rowena. Mrs MacDonald. All night he'd been thinking about the lovely pale skin glowing in candlelight over dinner, his memories of the challenge her slender curves and hollows presented to his own desires and cursing himself.

He'd made very sure the servants had seen him leave her room. He'd sent the maid up to help her ready for bed, too, so she would know nothing untoward had occurred. He'd done all he could to protect her from gossip. He would have to make sure this lawyer saw only mistress and servant.

Once more he was dressed in her husband's second-best coat, pretending to be what he was not.

The atmosphere when he stepped into the room was tense. Mrs MacDonald sagged at the sight of him. He frowned. What had this lawyer being saying to her that would upset her usual calm?

He bowed. 'You sent for me, Mrs MacDonald.'

'Yes, Mr Gilvry. Mr Jones has some questions for you.'

'Indeed I do,' the dapper young man said. 'On what date did Mr MacDonald meet his end? The day and the month.'

Drew had expected questions about the circumstances of MacDonald's death. Dreaded them. But the date?

He hadn't known at the time. He'd spent too long living by the seasons and the rise and set of the sun to be aware of dates. But he knew it now. The date was carved in his mind by words that chilled him to the bone. *Unbelievable that any man would allow...* 'September fifteenth.' He forced the words out.

The lawyer's eyes flickered with some sort of emotion. Disappointment? He gathered himself so quickly it was hard to be sure. He smiled a prissy smile. 'Are you positive?'

'I am.'

The lawyer looked at him expectantly. When he said nothing, the man shook his head. 'You have proof?'

A deep dark cold entered his gut. 'My word should be enough.'

'Any statement made is subject to being contested without proof.'

The cold expended to fill his chest. He had the proof. But to make his shame public, a byword.... There had to be another way. 'If you dinna have the date, is it a problem?'

The lawyer tapped his chin with a well-manicured nail, making Drew aware of his rough weather-beaten hands. No longer the hands of a gentleman. Jones frowned down at paper before him. 'It is true the date is not so important, once his identity is established. Without proof it is best if we couch it in the most general of terms.' He looked up with a lawyerly smile. 'And remain within the bounds of the law, you understand. Yes. Yes. It will serve very well.'

The man talked in such flowing periods, Drew wanted to hit him.

He picked up his pen and filled in some blank spaces on the document. 'Hmm. Date of death, sometime in late September.'

Drew looked at Rowena. She was pale, worrying at her bottom lip and looking tense. She clearly sensed something was wrong and, damn it, so did he.

The lawyer pushed the paper across the desk. 'Make your mark there,' he said, pointing. 'I'll witness it.'

His younger brother Niall had always wanted to study the law. One of the things he had said when they talked around the dinner table was that it was a foolish man who signed anything he did not understand. And it was clear the lawyer thought he couldn't read. He picked up the pen. 'Why not write the fifteenth as I told you?'

'You cannot put a date if you cannot prove it,'

the lawyer said. 'It would not be right.' He moved
the paper out of Drew's reach with a frown. 'And
as I said, it is not all that important. As long as
we have the proof of his death.' He gave a sly
little smile. 'As we will do, once the remains are
carried to Mere.'

'Then let us omit any mention of the date at
all.' Drew replied.

'Will that be sufficient?' Rowena asked, her
posture stiff, her expression remote, yet stern.
Drew sensed her anxiety.

The lawyer pulled his legal superiority around
him like a shield. 'If more is required, we can return to the matter at a later time.'

It seemed reasonable to Drew. Then why did
he have this odd sense of worry? He glanced at
Rowena. She also looked troubled, but she met
his gaze and nodded.

He pulled the paper back across the table,
scratched out the line and signed the document.

'Mr Jones,' Mrs MacDonald said sharply, 'there
are other matters pressing upon me at the moment with which I require your assistance.'

His gaze sharpened with wariness. 'Matters,
madam?'

'Matters such as my husband's will. His estate.'

'My dear Mrs MacDonald,' the man said with a condescension that again made Drew want to hit him, 'probate of a will takes time. There are many formalities to be undertaken, as I have already explained.'

She gazed at him coolly. 'I understand. But you must know something of his affairs. I am a governess. I must return to my position at once.'

His eyes widened. 'Oh, most certainly not. You and Mr Gilvry must travel to Mere.'

Drew stared at him. 'I have no intention of going to Mere. My own affairs take me in quite another direction.'

The lawyer shifted in his seat. 'It was my understanding that you were to accompany Mr MacDonald's remains to his final resting place. That is Mere.'

'I prefer to leave that to you.'

The lawyer shook his head. 'Until a third party has confirmed that the deceased is truly Samuel MacDonald, at which time the court will no doubt accept your information, Mr Gilvry, I cannot release you from your obligations.'

He turned to Rowena and, if anything, his

smile became more oily. 'I should not be saying this, but before he left, Mr MacDonald changed his will. Everything is left to Mere's estate. Any settlements will be at the discretion of the new duke. You will not find him ungenerous, I assure you, once your claim is established.'

Drew's hackles rose. The longer he spent in this man's company, the less he trusted him. While at first glance he seemed charming, with that ready smile, his eyes drifted away when met head-on, even taking into account that no one liked to look Drew full in the face.

Rowena visibly wilted as if the stuffing had been knocked out of her. 'He left everything to Mere? He indicated to Mr Gilvry that he made a settlement—'

Jones shook his head. 'It is in Mere's hands now. I am merely his representative. You will have to take your case directly to him.'

Drew glared and the man shifted his gaze to the documents on the table. 'MacDonald told me his wife would be cared for.' The dying man had said it with such bitterness, Drew had been shocked, but he had not doubted his words.

Jones frowned. 'The duke takes his responsibilities seriously, I can assure you.' Again that tight little smile at Rowena. 'As you will discover, Mrs MacDonald, if you will allow yourself to be guided by me.'

Rowena took an unsteady breath. 'It would be enough if I am relieved of his debt.'

The defeat on her face made Drew's chest feel as if it was weighed down with a rock.

'If there are assets, they should be passed on to MacDonald's widow,' he said firmly.

The lawyer was tapping his chin again. A sign he was thinking on his feet, perhaps. 'I see you are not satisfied with the word of a duke,' Jones said in an exasperated tone. 'Very well. If your claims are proved—' he inclined his head slightly '—as I am sure they will be, dear lady, there is a house set aside for you, at Mere, and an annuity.'

She perked up. 'The house would be mine? Something I can sell?'

Jones shook his head. 'It is on land that is part of the estate.'

'So the duke will continue to own the house.'

He nodded. 'Indeed. But once your husband's will has gone through probate, there may be more. You did mention debts?'

She looked down her autocratic nose and the lawyer visibly wilted. 'Yes, but none of my making.' She let go a little breath. 'But Mr MacDonald realised a large sum from the sale of my half of McFail's. I cannot believe there is nothing left.'

'Let us hope you are right. In the meantime…'

'In the meantime, it seems I have no choice but to accept the duke's generous offer. I will travel to Mere and learn the outcome of my husband's business affairs.'

Jones turned his gaze to Drew. 'I do hope I can prevail upon you to finish what you set out to accomplish. The return of Mr MacDonald to the bosom of his family. You will, of course, be rewarded for your time.'

'I would prefer to leave it to you,' Drew said. 'I have another engagement.' Ian. His gut clenched painfully.

Jones gathered up his papers. 'My first duty is to ascertain this lady's claim of marriage, which takes me in a different direction, after which I will then make post-haste to Mere. But you must allow it is vital that the poor dear departed be taken swiftly to his final resting place. Who knows what ravages may have occurred during shipment? If it is not possible to prove his identity...'

Rowena paled. Drew felt slightly nauseous, though the undertaker had assured him all would be well.

Rowena looked at him and, while her expression was one of serene indifference, he knew from the pleas deep in those soft grey eyes that she wanted him to say yes. 'Verra well. I will accompany Mrs MacDonald to Mere.'

The lawyer looked far too relieved at his words, but Drew could hardly change his mind, because Rowena had looked equally relieved.

'Excellent,' Jones said. 'You will make your way to Penwood House. No doubt his Grace will be delighted to receive you at the castle once you are established there.'

Drew didn't like the glint of triumph in Jones's eyes. 'And a conveyance?' Drew asked.

'I will arrange for a cart for the transportation of the...luggage.'

Rowena's face shuttered. 'I am to travel on this cart?'

'You may. Unless you prefer to ride. The driver,

a man by the name of Pockle, and his wife will serve your needs along the road, which regrettably is a difficult journey this time of year.'

Did the man hope she'd become lost on the way? Drew glared at him, knowing only too well the dangers of cross-country travel. 'How long will it take?' Drew asked.

'Two or three days. Longer if the weather is bad.'

'And where is Mrs MacDonald to spend the nights?' Drew asked. He could not get away from his sense of danger. 'You surely don't expect her to camp out in the hills.'

'Certainly not. There are inns along the way. Please be ready to leave in the morning. I will take care of all the arrangements before I leave later today.' He gathered up his papers and packed them away. 'I look forward to our next meeting at Mere, Mrs MacDonald.'

He bowed and left.

Rowena frowned. 'He was so keen on a date at first. Why do you think he changed his mind so quickly?'

The lass had a very sharp mind.

He shook his head. 'That's a tricky wee fellow, I'm thinking. You are right to seek out the duke.'

'Are you sure you don't mind going, too? While he seemed to want your presence at Mere, I could probably manage with the driver and his wife, since it is not too far distant.'

It was madness to agree to it. To spend more time in her company. To feel the call of her milk-white skin and find himself falling into the depths of her clear grey eyes. Madness and torture for the sake of a promise no one had heard but himself. 'Once I start on something, I have to see it through.'

No matter how long it took.

A soft breath came from her parted lips and he wanted to capture it in his mouth. 'Thank you.'

He turned briskly for the door. 'It seems I must find some sort of nag for the journey.'

His business with Ian could wait. A week. A month. A year. It made no difference; it had waited so long already.

Yet he could not help feeling he might be making the worst mistake of his life. And he'd made some bad ones in the past.

Chapter Three

Why on earth did Mere have to reside in such an inaccessible place in wintertime? Rowena thought, huddling deeper into her cloak. Why couldn't he live in Edinburgh like any civilised person? This was their second day since leaving Dundee and Rowena was already exhausted by the journey. The roads were so abysmal, the cart travelled at less than walking speed and, this afternoon, the sky had turned a lowering grey just skimming the hilltops.

The cold, damp air wormed its way through every fibre of her clothing. Worse was the way Mr Gilvry, riding ahead of the cavalcade, glanced up at the sky from time to time.

She urged her horse forward. 'Is it going to rain?'

She was on his left side and the beauty of his

features struck her anew, though she hoped she managed to hide the sudden hitch in her breath.

'Snow,' he said with such assurance, she did not doubt him.

Lovely. She shivered. 'How long before we reach the next inn?' She could just imagine a warm fire and a hot bath.

Mr Gilvry glanced back over his shoulder at the cart, where the driver and his wife sat pressed close together for warmth. 'Our next stopping place is fifteen miles from where we stayed last night. Since we havena' made more than ten miles, I would say we have another five to go.'

'Can we make it by nightfall?'

'Aye.'

He sounded confident, but she wasn't fooled. These one-word answers were meant to disguise his concern. 'You mean, if it doesn't snow and if the cart doesn't get stuck.'

He gave her a quick sideways glance and she could have sworn the corner of his mouth curled up in a smile. The effect was more than charming, it was wickedly seductive. Her inner muscles gave a little squeeze. Not the sort of reaction one should be having sitting on a horse. Or at all. But at least a new kind of warmth was now pulsing through her body.

'Aye, that is just what I mean,' he said.

To hide her flush, she also looked over her shoulder at the cart and its occupants. Twice it had become stuck in a muddy rut on the previous day. On both occasions, she'd been impressed with Mr Gilvry's strength and his whipcord leanness when he had removed his coats and heaved with all his might.

'I'm beginning to wonder if I shouldn't have just gone back to my place of employment and forgotten all about ever being married.'

His amusement faded. 'Would you let that wee mannie Jones have the best of you? I don't know what game Mere is playing, but your husband was telling me the truth. He made some sort of settlement for you.'

'It won't make any difference if I freeze to death out here.'

'I'll be certain that doesna' happen.'

From anyone else she might have taken his words as bravado, but the determination in both his voice and his face gave her a modicum of comfort, even as her heart sank at the sight of the next hill rising before them. The track disappeared up into the clouds. Who knew what lay ahead.

It was the steepest hill they'd encountered so far. 'We'd best walk the horses again,' Mr Gilvry said, dismounting in a swirl of coat. 'They need to rest, but we canna stop if we are to make shelter by nightfall.'

He reached up and lifted her down as he did each time she needed to dismount. Again the heat of his touch warmed her through and through. It was all in her mind, of course, there were layers and layers of clothing between his skin and hers, but it was the only bright spot in a very dreary day.

She smiled her thanks when he set her on her feet and received a nod in reply. A very cool nod, indeed. He was clearly regretting his agreement to escort her to the duke. But he'd given his word and he would keep it. Knowing he at least was a man of his word gave her comfort. A sense of security she had not known in a long time.

And that was a mistake. She'd thought the same about Samuel and look how that had ended. And if this trip to Mere ended the same way, she was going to be in dire straits indeed since Mrs Preston, rather than extending her leave of absence, had terminated her employment.

All her reliance was now on the generosity of the Duke of Mere.

They walked in silence, one behind the other for a while. Rowena turned to look back down the hill. There was no sign of the cart in the mist that had closed in around them.

'Shouldn't we wait for them?' she called out.

'They'll catch us up at the crest,' he replied. 'I'll make tea to warm us and have it ready when they arrive.'

That was the other thing she found strange about him. The way he carried an assortment of objects in his saddlebag, as if he was used to living in the wilds. A handful of oats. A tin kettle to make tea. And of course the leaves. No milk, though. Just a flask of whisky from which he added a splash to the brew. It certainly warmed her from the inside out and she found herself looking forward to their arrival at the top of the hill.

The Pockles also carried supplies in the cart—

bread, cheese, some oatcakes—but Mr Gilvry's tea was the best of all of it.

They had plodded upwards for what felt like a good half an hour. At this rate they would be lucky to make the last five miles to the next inn before it was dark.

At the top, catching her breath, Rowena looked around her, but there was nothing to see. Just a rolling blanket of white and a barely visible track disappearing downwards. Disappointing, really. She'd been looking forward to seeing the Highlands in all their glory. But it really was the wrong time of year for travel. She shivered and pulled her cloak tighter around her.

Mr Gilvry set about making a fire from a clump of peat he had picked up somewhere along the way, or perhaps taken from the inn where they stayed the previous night. The inn had only one bedchamber. Everyone else was expected to sleep in the commons. Mr Gilvry had preferred the stables. She didn't really blame him. The driver and his wife were a nice enough couple, if a little dour, but they were not as particular about their cleanliness as they might have been. She would not have wanted to spend a night with them in close quarters.

It didn't take him long to get the fire started and, while the small can heated over the flame, she bent to warm her numb fingers against the heat.

'I wish I understood what game the duke is playing,' she said softly. He crouched beside her on his heels. He looked so comfortable she thought about trying it.

'The only way to find out is to meet him face-to-face,' he said.

'If he will meet with me.'

'I canna see why he would not?'

No, she could not either, but there was something odd about the way Mr Jones had insisted they make this journey. And then there was the issue of the date of Samuel's death. Not just the lawyer's swift change of mind, but the way Mr Gilvry had stiffened at the mention of proof.

The water started to boil and she stepped back from the fire to give him room to brew his concoction. A few moments later, he held out a small pewter mug. She wrapped her gloved fingers around it and breathed in the steam. Bitter tea and whisky. While she sipped and felt the warmth slide down her throat, she stared into the mist. What sort of house would a duke have set aside for the wife of a distant relative? If she couldn't sell it, and Samuel had not after all left her some money, would she be stuck out here in the Highlands for the rest of her life?

It seemed likely. Unless she married again.

She glanced at Mr Gilvry. He was looking back the way they had come with a frown. And then the jingle of a bridle pierced the muffling mist and the next moment the cart and its occupants came into view.

Mr Gilvry collected the Pockles' mugs and filled them from the kettle. He kicked out the fire and stamped on the embers. 'We'll keep going, aye?' he said to Pockle. 'We don't want to be out here at nightfall.'

'That we don't,' said Pockle, cradling his mug just as Rowena had done and blowing on it to cool it. 'Old McRae willna' open the door to us if we arrive after sunset.'

Mr Gilvry glared at him. 'Why did you say nothing of this before?'

Pockle shrugged. 'We were making good time. Nae need to distress the lady for naught.'

Mrs Pockle took a deep swallow from her mug and made a little sound of satisfaction. Rowena had the feeling she cared more about the whisky than the tea. 'Auld McRae is afraid of the piskies hereabouts,' she announced. 'Locks up tight come the dark.'

Mr Gilvry made no comment, but she could see the irritation in his expression. Not a man to believe in piskies, then.

'We'd best be moving on,' he said. He took her mug, tossed the dregs and wrapped it in a cloth, before throwing her back in the saddle. 'We'll make the best use of the downhill slope to make up a little time.'

'I'll catch ye up,' Pockle said. 'I've a need to empty my bladder.' He handed his empty mug to his wife and jumped down.

'Dinna be taking too long, man,' Mr Gilvry said. 'We'll wait for you at McRae's place and I'll be sure of letting ye in, dark or no.'

Pockle touched a hand to his cap.

'Don't you think it would be better if we all

stayed together?' Rowena said. 'What if we get lost? Pockle knows the way.'

'I won't get lost.' Mr Gilvry growled. 'I looked at the map before we left.'

He mounted up and grabbed for Rowena's reins. 'But you might.' He glanced up at the sky. 'The sooner we get going, the sooner we will arrive.'

Normally she would not have considered letting a man lead her along like a child, but the worry in his eyes made such pride a foolish luxury. 'Just be careful, Mr Gilvry,' she said coolly. 'I would not like to follow you off a cliff.'

His sharp stare said the prospect was not out of the realm of possibility and her stomach dipped. So much for trying to strike a lighter note. Something that actually never seemed possible with this particular man, any more than it had been with Samuel.

She sighed. *Say nothing, and then you can't possibly go wrong.*

His horse moved ahead and hers followed at his tug on the bridle. After a few minutes of them heading downhill, big wet flakes drifted down to settle on her shoulders and her horse's neck. They melted almost at once.

Mr Gilvry muttered something under his breath. A curse, no doubt. She felt like cursing herself. Instead, she ducked deeper into her hood.

After a time, the numbness in her fingers and toes spread inwards. She blew on her fingers with little hope it would help and lifted her head to peer ahead, then she wished she hadn't. A gust of windblown snow stung her cheeks. But even that swift glimpse told her night was closing in fast.

Mr Gilvry stopped. Were they lost? Her heart began a sharp staccato in her chest.

She let her horse come up alongside his.

'Lights,' he said, leaning close so she could hear him through the muffling scarf he'd pulled up around his face.

The breath left her body in such a rush, she felt light-headed. 'McRae's?'

He nodded and urged his horse forward at a trot. Her mount followed suit.

He'd been right. He did know the way. She'd have to apologise for her doubts once they were warm and dry.

The inn stood alone, off to one side of the track they'd been following, a lantern lighting its sign. A golden glow spilled from the windows, making square patches of snow glitter as if dusted with stars.

Mr Gilvry helped her down from her horse. Not only light issued forth from the inn, there was sound, too. The sound of men talking and laughing. She glanced up at Mr Gilvry and, while she could not see his face, she could see his eyes narrow.

'It seems we are not the only company tonight,' she said.

'Aye. Wait here. I'll see the landlord about a room.' He thrust the reins into her hands and ducked as he opened the door.

'*Duin an dòras,*' someone shouted.

Gaelic. Someone not pleased about the draught from the door being opened. The door slammed shut. Rowena glanced around. The stables must be at the back of the inn, but no one had come to take their horses. Perhaps she should take them herself. She was so cold, the wind biting through her cloak, even the thought of a stable was a lure.

Before she could make a move, Mr Gilvry returned with a man and a woman with a shawl over her head in tow. The man, a spry fellow, regarded her with interest before relieving her of the reins. 'While I help yon lad with the horses, Mrs McRae will see you upstairs.'

The woman gestured for her to follow. 'This way, ma'am. There's a nice warm fire ready and waiting.'

Warmth. What more could she ask? She started to follow.

Mr Gilvry caught her arm, turned her around and brought her close, grasping her by her elbows and lifting her on her toes so she could see the glitter of the lamp over the door in his eyes. 'The men in there are a dangerous lot,' he murmured close to her ear. 'Do not look their way.'

Then he kissed her. Full on the lips. A warm dry pressure on her mouth. The heat of his breath on her frozen cheek, the thud of his heart beneath her fingertips where they rested on the side of his throat.

He broke away, gazing down at her, his expression dark, his mouth sensuously soft. She must have imagined it, because he set her away from him with a laugh as if it was she who had kissed him.

Stunned, she stared at him and her hand fell to her side.

He swung her around, pushing her forward with a tap on the rump. 'Ye'll be saving that for later, lassie.' He turned away, dragging her horse behind him.

Lassie? Later. What on earth...? She touched her lips still tingling from his unexpected kiss.

The landlady laughed. 'That's one cheeky lad ye have there for a husband.'

Husband? And so the goodwife might think after such a display. Her heart knocking against her ribs, whether out of fear for what she would find inside that he needed to warn her in such an odd way or the effect of that kiss, she didn't quite know.

Right now she didn't care about anything as long as she ended up close to the warmth of a fire. Later, though, when she wasn't too cold to think—cold on the outside, that was—she intended to discover just what sort of game he thought he was playing.

As she entered the inn, she realised he was right about the men in what must be the only bar-room in the house. She had a brief impression of three burly males filling the low-beamed room, all looking at her. She kept her gaze firmly fixed on the landlady's back and mounted the stairs to a low rumble of male appreciation.

'Dinna mind them, missus,' the landlady said in comfortable tones, opening the door to a chamber at the end of a short corridor at the top of the stairs. 'McRae won't put up wi' any o' their nonsense.'

She hoped not.

Mrs McRae ushered her into a chamber that barely had room for a bed, a settle by the hearth and a table with two chairs in the corner.

The woman turned down the sheets and gave the bed a pat. 'And that man of yours is more than a match for them, aye?' She chuckled.

Rowena narrowed her eyes at the woman. Now, what should she say to that? Deny that Mr Gilvry was her man, or wait for his explanation? Discretion was no doubt the better part of valour in this circumstance.

'Take off your cloak, my dear,' the landlady urged. 'I'll send up my Sin to help you out of those wet clothes in a minute or two.' And with that she whisked out, shutting the door behind her.

Sin. Well, there was an interesting name. She

removed her bonnet and tossed it on the bed, then unfastened her cloak and hung it over the settle where it could dry. She held her hands out to the fire and watched the steam rise off her skirts.

A knock at the door heralded the arrival of Sin, who turned out to be a pretty, blue-eyed, auburn-haired girl of about eighteen. As pretty as sin indeed.

She bobbed a curtsy. 'Mam says I'm to help you undress, mistress.'

'I'm afraid my luggage is still somewhere behind us on the road. I have nothing dry to change into.'

The girl gave her a grin. 'Your man said as how you was to take off your wet things and wrap yourself in the quilt.' She pointed at the bed.

'My man,' Rowena said drily. What on earth were the Pockles going to think when they arrived with the landlady calling Mr Gilvry her man? And what if it came to the duke's ears? She pressed her lips together against the urge to deny that Mr Gilvry was her man. She would let him explain, before she took him to task.

The girl scurried around behind her and began attacking her laces. 'Very positive he was about it, my lady, you being so damp and all. He feared you might take a chill. Said I was to get you out of these wet things, no matter what you said.'

'How very forceful,' Rowena said, wryly imagining Mr Gilvry dishing out orders and feeling a little shiver pass down her spine.

'Oh, yes,' the girl said, coming around to the front to help her unpin her bodice. 'Very forceful he was.' She giggled.

A strong urge to bash the girl over the head with a poker arose in Rowena's breast. Though why that would be, she had no idea. She didn't care in the least if Mr Gilvry made an innkeeper's daughter giggle. She probably hadn't seen his face. Oh, now that was mean.

'Was it a duel?' the girl asked. She sounded breathless. Too breathless for the effort to undo a few tapes on a gown.

'Was what a duel?'

'The scar. Was it a duel over a woman?' She sighed in the most nauseating way.

'I have no idea,' Rowena said repressively and stepped out of the gown. 'I have never asked him.'

'He must have been a right bonnie lad before...' The maid's voice tailed off.

Furious, and not knowing why, Rowena turned her back to give the maid access her stays. 'Do you think so?' She could not keep emotion from colouring her voice.

'I beg your pardon, ma'am. Not that he isn't bonnie now, of course. Lovely wide shoulders and those green eyes of his. They almost make up for the scar. We don't get many handsome young gentlemen passing through these parts.' The girl sighed.

'Are you done?'

The girl dropped the stays on top of the gown and picked up the counterpane. 'If you will just wrap this around you,' she said, 'I'll unpin your hair and gi' it a good brushing.'

Chapter Four

Drew followed the stableman, his head reeling. What the hell had he been thinking, kissing her like that? He'd just wanted to impress on her the importance of his words, and then the way she'd looked up at him, so sinfully tempting and ready to argue, it was all he could think of.

No doubt she'd be having his hide for that piece of foolishness. And for saying he was her husband. But the moment he saw the men inside the inn, he'd known they were trouble. His suspicions were confirmed by what he saw around him. The stables were full to the brim with ponies and stacked with barrels.

The three men in the common room were smugglers, and a rougher-looking lot he hoped never to see. The storm must have brought them in, because if things remained as they had been before he left for America, they would usually avoid any place where the gaugers might visit. There would be no excisemen out on a night like tonight.

It was a damnable nuisance that Pockle had been unable to keep up. It would have evened the odds.

Drew jerked his chin in the direction of the inn. 'Where are the men from?'

The little man's face closed up tighter than a Scotsman's purse. 'You'll find no loose tongues here, sir, but since you are a true Highland gentleman, I can tell you they work for McKenzie out of Edinburgh. A rough lot, I can tell you that. You would do as well to keep an eye on that wife of yours.'

Drew nodded and made a show of pulling his pistol from his saddle holster and tucking it in his belt along with powder and shot.

He glanced up to find the man watching him. 'Aye, well, I'm a man who kens how to look after his own.'

The little man grinned. 'As well to be safe as sorry, they do say.'

The cold feeling in Drew's chest expanded.

Pockle should never have suggested they stay at a known smugglers' haunt. They should have stopped earlier in the day.

'You can leave the horses to me,' the groom said. 'I'll look in on them later. You'd best keep an eye on that woman of yours and get yourself warm.' He gave Drew a nudge in the ribs.

Drew gritted his teeth at the thought of the impending chilly reception. He should not have let himself be tempted.

'Is there a back door into the inn?' he asked the groom.

'Aye, straight across. You'll go through the kitchen.' He winked. 'There's but one set of stairs.'

Drew didn't much like the sound of that. It was always good to have more than one way out. He picked up their saddlebags and heaved them over one shoulder, leaving one hand free to use his pistol. He just hoped he wouldn't need it.

He crossed from the stables to the back door of the inn. The goodwife was busy at the hearth, a pot bubbling with stew. It didn't smell too bad and right now he really didn't think he cared what was in it as long as it was hot and filling.

She waved her ladle at him. 'I'll be up wi' your dinner in a minute or two.'

He entered the taproom. Only one man seemed to be taking any real interest. His eyes narrowed when they caught sight of Drew's pistol. A grim sense of satisfaction filled him. At least they knew he was not easy pickings. Still, he didn't trust them an inch.

He had nothing against smugglers. He'd dealt with enough of them in the old days. He'd been one. But these men were different. Harder eyed and not Highlanders by their speech.

He sauntered between them to the bar along one wall. 'I'll take a bottle of whisky and two glasses,' he said to the landlord.

'Yes, sir,' the portly, red-faced fellow said, reaching under his counter.

One of the men behind him sniggered. 'Wi' that face you likely have to get her drunk before she'll have ought to do wi' ye.'

Drew turned and faced the room, fists loose but ready. 'If you have something to say, you can say it to my ugly face.'

The oldest man in the room eyed him for a moment, then nodded an acknowledgement. He shoved at a scrawny-looking fellow with a straggling beard. 'Yon Roger's had a wee bitty too much to drink,' he said. 'Haven't you, Roger?'

Roger looked sullen, but at another shove nodded and disappeared into his tankard.

'You'll have your men keep a civil tongue in their heads, man,' the landlord said from behind Drew. 'Or I'll be sending you back out in the snow.'

Drew grinned. 'I wouldn't be asking a dog to go out in that, lads.' He turned back to the innkeeper. 'Give them all a dram on me.'

The mood in the room lightened considerably. Drew picked up the bottle and glasses and raised it in salute, strolling out of the bar as three men rushed forward. Sugar was better than vinegar any day of the week. Not that he'd trust any of them.

He didn't take his eyes off them as he climbed the bottom steps, just to be sure he didn't get a knife in the back. Roger turned and met his gaze. He had the look of a man who was trying to solve a puzzle.

Drew halted. 'Is something else wrong?'

The man shook his head. 'I just had the feeling I've seen you before.'

Drew raised a brow. 'People don't usually forget my face.'

The man grimaced with distaste. 'You never had the scar last time I saw you.'

The hairs on Drew's nape rose. Was it possible he had met this man in his smuggling days? 'You are mistaken, my friend. Sorry.' He continued up the stairs, but from the feeling between his shoulder blades, the man watched him until he was out of sight.

He'd known a lot of people in the trade in the old days. Him and Ian. But he could not think of a reason why any of them would hold a grudge.

He knocked on the door of the chamber assigned to him and Mrs MacDonald.

'Who is it?'

At least she had sense enough not to just open the door without checking. 'Drew.'

'Just a moment.'

A rustle of skirts, the door swung back, opened by a maid, but his gaze went straight to the figure kneeling by the hearth, wrapped in a cotton cover, and his mind ceased working. Her unpinned hair hung down her back, as sleek and as shiny a chestnut as would do a thoroughbred proud.

There was something extraordinarily intimate about seeing a woman with her hair down around her shoulders. And on her knees, too. His body responded as if she'd offered him the most personal of attentions. He almost groaned out loud at the blaze of heat scorching through his blood. At this rate, he wasn't going to need the fire to get warm. Disgusted by his reaction, he dropped the saddlebags off to one side and set the whisky and the glasses on the table.

'Out,' he said to the maid.

Mrs MacDonald rose up on her knees and turned to look at him, surprise on her face.

Drew looked at the maid. 'If you don't mind?' he said as politely as he could manage.

The little lass bustled past him.

Drew closed and locked the door, using the moment to repress the wicked images his mind had conjured up.

'Mrs McRae will be along shortly wi' our supper,' he said, annoyed by the hoarseness in his voice.

She put her hands on her hips. 'Well, well, if it isn't my dear husband.' Her eyes sparkled like water running over pebbles in a brook. Anger or amusement. Whichever it was, it made a breath catch in his throat; she looked so lovely with her hair hanging about her shoulders and her cheeks flushed by the warmth from the fire.

He strode for the window and opened it.

The wind gusted in, bringing with it a whirl of snowflakes and a chill to his overheated blood.

'What on earth are you doing?' she asked, her voice rising in pitch.

'Admiring the view,' he said over his shoulder. And checking for a way out should it be needed. The kitchen roof jutted out a few feet below. An easy climb down to the ground.

He took a deep breath, closed the window and turned back to face her. 'I'm sorry I had to tell them we were wed. I couldna' leave you up here alone with that lot staying below.'

Her lips thinned. 'And I suppose you are sorry you had to kiss me, too.'

Heat travelled up his neck. 'It was necessary, but, aye, I'm sorry.'

The apology didn't seem to mollify her one little bit.

He jerked his chin at her saddlebag. 'Is there something dry in there you can change into?'

She glanced down at the bag and then up at him. 'Only my nightgown. I wasn't expecting to put up at an inn without my luggage, which is now with the Pockles who, by the way, will be surprised to find us calling ourselves man and wife.'

The Pockles were another worry. They could not have been more than a half hour or so behind them, so they should have arrived by now. He didn't see any reason to let her know his concern, though.

He shrugged. 'We'll cross that bridge when we come to it.'

A rap sounded at the door. 'Who is it?' he asked, one hand going to his pistol.

Rowena's eyes widened and he cursed himself for a fool for putting fear in her eyes.

'Mrs McRae, dearie,' the landlady called out. 'With your supper tray.'

'Leave it outside the door. I'll fetch it in when I'm dressed,' Drew said. He moved to the door, listening first to the sound of the tray hitting the floor, then the woman's footsteps moving away. He pulled his pistol and unlocked it with his left hand, ready to leap clear.

Slowly he opened the door. The sound of men's laughter wafted up the stairs.

His instincts told him there was no one there, but still he glanced up and down the hallway before tucking away his pistol and bending to pick up the tray. He set it down on the nearby chest of drawers.

Thank goodness the common room was in the front of the house and this chamber was at the back or, with that racket, there'd be no chance of sleeping.

Rowena gave him a narrow-eyed look. She nodded at the pistol. 'You really do think we are in danger, then?'

'Aye.' He kicked the door closed and turned the key.

The look on her face said it wasn't enough to make her feel safe. He breathed out through his nose, summoning calm. 'They are smugglers.'

'Oh,' she said. 'Not good.'

'As a general rule, I would no' be concerned.

They go about their business and as long as no one interferes...' He shook his head. 'These men have a different look about them.' Not to mention the one who thought he knew him.

'Not your normal run-of-the-mill smugglers, then.'

He couldn't help but smile at the no-nonsense tone of voice, as if she dealt with such criminals on a daily basis. And he had the feeling, if he was truthful, she wouldn't flinch if they did turn up at the door. 'No. Not run-of-the-mill at all. And when I explain why we are sharing a room to the Pockles, they will understand.' He hoped, because if they didn't he was going to find himself with a duke who might feel vengeful. An angry duke might be worse than an inn full of smugglers. And they were quite bad enough.

Another tête-à-tête meal with Mr Gilvry. Rowena felt a rush of warmth in her belly. This time, he rearranged the table so he sat beside her, instead of opposite, presenting his profile. Unlike last time, when she had dressed in her best, she was wrapped in a blanket and he was posing as her husband.

Why?

Was it possible he had deliberately separated her from their escort? After that kiss she might almost believe it, if it wasn't for his mortifying apology.

She was not the sort of woman a man wanted to kiss of his own free will. He'd used it as a pretence to give her instructions. The logical side of the brain applauded his cleverness. Her foolish heart contracted painfully every time she recalled his harsh apology.

Perhaps he wished he could be downstairs, kissing pretty little Sin.

Anger and disappointment rose in her throat, threatening to choke her. Anger at her own stupid thoughts, surely.

But she knew she was lying to herself. She found him attractive.

No matter. There was no use in feeling wounded. It hadn't done any good with Samuel, or her cousin. It would be no different with this man. She just wasn't the sort of woman to engender strong feelings in a man. Instead of worrying about such nonsense, she would use the opportunity to find out more about her escort. Mr Gilvry could hardly walk away, given he had taken it upon himself to remain on guard in her room. And while she didn't dare trust him completely, she trusted the smugglers a whole lot less.

Pulling the counterpane tight around her shoulders, she let him seat her at the table. 'It does smell surprisingly good.'

'Aye.'

'Will you say grace?' It was a habit to ask her pupils to do so, so it came naturally out of her mouth.

Surprise flickered across his face, then something that looked like embarrassment before he bowed his head. 'Thank you, Lord, for this food and for bringing us safe to this place.'

She added a silent prayer that they might leave it in one piece. 'Amen.'

He picked up a bread roll.

'Do you think the duke is aware that one of his tenants entertains smugglers?'

He glanced up, his expression unreadable. 'Probably.'

She huffed out a breath and picked up her own spoon.

'What?' he asked, still looking at her.

There was no point. When a man didn't want to tell you something, asking questions only made him more determined to remain silent. 'Nothing.'

He gave her an irritated look and broke the roll apart with long strong, fingers. 'You asked and I answered.'

'You said *probably* as if you meant *of course*.' Dash it, why was she explaining? Giving him the opportunity to put her in her womanly place?

His sideways glance showed surprise, as if he hadn't expected her to realise he was trying to protect her. 'Smuggling is a matter of survival in the Highlands. A great lord might not admit to it, but he'd be a fool if he didn't know. He probably buys his whisky from them, too.'

The truth. 'But why, if it is such a normal thing, do you think they mean us harm?'

He sighed. 'One of them thinks he knows me. And it is no' a happy reunion.'

'Does he know you?'

'No.'

This time she believed him. She glanced at the door he had locked so carefully and recalled the pistol he had to hand in his waistband. 'Do you have another gun?'

His eyebrows shot up. 'Can you use a pistol?'

'No. Surely it can't be so very difficult?' Even the stupidest men seemed to manage it.

He gave a short laugh, but there was no humour in it. 'I have no wish to be shot by mistake, thank you verra much.'

'But you are worried about their intentions.'

'Persistent wee thing, aren't you?'

She should have been a bit more persistent in her refusal to accept Samuel's suit. If she hadn't been so unhappy in her cousin's house... Not true. After her first refusal Samuel had made it his mission to gain her hand. She'd never had a chance. The lure of marriage and what she took for love had been far too tempting. But she had learned her lesson. Hadn't she?

'Do you think they will attack us?'

'Honestly, I dinna ken.'

Her jaw dropped. What a surprise. A man admitting he was unsure about something?

He touched his cheek and shook his head. 'I canna understand why this man thinks he knows me.'

'What happened to your face? Were you attacked by some sort of animal?'

His face shuttered.

She winced. 'I beg your pardon. It is none of my business. It is not so bad, when one becomes accustomed—'

'I am in no need of soothing words, ma'am. I see how I look every time I shave.'

'Then we are both accustomed,' she flashed back.

He gave her a look that was neither irritated nor friendly and resumed eating. He ate quickly, something she had noticed before, as if it might be his last meal.

Taking a chance on his apparent lack of ire, she decided to plunge on with her questions, albeit in a different direction.

'Mr Gilvry, you never really said what it was that you were doing in the mountains of North Carolina when you met my husband.'

His expression darkened as if the question was unwelcome, yet not unexpected. He glanced at her face and then her bowl of untouched stew. 'Eat first and I will tell you.'

Or would he find yet another excuse to avoid her questions? 'I find I am not all that hungry.' Her stomach growled, giving her the lie.

He gave her an I-told-you-so look. He was very good at looks that spoke volumes. She tasted the stew. It was as good as it smelled. Thick rich gravy. Tender meat and plenty of vegetables. 'The inn must be doing well to provide such an excellent meal.'

'Likely it's a regular stop for those in the trade. They pay well for silence.'

'You know a great deal about the smuggling trade.'

She was surprised when he answered, 'Aye. I used to be one. Before I went to America.'

She closed her mouth on a gasp. 'I am surprised you admit to it so freely,' she said as calmly as she could manage. 'Were you... I mean, is that why you went to America?'

'Was I transported there, you mean?'

So much for being tactful. 'That is precisely what I mean.'

He leaned back. 'I wasna' transported for any crime by the government.' His tone was bitter. 'I had no choice but to go, however.'

'Oh.' His tone did not encourage further questions. But that didn't mean she wasn't going to ask. Not at all.

He pushed his chair back from the table. His roll had disappeared and so had his stew, whereas she had eaten only a few mouthfuls.

'Well?'

'Eat your meal, Mrs MacDonald.' He got up and went to the hearth, crouching down and poking at the fire as if it had gone out, instead of being the merry blaze it was.

He was no doubt regretting saying as much as he had. And it really was none of her business. She ate the rest of her stew and finally sat back, completely sated.

'That was good.'

He glanced at her plate. 'Will you no' eat your bread?'

'I couldn't eat another bite. You can have it if you wish.'

He picked up the bread, but did not eat it. He tucked it into his saddlebag. 'Would you care for a dram?'

A splash of *usquebaugh* in tea to keep out the cold was one thing, but it was a long time since she'd enjoyed a glass for its own sake. Her father had never drunk anything else and had often invited Rowena to join him in a wee glass after dinner. As a governess, she never drank.

'I would love a dram.' She got up, drew the counterpane carefully around her and went to join him at the fire, taking up residence on the settle. She couldn't help thinking of those evenings with her father. He had been such a kindly man and had never belittled her abilities. While he was ill, he had come to trust her with his business. All that had changed when he died. She'd become nothing but a spinster relative to be accommodated under her cousin's roof.

If she had known what Samuel would do with her half of the factory, she would have run a mile. She should have listened to her head instead of her heart. Well, she certainly wasn't going to make that mistake again.

He poured them both a drink and lifted his glass in a toast. *'Sláinte.'*

'Good health.'

They sipped their drinks in silence.

Steam was rising from his trousers below his knees, just as it had risen from her skirts. 'You are still wet,' she said.

He glanced down and shrugged. 'Looks like

I'll be dry soon enough. My change of clothes is also in the wagon.'

Now mist was curling up from his coat. It would take for ever to dry. 'Perhaps the landlord could loan you his shirt.'

He shook his head.

'What if you take a chill? You can't sit there soaking wet.'

'Surely you aren't suggesting I strip down to my skin?' There was a mocking note in his voice, but the very thought of it made her insides melt. How infuriating that he would plant such a picture in her mind.

'At least take your coat off and get nearer to the fire,' she said crossly.

He huffed out a breath, stripped out of his coat and went to fetch one of the dining chairs, which he set on the other side of the hearth. He hung the coat over the back. 'Will this do?'

'And the waistcoat.'

He took that off, too, hung it up and came back to sit beside her.

'Satisfied?'

She eyed his trousers. 'You really should…'

He put up a hand. 'No, I really should not.'

'Stubborn man.'

'Aye, that may be so.' He breathed deeply through his nose. 'I thought you wanted to hear my story?'

She stilled. 'I do.'

'Then cease your fashing and I'll tell you. Though there is little to tell, Mrs MacDonald.'

'Would you very much mind calling me Rowena? It is dreadfully hard hearing Samuel's name every time someone speaks.'

He looked...guilty. What reason did he have for guilt?

He turned his face away, staring into the fire, his sculpted jaw softened by its glow, and flames flickering in the depths of his eye as if he was peering into hell.

'Verra well. Rowena,' he murmured.

It sounded beautiful the way he said it. Softly. As if he was tasting the syllables on his tongue. Her insides clenched, sending a wave of desire rippling through her body. And now he was looking at her with something akin to horror. Self-disgust washed through her and she looked down at her hands. What on earth was wrong with her?

She'd never had trouble containing her desires before now.

She clasped her fingers to keep her hands steady.

In the ensuing silence she glanced up at him and saw that his gaze was very far away. He seemed to be gathering his thoughts. His expression said they were painful. It was hard to imagine such a hard man feeling emotional pain.

She held her breath and waited for him to speak.

'I had been living in the mountains for some time. I made up my mind it was time to leave. To take control of my life.' His voice sounded a little strained. As if the memories were painful.

At her look of puzzlement, he shrugged. 'When an opportunity presented itself, I headed for the coast. Then I heard sounds of the Indians attacking your husband's camp. By the time I got there only your husband was alive. He told me he was on his way back to Scotland when he'd heard that this group of Indians had gold and knew where to find it.'

He looked her straight in the eye. 'As I understand it, he thought to trade brandy for information.'

At her blank look, he shook his head. 'Even a dolt knows that Indians have no head for strong liquor. They become wild and aggressive.'

'So they attacked him?'

'Not at first. They were too drunk to do more than pass out. But the next day, when they saw he had left, taking the rest of the drink with him, they were no' verra pleased.'

An understatement if ever she heard one. 'They followed him?'

'Aye. I arrived too late to be of any assistance. I'm verra sorry.'

'His foolish actions were hardly your fault.'

Her words, intended to absolve, seemed only to add to the pain in his eyes.

'If I had arrived sooner—'

'They might have killed you, too,' she said.

He blinked and looked as if he thought that might have been preferable.

A pain stabbed at her heart. 'I won't hear another word of you taking the blame for my husband's stupidity.'

He turned his head away and looked into the fire as if he could see the events playing out before his eyes. 'By the time I got to the camp, the

Indians had taken what they came for and left everyone for dead.'

'The brandy,' she whispered.

'That they drank as soon as they found it. They took the horses, clothes, money, trinkets. Anything that took their fancy. They are a bit like children in that regard. They left some things. Mostly papers. They were crazy with drink again by then. Everyone in the camp was dead, I thought.' He shook his head. 'I was leaving when I heard a noise from the bushes. Somehow, they'd missed him. I pulled him clear. The wound was in his belly.' He glanced at her. 'There was nothing I could do. I thought if I could get him to a white...to a doctor... Charlotte was closest. I carried him. It was slow going. I could hardly believe he was still alive when I made camp that first night.'

She sighed. 'Go on.'

'We talked. He was in a lot of pain. Mostly he talked and I listened. He spoke about his wife.' He gave her a sideways look.

'What did he say?' She steeled herself.

'Your name. That he had some regrets.'

She gave a small laugh at that statement. Samuel had suffered regrets from the moment the knot was tied.

'He was determined to get back to Scotland. To make amends, he said. I swore I would see that he did.'

It was hard to believe that Samuel would have cared one way or the other about her. And in his last moments, too. The thought brought tears to her eyes. Tears of regret that she hadn't been the kind of wife he had wanted.

'The rest you know,' he said.

Looking at his expressionless face, she was certain he was holding something back, telling her only what he thought she needed to know.

Out of kindness? Or was there something more to his reticence? And did she really need to know all the gory details? It couldn't possibly impact on her current predicament.

He pushed slowly to his feet, as if he carried a heavy weight. 'I am thinking it is time to sleep. Tomorrow will be another hard day.'

Suddenly suspicious, she frowned. 'Where will you sleep?'

'In here. As your husband, I can hardly bed down in the common room or outside your door.

And besides, I've no intention of leaving you alone, even with the door locked.'

Her gaze strayed to the bed and her heart started to race. What would it be like to lie beside a strong virile man like him? Would he let her see him naked? Touch him. She put a hand to her throat.

'I'll be sleeping on the floor,' he said harshly as if guessing her thoughts and being repulsed.

He bent and picked up her saddlebag and tossed it beside the screen. 'Change behind there.'

'Yes,' she said, breathless. 'Yes, of course.' Flustered by the heat generated by her wayward thoughts, she ducked behind the screen and changed. When she came out, face washed, teeth cleaned, dressed in her nightgown and wrapped in the counterpane, he was standing at the window, staring into the dark.

It was almost as if he'd forgotten her presence.

She hopped into bed and drew the covers up to her chin. 'I left some clean water in the jug,' she said. 'And you might as well have the counterpane as a cover.' She hesitated. 'If you would like.'

'Thank you.' His voice was grim. He must really be regretting agreeing to this journey, she thought dismally. She tossed the cover on to the floor and pulled the sheet up over her head. The least she could do was give him some privacy.

And she didn't dare let him catch her peeking.

Chapter Five

Lying on the hard floor beside the bed in the dark, Drew didn't know which was worse, listening to her get ready for bed and imagining her baring the slim body that he'd felt pressed against him for one brief instant out in the yard or glimpsing her chestnut locks spread out over a white pillow before she disappeared beneath the sheets.

And now there was the sound of her breathing inches from his head. His body ached at the thought of those sweetly curved lips and the image of soft little breasts rising and falling beneath the covers.

He couldn't believe how much his body wanted more of those swells and hollows. The sparks prickling along his skin every time he came within just a few feet of her were one thing. This more intimate sensual knowledge had added a new and higher pitch to his lust.

He clenched the counterpane tight in his fists and rolled on his side, facing away from her. He didn't want to find her attractive. He was his own man now, with no fetters or ties. That was how he wanted his life, and the sooner he left her with the duke, the better.

If he hadn't said he was her husband, he could have spent the night in the common room, drinking with the other men. And fighting if he had to, though he had no recollection of the man who had looked at him with such rancour. It might be a case of mistaken identity. He rubbed his fingers over his scar, feeling the raised and twisted welts. Hardly likely.

No matter what, their kind of trouble was far more welcome than what he risked in this room. But if he was busy defending himself, there would be no one looking after Rowena. He didn't dare take the chance of leaving her alone with a gang of cut-throats nearby.

He huffed out a breath. No doubt he'd have some explaining to do when he left her with the duke. There was no way around it, given that the innkeeper was the duke's tenant, not to mention what the Pockles would hear when they arrived.

Thank goodness she was a widow. At least he wouldn't be facing down an angry husband. Or worse yet, the father of an unmarried lass with a wedding on his mind. But the knowledge that she was a widow, an experienced woman, was a temptation he didn't need. Disgust at his weakness writhed like a monster in his gut.

He forced himself to breathe deeply. To listen to the sounds of the night, the way he had done so often in the vast forests. The sounds of the men below filtered through the floorboards. The carousing seemed to have tapered off. There was only the occasional mutter or shout of laughter. No doubt they would slip beneath the tables as drink overcame them. It was why he had ordered the whisky. The inn's comforting warmth would also do its work, since this sort of man usually slept out of doors. He could remember his own nights travelling the Highlands with contraband. He and Ian had thought it such an adventure, they hadn't cared about the cold and the damp. But they'd been young then, and carefree.

Was Ian still smuggling brandy for Carrick? The men downstairs would likely know. McKenzie's men from Edinburgh, the stableman had said. He wasn't familiar with the name, but no doubt the people involved had changed over the years. What they did was the same as it had always been.

He had been tempted to go back downstairs and ask after his brothers, but it seemed he'd already aroused suspicions enough. And besides, what was the point of torturing himself with thoughts of a family who had banished him out of their lives? Aye, or with recollections of an older brother who had arranged for his death? He gritted his teeth as the old pain of it squeezed the air out of his lungs.

No, he'd find out soon enough what was happening with his family when he had delivered Rowena and her husband's remains to Mere.

He forced himself to relax, to let the dark enter his mind, to welcome the oblivion of sleep.

A soft sound brought him upright, hand on the pistol he had primed and placed at his side before lying down. A whimper. From the bed. She was dreaming. No doubt she was seeing his face in her dreams. It would be enough to make anyone cry out.

She turned over.

He could see only her outline in the light from the candle, a lock of hair hanging over the side of the bed. His fingers itched to stroke its silky length.

She screamed.

He leaped to his feet and leaned over her. She was panting and fighting the bed sheets.

'Rowena,' he said, his mouth close to her ear, his nose filling with the scent of soap and warm woman. Lust surged. He bit back a curse. 'Rowena.' He shook her shoulder.

She opened her mouth. He cut off the scream with his palm. Her head thrashed back and forth, her fingers clawed at his hand. Scratching at his wrist.

'Rowena,' he said in an urgent whisper. 'Stop. It's me. Drew.'

Her eyes opened, dazed, confused. Her breathing rapid, her body trembling with fear.

Slowly he lifted his hand.

'It is you,' she murmured. Her voice cracked on the last word, tears welling.

'Yes,' he said, 'You were having a bad dream.'

Staring at him, she took a few deep breaths and sat up. 'You were trying to smother me.'

He reared back at the accusation in her voice. 'You screamed. Another one and we'd have had that lot from downstairs knocking on the door offering assistance.' Or asking to participate. 'You didn't want that, did you?'

'Oh.' Her eyes cleared as if she was only now coming fully awake and conscious. 'No. Of course not.'

He let go a breath he didn't know he'd been holding. For a moment, when she'd looked at him in terror, it had given him an unpleasant, sickening sensation in the pit of his stomach. It receded and left a very fine appreciation for the way her breasts created two snowy mounds beneath her flimsy nightgown. Under his gaze, the peaks pearled, little hard nubs at the crest of high firm breasts the size of peaches.

She followed the direction of his gaze and her face flushed bright red.

He bit down hard on a string of curses and moved away from her, going to the hearth to rake at a perfectly smoored fire. After such violent treatment, he'd be lucky if it lasted until morning. He set to work putting it right, banking it so it would once more give off enough heat to keep the chill off the air, but not use all the fuel before it was time to rise.

'I'm sorry I woke you,' she said softly from the other side of the room.

'It must have been a pretty bad dream,' he said, standing up, satisfied with his efforts. He glanced her way and was surprised to see she had not pulled the sheets up, but instead was sitting with her arms around her knees, watching him with those cool grey eyes.

Blood stirred in his veins. His shaft responded to the quickening throb of his pulse. How did a woman who looked as stern as an angel of retribution able to see a man's sins rouse his passions so easily?

Because he was little better than an animal, he thought bitterly. *She* had roused him, too. Made him a slave to her desires. It had been the only way to survive.

He turned away, running a hand over the beard forming on his chin. *She*'d hated those bristles almost as much as he had hated her. But if he'd stayed with her, Samuel MacDonald would still be alive and his wife wouldn't be having nightmares likely brought on by all the details he'd revealed. And by hours of seeing nothing but his ugly face.

'I think you'll sleep better alone.' He picked up the cotton cover and headed for the door. 'I'll be right outside the door.'

'Drew,' she said, and while she spoke quietly there was a note of panic in her voice. 'Please. Don't go.'

Stunned at the sound of his name on her lips, he stared at her. She looked away, twisting the sheet in her fingers. 'I don't want to be alone right at this moment.' She lifted her gaze. 'Talk to me. I've slept enough.'

She'd slept all of four hours. But she was still upset. Those restless hands were trembling.

She gave a small self-mocking laugh. 'I'm sorry to make such a fuss about a dream. You need your rest. Please take no notice of my foolishness. And please don't go sleeping in a draughty corridor on my account. Indeed, take the bed. I will be quite happy to sit in the chair.'

She was babbling like a nervous child, but she

was smiling at him. A smile that made him think of kindness and courage. A smile that pushed back at the shadows he saw in her eyes.

'I'll no' be putting you out of your bed,' he said. 'But I'll stay, if that is your wish.'

'You are very kind, Mr Gilvry.'

So they were back on formal terms. As they should be, but he couldn't help liking the way his name sounded on her lips. It was a long time since anyone had called him Drew.

She had always called him her yellow dog. The others in the band had followed suit, when they called him anything at all.

Sometimes, in his head, he'd begun to think of himself that way, too.

He brought a chair from the table and set it near the bed. 'Do you want to tell me about your dream?'

She frowned. 'Something or someone was chasing me. That is all I remember.'

A common enough dream. A shaman might have read something into it, but Drew didn't believe in their heathen superstitions. Or not much anyway.

'What would you like to talk about?' He prayed

it wouldn't be more questions about her husband. He'd revealed far more than he intended over dinner. The lingering death. Their conversations. The man had been utterly callous with respect to his wife, only caring about the prospect of wealth. Nor did he want to reveal how he had slipped away from the band who had held him prisoner for two long years. It was their drunkenness that had given him the chance to escape. But he should have known that *she*'d want him back. They must have thought he'd try to join up with MacDonald. He'd known better, but it hadn't made any difference.

'Tell me more about you,' she said. 'Where you grew up. Your family.'

His blood ran cold. 'I'm no' a very interesting topic of conversation, I'm afraid.'

He slouched in the chair, trying to look at ease. It wasn't easy when he was still as hard as granite. 'Where to start?'

'Where in Scotland did you grow up?'

As topics went it was fairly neutral. 'My family is from Dunross, a small village north of Inverness. My father was the laird. And my brother after him.'

She straightened. 'You have a brother? I had the impression you were alone in the world.'

Curse intelligent females who listened to what you said. 'I have family, but they are not looking for me to return.'

'Why?'

Well, here was his chance to confess just what sort of man she'd been trusting. A way to serve up a bit of reality to keep her at a distance. Yet something held him back. Pride. He did not want her to think worse of him than she already did. And a measure of lingering shame. He had hurt Alice badly. He couldn't think about it without a nasty lurch in his stomach. He'd deserved his punishment. But he had not deserved to die for his mistake.

He shrugged. 'Let us say it was better for all that I left.'

'How long ago did you leave?' she asked softly.

Hell, if it was the year 1822 now, then it had to be... 'Six years.'

'And you haven't seen your family since?'

Hadn't seen them or heard from them. There had been no way to get in touch even if he had wanted to. And he hadn't. And when he did, it wasn't going to be pleasant.

He shook his head.

'And your parents?'

He winced inwardly. 'My father died years before I left. My ma—' It was hard to say it. He forced the words out. 'Ma was alive when I left.'

'She must be terribly worried.'

That was females for you. Straight for the kill. Rip out your throat or your heart. 'I doubt it.'

A lie. His mother had been devastated when he had told her he was leaving. Had begged him to write. He hadn't sent one letter. Ian had made sure of that.

They must all assume he was dead. He steeled his heart against a surge of longing. He'd made his decision. He'd see Carrick first. Confirm exactly what favour Ian had asked of him. And then he'd send Ian to the same kind of hell as he had endured.

Her face softened. 'And your injury?' She touched her own cheek. 'If it is not too difficult a topic.'

He inhaled a breath though his nose. He could slough her off, but it would come up again. It wasn't as though he could hide it, not really. And every time she looked at him, she would wonder. A deep longing filled him. The need to tell someone. To tell her. Something about this woman made him want to be rid of the weight of his past. To unburden himself. But he couldn't. The shame of her knowing would finish off what was left of his soul. But he must tell her something.

'I had been in America less than a week. I went hunting. It seemed like a grand adventure, ye ken.' He paused to gather his thoughts. 'There was an accident.'

It wasn't until his fingers encountered the welted, knotted skin that he realised he had touched the scar. He grimaced, then smoothed out his expression. Any sort of emotion only made him look worse.

'What sort of accident?' she asked.

'A stray bullet.' It had strayed off its target. Either his brain or his heart, he didn't know. His foot had slipped at the same moment the shot had been fired. 'It knocked me off my feet and I fell into a river. An Indian band found me downstream in verra poor shape.'

At her wide-eyed gasp, he shook his head. 'Nae

those who killed your husband. A small, peaceful family. They did what they could. Fed me and cared for me. And when I was well...I just stayed.'

He'd been unable to face going back as he was. Scarred. Angry, yes, but also hurt that Ian had wanted to be rid of him in such a final way. He'd decided to try to forget the words he'd heard before the shot was fired. To let his brother think he had won. Then anyway.

'You lived among them for six years?'

Not for the last two. But she didn't need to know that. 'It was a simple life. Almost spiritual. They are verra close to the natural world. It reminded me of the Highlands.'

He winced at how stupid that sounded, but her expression held only interest.

'How fascinating,' she said. 'But you decided to leave? You weren't satisfied with such a simple life?'

That life had changed. Later. When they were attacked by a band of renegades. The warriors had wanted to kill him, but their *woman of magic* had been fascinated by his yellow hair. She stopped them. And because she'd saved his life she considered him her property. He froze out the images that seared though his brain.

'It was time to leave.' Hundreds of miles from where he'd first been taken, when her husband had showed up with the firewater and given him the chance he needed. And her husband had paid the price.

'What about you?' he asked, changing the subject, hoping she wouldn't delve any deeper. He didn't want to lie to her, but he would not tell her the worst of it. 'Where is your family?'

'I was an only child. My mother and father are dead.' Sorrow coloured her voice. 'There is a cousin, of my father's, but we are not close.'

He frowned. 'The duke—'

She shook her head. 'That is what I don't understand. Samuel never mentioned Mere. He told me he was alone in the world apart from very distant relatives who would not approve of him marrying into the *bourgeoisie*.' She lifted her chin. 'It didn't matter that Mother's grandfather was an earl, of course, since she'd married into trade.' She sighed. 'I really thought he cared for me. But it turned out he just needed my money.'

What she was saying accorded pretty well with

what her husband had said, and part of him was glad the man had died. Another part felt guilty, that he'd been the one to cause his death. She'd be a great deal better off if MacDonald had lived. 'I'm sorry.'

She sighed. 'It was my own stupid fault. I thought he was my one chance for happiness. It turned out that it only made things worse.' She gave a small laugh and buried her face against her upraised knees. 'Pride comes before a fall, doesn't it?'

The pain in her voice was like a blade of steel pressing into his temple. It was as if her vulnerability called out to him. He couldn't help himself, he leaned forward and touched her shoulder, felt the bone smooth, round and cool to his palm through the fine linen. 'Any man would be proud to have you for a wife.'

Her short laugh was hard edged. 'Mr Gilvry, please do not insult my intelligence. If he could have had the money without me, he would have been the happiest man alive. He couldn't wait to escape, once he had my fortune in his pocket.'

He could hear tears in her voice and for some reason he couldn't bear to think of her crying. He moved to sit on the edge of the bed. 'Hush now. You've had a bad dream. It's the blackest part of the night. Things will seem better in daylight.'

She sniffed, a small sound that made his chest clench painfully. He wanted to hold her in his arms, protect her, but he didn't dare—even sitting this close had him hard with wanting. Something he could and would control. Besides, she would never consent to give him what he needed.

'You must think me a fool.'

'Not at all. I think you should sleep now, though. With the snow and all, it will be a long, hard day tomorrow.'

A small laugh shook her frame. 'And the sooner we get there the sooner you can be about your own affairs.' She looked at him, her grey eyes misty, but a brave smile pinned to her lips. Lips he wanted to kiss. He pushed the thought aside.

That was her, though, he thought. Brave. Full of courage. And no matter what she said about her marriage, she would be worse off as a widow if the duke did not treat her right. For a moment he considered confessing the whole of it. Unburdening his soul. What then? Likely she'd scream bloody murder and he'd find himself behind bars. Imprisoned yet again.

He stood up. 'Try to get some sleep.' He picked up the candle and blew it out. With the glow from the fire and the moonlight from the window now the storm had blown over, there was more than enough light for him to see his way to his blanket.

The bed ropes creaked as she lay down with a sigh. 'Thank you, Mr Gilvry,' she said softly.

'For what?'

'For listening to a foolish woman.'

If there was anything she was, it was not foolish. Anyone would be troubled with nightmares after the story he'd told her of what the savages had done to her husband and his party. He wrapped himself in the counterpane and settled into his spot on the floor. He put his hands behind his head and stared up where the ceiling would be, if it wasn't hidden in the dark.

Tomorrow they'd reach the duke's estate where he'd be questioned very closely. The thing was, would he tell the duke all of it? For her sake? Would it help? The lawyer had said since there was no proof, the date wasna' important. His eyes said he was lying.

Drew listened to the sounds of a house breathing as his mind grappled with the question. The soft sounds of a dwelling at rest.

A creak. Outside the door. Heavy weight pressing down on wood. Metal against metal. He sat up. So did Rowena. Silently he rose, pistol in hand, leaning over her, once again pressing his palm to her lovely mouth. 'Hush,' he breathed softly in her ear.

She nodded. Not only brave, but trusting. Of him. Too trusting.

The thought was a sickening lurch in his stomach he could not afford to acknowledge. He crept to the door, careful to avoid the loose board in the middle of the room and another in front of the door.

The latch lifted, the door moved in the frame, just a wee bit. As far as the lock would allow. Now, who would be trying the door in the middle of the night? And what sort of idiot would expect it would not be locked?

He glanced over his shoulder. Rowena was watching him, her profile outlined by the glow of the fire, her body rigid.

The pressure against the door ceased and it returned to its former position in the frame, but he could hear the sound of quiet breathing on the other side. A sound of metal against metal. Whoever was out there was determined to get in and, if he wasn't mistaken, they had another key.

All Rowena could see was the dark bulk of Drew's shape in the shadows near the door where the moonbeams streaming through the window did not reach. Breath held, she watched, her stomach clenched tight, her throat aching with the urge to say something to break the tension she felt in the room.

Was someone really trying to break in?

A sharp sound. Something dropping to the floor. Drew picked it up. In a flash, she realised it must be the key from their side of the door. Startled, she threw back the covers.

At the same moment, Drew flung open the door to reveal two burly men, one holding a lantern. Rowena, half out of bed, covered her eyes against the sudden glare.

Someone—one of them, she thought—cursed.

When she looked again, she could see why. Drew was holding them at bay at pistol point. The man with the lantern was backing up, struggling to free his pistol from his belt, the other one had what looked like a lump of wood in his hand.

'Leave that where it is,' Drew said calmly to the man with the lantern. The man held still.

Drew narrowed his eyes. 'Planning on robbing us while we slept? Who gave you the key?'

'We just wanted to ask a few questions,' the man with the cudgel said, his voice hoarse. He looked at the pistol and licked his lips.

Drew glared at him. 'You could have asked me in the morning.'

'We won't be here come morning,' the man with the lantern said. 'I do know you. I've seen you afore.'

Drew stiffened. 'I have never met you in my life.'

He frowned. 'Gilvry your name is. Not Mac-Donald. Led us a pretty chase in Edinburgh last summer, didn't he, Morris?'

'Aye,' the man called Morris said. 'Caused our boss a load of trouble.'

An expression of shock passed across Drew's face. He masked it quickly, but Rowena knew the man's words had hit home for some reason. But how could he have been in Edinburgh last summer? It didn't make sense.

'You are mistaken,' he said. 'I am Samuel MacDonald. And this is my wife.'

The man with the cudgel, the one who seemed to be in charge, shook his head. 'No, laddie. You might have fooled us poor folks, what ne'er meet with the nobs, but you can't fool McRae. He's met Samuel MacDonald. You're a Gilvry. A spy. You ruined McKenzie's business once—he'll no' be very happy if you ruin more of it. So what I wants to know is, what game are ye playing?'

Comprehension dawned on Drew's face. 'Whisky,' he said. 'You think I'm here because of the whisky. Well, I'm not.'

The man shook his head. 'Not good enough, laddie. You'll need to explain to McKenzie. We'll be takin' you to Edinburgh.'

Rowena gasped.

Drew smiled tightly. 'I see. Well, if we are going on a journey, I hope you won't mind if my wife gets dressed.'

The man with the lantern leered. 'She is more than welcome to come as she is.'

'Rowena,' Drew said.

The word was a command. Legs shaking, she scurried behind the screen. Stays were impossible, but she could manage her shirt and riding habit. With a bit of a struggle she got dressed. If only her hands would stop shaking. And her throat was so dry, she couldn't swallow.

She pulled on her boots and sidled around the screen.

'Are you ready?' Drew asked.

'Yes,' she croaked and tried swallowing again.

Drew smiled and cocked his weapon. 'This pistol says I am no' going anywhere with you.'

The men at the door gaped at him.

Then there was a noise beyond the window. A sort of scraping sound. From the cocking of his head, she knew Drew heard it, too. He jerked his head in that direction and she ran to look out.

And screamed, leaping back. There was a bearded face on the other side of the glass, grinning at her.

In that second, all hell seemed to break loose. The door slammed shut. The room went dark. A pistol fired with a blinding flash and deafening bang. Glass shattered. The smell of black powder hit the back of her throat. She threw herself to the floor.

'Get up,' Drew said, his voice cold, his hand gripping hard on her arm as he pulled her to her feet. 'Get your cloak.'

As ordered she grabbed her cloak from the settle and wrapped it around her. Still damp, but warm from the fire.

Shouts and bangs came from beyond the door. Then the sound of someone running downstairs.

'Come here,' he said. He flung something out of the window and then knelt by the bed, tying something to the leg. A rope.

Then he picked up their saddlebags and threw them out. 'What are you doing?' she cried.

'We're leaving.' He picked her up, flung her over his shoulder and climbed out of the window.

It was a short drop to a roof just below the window. And another to the ground. He landed in a shower of snow. Another bang and a flash. She ducked. Someone was firing at them from the window they had just left. A scream lodged in her throat.

'Run,' Drew said. 'This way.' He grabbed her

hand, snatching up the saddlebags on the way past. They charged into the stables.

The horses stirred.

'No time for saddles,' Drew said hastily untying the horses. 'Can you ride astride?'

She had no idea, but, too breathless to speak, her heart thundering too loud, she nodded.

He threw her up on her horse. 'Tuck your skirts between your legs, aye.'

Her jaw dropped, but he'd left her to mount his own horse at a leap. Assuming he knew whereof he spoke, she did as he suggested. He grabbed her horse's reins and they charged out of the stable door at a gallop.

A shape holding a lantern darted towards them, but when he realised they were not going to stop, he dived out of the way.

A gun fired. She half expected to feel a searing pain in her back. But no, it seemed whoever was shooting had missed. And then they were fleeing into the night, leaving behind them the sound of curses.

They rode uphill, sometimes walking the horses to give them a brief rest, sometimes breaking into a bone-jarring trot. Moonlight reflecting on snow made the landscape featureless and ghostly.

Ahead of her, Drew kept looking over his shoulder. She looked back once, but almost lost her seat, so contented herself with clinging on desperately and praying that they were not going to stumble off a cliff or fall into a burn. The cold bit into the bare flesh of her legs above her boots and stockings and the rough horse blanket rubbed against the insides of her lower legs. She could not deny she was glad of the fabric of her skirts between the blankets and her thighs, but even so she did not know how long she could ride without a saddle.

Soon it was clear the horses were blown and about the time she was going to suggest they stop for a rest, he halted. Once more he looked back.

Her heart tripped and stumbled. 'Are they coming?'

'No.'

The hoof prints in the snow would be hard to miss. 'Do you think they will follow?'

'Lucky for us, they only have ponies. The wee beasties canna follow us through the drifts.'

'Well, that's a relief.'

He looked at her, then laughed.

'What is so funny?'

'Nothing. I'm just relieved you are no' having a fit of the hysterics.'

'Do you think it would help?'

'Not at all.' He looked up at the stars. 'Northwest is where we need to go if I remember right from the map.'

She looked up. 'You can tell where we are from the stars?'

'Aye. Something I learned from the Indians. It works the same on land as it does on the ocean.'

He turned away.

She grabbed his arm. 'Wait. What on earth was going on back there? Why did they attack us?'

Even with only moonbeams to light his face, she could see his jaw harden. He touched a hand to his scars. 'It seems they mistook me for one of my brothers.'

'I don't understand.'

'My brothers smuggle whisky for a living. I assume they are competitors.'

His brothers were criminals. Like those men at the inn. Her heart raced. An overwhelming sense of danger flowed through her. The same feeling that had woken her earlier in the night.

'Come along,' he said, pushing ahead.

What choice did she have?

Chapter Six

It had been getting colder as they climbed upwards, as Drew had expected. It might not be snowing, but the wind was raw and biting. Neither of them were dressed for it. It didn't matter to him. He was used to being cold and hungry, but Rowena was a whole different matter.

They had to find shelter, and soon. He was just hoping that by climbing, he would make it harder for the smugglers to follow. Hoping they wouldn't bother.

Damn Ian and his bloody smuggling.

What the hell had he been up to in the years Drew had been gone? Starting a war, by the sound of it. And then there was the Pockles. They were bound to reach McRae's some time the next day and their ears would be filled with the account of him and Rowena posing as husband and wife. He just hoped he could speak to them and explain before they reached the duke.

Right now, though, that didn't matter. What mattered was finding somewhere to shelter until it was light, which wouldn't be until around nine in the morning these short winter days.

He glanced back at Rowena hunched into her cloak, her horse struggling through the snow. The lass was as valiant as a soldier. She hadn't offered one word of blame for what had happened back at the inn, but she had been very quiet. Withdrawn.

Likely in fear for her life.

And it was his fault. His lack of judgement about those men at the inn. He'd not trusted them, but he had not really expected an attack. He turned and looked ahead, keeping his gaze fixed on a small break in the vegetation, almost disguised by snow. He was sure it was a track and plunged ahead. The horses were beginning to flag. If they didn't find shelter soon, they'd be forced to dismount.

He'd done a lot of walking in snow in the winter these past few years. After spending a good few days floundering along behind the rest of the band, much to their amusement, he'd learned to fashion the snowshoes they used. This snow was nowhere near as deep and difficult. Not yet anyway.

A dark shadow loomed out of the hillside. He halted. Pleased could hardly describe his emotion at that moment.

'What is it?' Rowena called out from behind him. 'Is something wrong?'

Was that an edge of panic he heard in her voice?

'Nothing's wrong. We have shelter.' A lowly building to be sure, with a low-pitched peat-covered roof, no windows, no outbuildings. And there was no doubt it was deserted.

Rowena brought her horse up alongside him. 'What is it?'

He pointed. 'A bothy. We'll stay here for the rest of the night and continue on in the morning.'

She looked puzzled. 'Will they mind if we get them out of bed at such a late hour?'

He almost laughed. 'There is no they. No one lives here. It's used in the summer by shepherds. We'll be lucky if I can make us a fire.'

She glanced around. 'Do you think the smugglers know about this place?'

'They might, which is why we will need to be

away early. And if we are lucky, we'll have a wee bit more snow and they won't be able to follow our tracks.' He got down and helped her off her horse.

Luck didn't seem to be something he had much of, but he saw that his words had cheered her up. A little.

He tried the door. As he expected, it swung open. Bare stone walls, a dirt floor, an open hearth, a flat lump of granite balanced on rocks for a low table. It was better than he had expected, worse than he'd hoped. He'd hoped for a cot or two. Some blankets to keep out the cold.

'Oh, dear,' she said as he ushered her into the small stone chamber.

At least they'd be out of the wind. And against the wall was a small pile of peat. They would have a fire after all. And hot tea. He fumbled around the walls until he found what he was seeking. Tallow candles. He lit one, dripped wax on the table and it stood there, a small warm glow.

'I'll see to the horses, then light the fire,' he said.

She rubbed her hands together, the candlelight showing her face, calm and accepting. No anger.

Not even worry as she looked around at the bareness of the place, which made him feel somehow worse. He'd been an idiot for not following up with the fellow who had stared at him so hard at the inn. A sensible word with the man might have prevented what had happened tonight.

Angry at his failure to protect the woman in his charge, he stomped out to see to the horses, who were standing patiently outside. He hobbled them, rubbed them down with one of the blankets and hoped for the best. They'd already been fed, so they should be fine outdoors for a few hours.

He removed the saddlebags and blankets and took them inside. It was little enough to offer comfort, but at least the blankets wouldn't take long to dry.

He was surprised to find Rowena piling peat in the central open hearth. She looked up at his entry. 'I thought I would help get it started, although I am not sure I have laid it correctly.'

'Is there kindling?'

She shook her head.

Without kindling it would be difficult to make it catch. He tried not to let his concern show. No sense in worrying her about something until it was a real problem. He cast his gaze around the room for something to get the peat started. 'I expect they use gorse or heather in the summer.'

Rowena held up a small book. 'My journal,' she said at his glance of enquiry. She ripped out the small sheets of paper and twisted them into spills. 'They will light very nicely, I think.'

Smart as paint, this woman. He had a journal, too, buried deep in his saddlebag. Not his, though, and he was loath to dig it out, fearing she might recognise it. It had been one of the few personal things the Indians hadn't taken or destroyed when they attacked MacDonald's camp.

What he had read of its contents on his way down from the hills had revealed it to be a document he would never want another living soul to see, but since MacDonald had written his authority to use his money and property to get him to Scotland on one of the pages, he'd had no choice but to keep it, in case anyone asked. Not that MacDonald had expected he would be transported in a barrel. The man had had no idea of the extent of his injuries.

And as soon as Drew was free of this duty of

his, he would burn the journal. But not to keep out the cold.

'Will it be enough, do you think?' Her hands were trembling with cold as she worked and her teeth chattered every now and then.

They had to have heat.

He arranged the blankets close to the hearth. 'It will do very well,' he said and let her hear his admiration.

She glanced up at him and their eyes met and lingered. There was warmth in her gaze.

It sparked a fire inside him. His throat dried. 'I'll see if I can find some brush, as well. To make it burn better.'

Cold air was what he needed right now. Or better yet, a dip in the nearest loch and the more ice, the better.

Rowena poked the few twists of paper deeper into the overlapping slabs of peat. They had never used peat in her father's house in Edinburgh. Coal had been plentiful, but it seemed to her that fuel was fuel, and the maids had used paper spills to light the fires.

She stood up, rubbing her hands together trying

to get some feeling back in her fingertips, then strode to the slab of rock that served as a table, cupping them around the candle flame for a moment before slipping her gloves back on.

Even frozen as she was, she could still feel the warmth of Drew's intense gaze in her belly. It had been better than a shot of whisky. Not that he seemed to notice. To him she was just a responsibility. There had to be something wrong with her, being attracted to such a man. He was no different from Samuel, using her for his own gain. No doubt he expected the duke to reward him handsomely for delivering his relative's remains. And her.

The duke might not feel so generous when he learned he was naught but a smuggler. She sighed. Not that she would tell him, but it would be hard to keep it a secret. The Pockles were bound to arrive at the inn and hear the whole story.

Drew brought in a rush of cold air. And she'd thought the air in the bothy was freezing before. She clenched her jaw to prevent her teeth from chattering while he, with his arms full of brush, stamped the snow off his feet in the doorway.

Without a word he crouched before her peat pile, rearranging the earthy slabs, lifting them, inserting clumps of heather. She was pleased to see that he also took care with the placement of her little bits of paper in the heart of the pile.

She freed the candle from its wax blob and held it ready. He looked up and met her eyes. Her heart tumbled over. Her hand shook, splattering hot wax on her glove. She could feel the heat of it through the leather, but it was nowhere near as hot as the flare of heat blazing a path through her veins.

She had no business feeling such things. Even if he had kissed her, it had meant nothing. His shoulders tensed, as if he sensed her dismay. Then he took the candle and touched it to each twist of paper.

Pinpricks of flame. He dropped cross-legged to the floor and nurtured each little lick of bright light, breathing on each tiny flicker, protecting them from the draughts that eddied around them.

'Ah,' he said softly as little curls of smoke rose up.

The peat caught. At first just a glow of tiny embers, like hair caught in a candle, then real flames. She breathed a sigh of relief. They were not going to freeze to death after all.

He pulled his little pot from his saddlebag and the tea and the whisky and she bit back a laugh. 'Too bad you don't have a loaf of bread tucked in there, too.'

'I have your roll left from dinner and something better,' he said. He pulled out the small muslin pouch of oats and dangled it in the air. 'Porridge, ye ken. We'll no' set out on an empty belly in the morning.'

'Porridge. The Scotsman's answer to everything.' She could not help but smile.

His face tightened as if with a painful memory. 'A Highlander never leaves home without one night's food in his sporran. Something my grandfather taught me.'

'Well, my thanks to your grandfather, where e'er he may be.'

'Aye.' He glanced up at the roof where the smoke was curling around in the low rafters. 'I'll open the chimney or we'll be kippered by morning.'

Smoked like fish. She couldn't help a smile at the vision.

He climbed up a series of larger stones set like steps in one of the walls and then up to balance on one of the beams supporting the thatched roof. He found what looked like a long piece of metal, hooked at one end, and used it to push at a trapdoor let into the thatch. It opened an inch or two. The smoke disappeared through the gap and into the night.

While he climbed down, she sank onto the nearest blanket, glad of the warmth of the fire. 'What do you think we should do about the Pockles?'

He dropped to sit beside her. 'Nothing we can do. We'll either meet them on the road or at our destination.'

'You think they will look for us?'

'They might.' His mouth tightened, one corner curling up as if to mock his words. 'I'd sooner they didn't.'

'You are thinking of those men.'

'Aye.'

'Did you know them, as they said?'

'No, but I have no doubt they know my youngest brother, Logan. As wild a wee scamp as there

ever was. He was a fair way to looking like me
when I left.'

Two like him. It seemed hard to imagine. 'They
don't seem to like him very much.'

'I can't imagine why,' he said drily, as if he
knew very well.

Under that sullen demeanour she sometimes
suspected he had a wry sense of humour. 'Business, I suppose.'

He raised his gaze to hers and she was right,
there was amusement glinting there, hidden unless you cared to look. Not that she thought he'd
be pleased that she'd noticed. He'd likely deny
any kind of warm feelings.

But right now there was one rather urgent problem she needed to deal with. 'I don't suppose
there is a privy out there?'

He winced. 'No.'

'But there are bushes.' She nodded at the few
bits of brush he'd kept back from the fire.

'Aye, but you canna go out there alone. It's too
dark. Too easy to lose your way. I'm afraid you
will have to suffer my escort.'

So much for modesty. But there was no sense to
being missish. She rose to her feet and he stood

with her. 'I am sure you will not mind turning your back.'

Outside, she couldn't see an inch in front of her face, once he shut the door. She looked up at the sky. The moon had either set or disappeared behind clouds. She would have been afraid to take one step farther if it had not been for his strong hand beneath her elbow.

They went around the side of the house where the wind was less fierce. 'This will have to do, I'm afraid.'

He stood with one hand against the wall, his back towards her. She followed the length of the wall to the furthest corner, putting the width of the house between them, and took care of her needs. It was at times like these that she found differences in rank more than ridiculous. People were people, no matter what they were called, and if they were above the animals in the fields, it was not by much. She stood, straightened her skirts and followed the wall back to Mr Gilvry.

'Thank you.'

He grunted, then put a hand on her shoulder. 'You're not like any lady I ever met.'

She couldn't see his face in the dark, but she

heard something odd in his tone. Criticism? The kind she'd endured from her husband.

'I'm sorry if you find me a disappointment, Mr Gilvry.' Head high, she stalked back to the front door and inside.

It seemed he'd unintentionally touched a nerve when he'd intended his words as a compliment. Apparently, he was out of practice in the charming of women. Not that he'd had to practise when he was last in Scotland. Or in London, for that matter. All he'd ever needed was a smile. A smile wouldn't do him a bit of good anymore, since it made him look like a gargoyle, the kind that terrified small children in the night. More than one had run away in terror after seeing his face.

As he'd do well to remember. So did he say he was sorry, or let it go?

Given their circumstances, their close quarters and his visceral responses to her presence, it was probably best if she was annoyed. It would keep them both at a distance.

While she seated herself cross-legged on her blanket beside the fire, he proceeded to heat the snow he had collected while waiting for her outside. A bothy usually came equipped with a couple of cooking pots and a trivet. Either someone had stolen them or the landlord was discouraging the bothy's use by itinerants. Lots of people had been cleared off their ancestral lands these past years, many roaming the hills looking for somewhere to settle. No landlord worth his salt wanted squatters on his land.

He balanced his tin pot on the peat and turned his attention to his pistol. He did not want to be caught unawares and unready if the men at McRae's had followed them. Her gaze followed his every movement as he primed the pan and loaded the ball.

'It is warming up in here already,' she said with determined cheerfulness.

An olive branch. A courageous attempt to be brave. Damp chill clung to the stone walls, making the room as cold as the grave. Still, he wasn't going to negate her courage, not when he could not help but admire it. But nor did he want to meet that clear steady gaze of hers. Every time he did, he found himself drowning in their cool depths, wanting more that he should, saying far more than he intended.

He'd already revealed more than he should about his past. Perhaps because it was the first time in a long time that anyone had shown the slightest interest.

He kept his gaze fixed on what he was doing. 'If we can keep the fire going, we shouldn't freeze to death. There's enough peat for a night or two.'

'A night or two?' She sounded horrified.

'Aye. If it snows again and we canna get out.'

'Oh, dear.'

He set the pistol aside, close to hand, pulled his knife from his boot and stirred the melting snow. 'It might not come to that.'

'I hope not.'

And so did he. Given the growing attraction he felt towards this woman, and not just to her physical being, but to her as a person, the next several hours would not be easy, no matter whether they stayed here or continued their journey.

The water in the pot began to steam. He tossed in some tea leaves. It would warm them through and perhaps she'd sleep for a while. And he could pretend he felt nothing.

He watched the water, waiting for it to come to a full boil, but could not help but feel her gaze upon him, or stop recalling to mind the shape of her body beneath her nightgown. There was no doubt about it. The sooner he was rid of her the better he would like it. She was too much of a temptation. No matter what his body thought, she was not the kind of woman he needed.

His mind went back to their discussions with the lawyer. 'I have the sense yon Jones didna' like the date of your husband's death. Do you think he had a date he preferred? A date later in the month?' he asked as a distraction from his carnal thoughts. 'I could make it whatever date he wanted if you thought it would help with the duke. I canna see that a few days here or there would make any great difference.'

She stripped off her gloves and held her hands out to the fire. They were capable-looking hands, he noticed. Hands that looked as if they knew their way around a man's body.

A wave of heat rolled through his blood. Hell and damnation, had his time in captivity made him naught but a beast? Even there, he'd had more control over his thoughts than he seemed to have now.

'I thought he said he didn't care about the

date,' she mused, seemingly unaware of his inner struggle.

'His tongue said he didn't care. His face said otherwise.'

Her eyes sharpened. 'Are you sure?'

'It's hard to be sure of anything. But he definitely winced at the mention of the date, then went to a deal of trouble to deny its importance.' He shook his head. 'It makes no sense to care about such a thing. Unless there's money in it.'

'A loan? Something in Samuel's will?' She blew on the tips of those long slender fingers. 'I can't make any scenario work that would tie to the date of his death.'

Nor could he. 'But there is something.'

'Perhaps the duke will be more forthcoming when I see him.'

A sound outside the door brought him to his feet and the pistol into his hand. He pulled Rowena to her feet and pushed her behind him.

'What is it?' she asked in a whisper.

'I heard something.'

'It's them. They've found us.'

Inside, he went still, cold, listening with his body as well as his ears, becoming at one with the air to feel any small disturbance. He lifted a finger to his lips and to his relief she nodded and remained utterly silent. There were only two smugglers left, if he was right about the one he'd shot, and the night was dark. He blew out the candle. He didn't want the light behind him, making him a perfect target. Too bad he didn't have the moon to help him see whoever was outside.

He moved slowly towards the door. Reached for the latch.

A bang. The door rattled in its frame.

Rowena gasped and clutched at his coat. She'd crept along right behind him, using him for a shield. He was glad of it.

But...

Another bang. Metal on wood. Low on the door. Heavy breathing on the other side. And another metallic sound like...

What the hell? He whipped the door open, pistol cocked.

Her horse huffed out a breath and made to come in.

Air rushed from his lungs. 'Yon beastie wants in.' He crouched and felt for her hobble. Still there. He gave her a push. 'Sorry, lassie. People only in here.' He shut the door in the animal's face.

Rowena, behind him, was making odd little noises. Crying? She must have been terrified. He found the candle and lit it from the ashes and held it aloft.

She was leaning against the wall, doubled over, her face covered by her hands and her shoulders shaking. Sobbing.

His stomach dipped. His heart lurched. He crossed the room and put an arm around her shoulders. 'It's all right,' he soothed, horribly aware of her body against his and the loud beating of his heart.

'It's all right. It was only your horse.'

Her shoulders shook harder.

Heavens, after all she'd gone through tonight so bravely, and now she was falling apart. He turned her in his arms, pressed her face to his shoulder, held her close, felt her soft curves and sweet hollows down the length of his body, felt her warm breath on his neck and wanted to groan with frustration.

'Please, *mo cridhe*, don't cry.'

'Oh,' she gasped, looking up. 'I'm not…crying.'

He looked down into her face. Her eyes had tears and her face was bright pink, but her mouth was…laughing. She was laughing?

'It was just your…expression. When you saw the h-horse.' She dissolved into giggles.

A laugh rose in his chest, bubbling up where no laugh should be. 'She was cold,' he said.

'She wanted a cup of tea.'

And then he did laugh. And laugh. Holding her fast, grinning like a fool. And laughing until they were both breathless.

'Oh, Drew, I thought we were done for.' She flung her arms around his neck and kissed him full on the mouth, still laughing.

He pulled her arms down from around his neck, holding her hands fast at her sides, intending to set her away, but as he gazed into eyes dancing with merriment, he found himself entranced.

And he moved his grip to her back and kissed her in return. And kissed her. Savouring the softness of her lips and the sweet way she opened her mouth and her tongue tangled with his. Nothing, not even the best *usquebaugh*, had ever tasted so good as her passion or warmed the coldness inside him so deeply.

Her hands strayed under his coat, caressing his back, while her hips arched into him in open invitation.

Deep in his bones he felt a shudder so strong he could have sworn the ground was shaking. And he didn't care if the stone walls crumbled around them, as long as she held him and stroked his chest, her thumbs teasing his nipples, her sweet soft belly grinding against his swollen shaft.

His mind was a hot dark pit of lust and torment. Yet her kiss, the dark slide of her tongue against his brought warmth to the deepest reaches of his heart, to the shivering creature that craved her heat.

The pain of it was too hard to bear.

Because somewhere at the edges of his consciousness he knew this was wrong, though he wanted her badly. He should not be doing this, taking advantage of a woman far too good for him.

On a wild groan he could not contain, he let her go and stepped back, panting and shaken.

'Rowena,' he rasped in a voice that sounded as if it was broken.

'Drew,' she said. 'I want this. I want you.'

He heard the demand in her voice. An order from the past he'd been forced to obey.

Resentment flared to life. 'I'm no' yours to command.' Not anymore. Never again. 'If you want what I have, you'll beg for it.'

Eyes hazed by desire, she drew in a hiss of breathy pleasure. 'Please,' she whispered. 'Oh, please, Drew.'

Heat blazed in his veins even as he stared at her, caught up by lust and shock as her words brought his every fantasy to the fore. Had she somehow guessed at the flaw in his nature and thought to mock him? He suffered a pang of shame.

Or could she...? No, it was impossible. She did not know what she was saying, what it did to him. It was the shock of the events of the night making her ask for comfort. And heaven help him, he wasn't sure he could resist that quietly spoken plea.

She dropped her gaze. 'Please,' she said again.

Heat blazed a trail across his skin. Desire ran rampant. 'You'll do exactly as I say.'

'Yes,' she murmured. 'Anything.'

The battle was lost.

He teased the seam of her lips with his tongue and they parted on a sigh. He stroked the inside of her mouth and she moaned, arching into him, responsive to each little flick of his tongue, her hands coming up to rest on his shoulders for support as she melted in his arms.

'No touching,' he muttered. She let her hands fall away.

He slid his fingers around her nape, angling her head to deepen the kiss, and felt the thunder of her pulse at her throat. He let the other hand drop to her shoulder, glide over her back, caress the dip of her waist.

Their lips clung and their tongues tasted, and their breath mingled until he was the white heat in the centre of the flame. And the demands of his body blazed into life.

Doubts assailed him. He broke their kiss. 'Are you sure?'

Heavy lidded, her liquid silver eyes gazed back at him. 'Positive,' she whispered.

God help him, those words undid him. He scanned the room, the cold dirt floor, the blankets, and he wanted to howl with frustration. Then his gaze took in the table behind her. He swallowed and backed her up to its edge.

She shivered.

Cold stone. He couldn't... 'Blanket,' he muttered, releasing her shoulders. He folded both blankets and arranged them on the table. Then he set his hands to her narrow waist and lifted her to perch on the rough wool. He kissed her again, his hips pushing between her legs, one hand pushing up under the full fabric of her skirt until it found the soft silken skin above her stocking. As his fingers stroked the delicate flesh of her inner thigh, she sighed into his mouth and shifted closer to the table's edge.

Lust hit his groin in a hot river of pulsing blood. He took her mouth in a brutal ravaging kiss, forcing her head back with his assault, and she tangled her tongue with his and made little sounds of encouragement. Urging him on with her fingers in his hair, then stroking his jaw, his scars with a feathery sweeps of her fingers. Trying to gentle him. To control him.

A feral growl ripped at his throat. The need for

possession, a beast on the rampage. 'You must do only what I tell you. Do you understand?'

She nodded.

'Do not touch me, unless I say you may.'

She licked her lips and opened her mouth to speak.

'Say nothing,' he warned.

Eyes wide, she gazed at him and said nothing.

One arm around her back, he lifted her, sweeping her skirts up and away until they were bunched at her waist. He gazed down at the wickedly delicious sight of her long slim thighs parted to embrace his hips and the soft dark curls at their juncture. A low groan broke free.

He fell to his knees, and she gasped. Surprise? Shock. He looked up to see her staring down at him, her lips rosy and swollen from his brutal assault on her mouth. But instead of fear in her eyes there was the heat of molten metal. And puzzlement.

Triumph settled deep in the pit of his stomach. He was not her first, but he would be the first to teach her this pleasure. He lifted her legs and hooked them over his shoulders. Her eyes widened.

Holding her gaze, he parted the soft folds of

her feminine flesh with his thumbs and stroked a finger over the already swollen bud hiding deep within. Her eyelids fluttered, then drifted closed, and she moaned sweetly.

He leaned forward and pressed a kiss to the hot centre, inhaling the deep rich scent of aroused woman, feeling the dampness on his lips.

She hissed in a breath, her fingers gripping the edge of the table as if afraid she might fall. He nuzzled deeper, using his lips and his tongue to sweep the sweet cleft of her body.

'Oh,' she cried out as his tongue flickered over the hot little bud deep in her folds.

Oh, yes, the beast inside him said. *Yes.*

Chapter Seven

The delicious wickedness of his mouth made Rowena's limbs feel boneless. The quick, light flicks of his tongue against her flesh were a constant torment. The sight of that dark chestnut hair between her thighs made her insides clench tighter.

The most salacious hedonism she could have imagined held her in its thrall. How had he guessed at her secret fantasy? Her dreams of ravaging pirates and marauding sheikhs who bound her and made her submit to their every whim. Who dominated and forced her into submission. She shuddered with the power of his masculine strength.

At any moment, it would happen. The waves of pleasure, followed by a rush of heat that she'd discovered as a girl and that were so shamefully addictive.

She loved the sensations storming her body. Never had she created any so powerful from her mental images as he created with his lips and tongue.

The end hovered just out of reach. She wove her fingers in the silky waves of his hair, opening herself wider, lifting her hips, pressing into him, seeking to break the mounting tension.

He jerked away, those incredible green eyes blazing up at her, his face a mask of agony.

'Lean back,' he ordered, his voice a low, feral growl. 'Palms on the table. Do. Not. Move.'

The command, the threat, lashed her with hot pulses at her core. Languorous with desire, she complied, leaning back, legs spread, completely at his mercy.

With a grunt of satisfaction, he renewed his assault, licking the little tiny nub that was the source of the pleasure she sought. Such a small thing to turn her limbs to butter, she'd thought when she peeked in a mirror. Hardly impressive compared to the male of the species.

He suckled.

Her hips shot off the table. That she had not expected. She moaned her pleasure. The ache inside her increased tenfold, making her tremble. 'Please,' she begged, seeking the tipping point just out of reach, which loomed in every dark, hot corner of her body.

'Silence,' he ordered, 'or I will walk away.'

She melted. Thrills chased down her spine at the power of command in the deep growl of his voice. This was her pirate. The man who prowled through her dreams, taking control of her body and soul. She closed her eyes in submission.

He eased one finger inside her and her inner walls clamped tight as he stroked within and without with his thumb. The ache intensified. Tears of joy leaked from the corners of her eyes as she let him do with her as he would.

And he lowered her legs to hang over the edge. Stepped back and left her, cold and bereft.

'No,' she moaned. She sat up, reached for him.

His gaze dropped to the place his mouth had so recently vacated, so raw and aching, the look on his face dark and sensual. 'Palms on the table,' he said roughly. 'Do as I bid or I'll end this now.'

The words made her quiver and shiver as if he was still touching her with his mouth.

She gasped. Lolling back, too weak and melting to do anything else. A jerk of a nod signified his approval.

His hand went to his breeches. He unbuttoned his falls. She wanted to offer to help. To touch him as he had touched her, but the darkness in his expression kept her hands glued to the table and her breath coming in little soft pants.

He dropped his coat to the floor and dragged off his boots and stockings while she watched, fascinated. No man had ever undressed in her presence before. She hadn't even seen her husband naked. The few times he'd coupled with her, he'd always blown out the candles before he removed his banyan.

Breathless with anticipation, she watched. She licked her lips as he peeled the pantaloons down his legs, but saw only a glimpse of his thighs as his shirt, released from its confines, fell to his knees.

She made a sound of disappointment.

He went still and her gaze drifted up to his face.

'Did you speak?' he asked in rough, hoarse tones.

She quickly shook her head.

His eyes narrowed, but his hands got busy with

his shirt buttons. The placket opened to reveal a narrow strip of chest with a dusting of crisp reddish-gold hair. What would it feel like, that hair, against her skin? Her palms tingled with the desire to touch. She kept them pressed against the cold stone while he pulled the shirt off over his head.

The breath left her body in a long sigh. A Greek statue had never looked so beautiful. Arms that she had known were strong were gilded by the sun and warmed by the light of the candle and the fire. They were beautifully formed. Lovely. And she longed to touch the smooth planes, the curve of muscle. She itched to curl her fingers in the crisp hair sprinkling gold dust across his chest, to trace the hard ridges of muscle beneath his ribs.

Fear held her back. The certain knowledge that if she did, he would not be pleased, and she desperately wanted to please him. To feel desirable.

And right now, he did want her. He was aroused. His male member standing erect from a nest of crisp reddish curls, its head dark and glistening.

It stirred under her gaze and she sucked in a breath, her gaze shooting up to his face.

His eyes were hooded, his mouth sultry, yet mocking her with its slight upward tilt at one corner. Her body trembled with anticipation. Ached for what he might bring her.

He stepped between her knees and she looked down to see their hips were in perfect alignment, his shaft brushing hot against her inner thigh.

'Wider,' he ground out through a jaw that was clenched as if he felt pain.

She inhaled a shaky breath and complied.

He clasped her hips and pulled her closer. He placed his knuckle beneath her chin, lifting her face with gentle but firm pressure. There was something in his expression she didn't quite understand. Shame?

'Are you sure?' There was no mistaking the desire in his hard-edged voice—it sent wild shivers all the way to her core, hot little pulses of wicked pleasure. An ache tightened inside her. The need for release from the tension of longing.

She swallowed. 'Yes,' she whispered. A shudder of anticipation rippled through her at the power he exuded. He made her feel feminine, desired and strangely—protected.

He reached between them, gazing deep into

her eyes as if to gauge her response, and guided his hot hard flesh to her core, pressing against her most private place, a hot, deliciously tempting pressure as he rocked his hips.

He stilled, looking down at her, watching her as if testing her resolve.

She panted, wanting to move, to arch into him, to make him... No. He was like a wild animal—one wrong move and he would walk away and leave her with nothing but the shame of being undeserving of what most women took for granted: male desire for an attractive woman.

She shook with the effort of remaining utterly still.

He leaned forward, his body coming over her, his hands unfastening her gown then trapping hers to the table, pressing her back onto her elbows, her breasts exposed to his mouth. She let her head fall back, eyes closed, exposing her throat. Offering her surrender to his will.

A deep dark sound rose up from low in his chest, a feral sound of possession, and his hot breath scorched her cheek, before he took her mouth in a soul-searing kiss. She melted beneath his assault, her thoughts giving way to the sensation of his lips on hers, his tongue exploring her mouth, the feel of his hard body against her naked breasts and the tantalising feel of him between her thighs.

How could she not have guessed how wonderful it could be? Why had she never known?

He raised his head, leaving behind her lips to trail hot kisses down her throat and then first on one breast, then the other. Sensations chased across her skin in rapid succession. The peaks ached and tightened as he licked and nuzzled the sensitive tips. It felt wicked and wildly exciting. Though she tried, she could not stop the sounds of encouragement coming from the back of her throat.

He teased at her nipples with his tongue, with his teeth, and then he suckled.

Inside and out, her body convulsed at the painfully sharp pleasure that arrowed straight to her womb. She cried out with the shock of it.

He raised his head and the chill air across her wet breast made shivers ripple across her skin to settle low in her belly. Then he suckled at the other breast and the delicious torture started all over again.

It was perfect, wonderful, his mouth was wonderful, an instrument of pleasure that worshipped her body. She lifted her head to look at him. Sensing her movement, he glanced up. For a brief moment she thought she saw a flare of heat in his eyes, of desire. But his expression was cold, remote, as if he was only doing this to please her and sought nothing for himself. Felt nothing.

Her arms trembled with the strain of holding herself in place, but before she collapsed, one hand left hers to support her nape, while the other went between them, stroking her centre in strong, slick motions that made her gasp and cry out. Gently he parted those folds and guided himself to the entrance of her body until she felt herself opening and flesh give way. She felt his flesh enter her a fraction, intrusive, hot and delicious.

He shuddered as if under some great strain. A warm hand stroked her thigh behind her knee, lifting it, and he pressed deeper inside, stroking her inner flesh with small rocks of his hips.

She wanted more. She lifted the other leg, wrapped both of them around his hips, opening herself fully, bringing him closer to her sweetly aching centre.

Without warning, he drove forward, hard, to the hilt. Uncontrollable pleasure washed through her in a searing surge. She cried out.

A growl of warning rumbled up from his throat, a feral sound laced with torment. He nuzzled at her neck first nipping, then soothing with his tongue. He nibbled at her ear all the while driving into her. He filled her and left no room for anything but raw sensation: the rhythm of their panting breaths loud in her ears; the sound of their bodies joining; the sensations of one hand on her breast, the other holding her up so his mouth could feast on her lips, her tongue; and the slapping of his hips against her inner thighs.

Then he swirled his tongue in her ear. His hand left her breast and went to the tiny straining numb buried in the soft folds of her female flesh, expertly rubbing and pressing and...

She shattered in a fountain of heat forced up from her core that blazed along her veins like a forest fire caught by the wind. Her body went limp and she collapsed backwards on to the table.

He groaned softly and withdrew from her body. He hung over her, his hands either side of her, his breath coming in harsh, raw gasps hot against her breasts and his head hanging low. He looked like a man in the throes of terrible agony.

Because… Because he had not found his release. Her heart slowed. Where there had been heat, there was ice.

He had been unable to… She had not been enough for him. She wanted to weep.

Instead, she took a deep breath and sat up. With unsteady fingers, she eased her gown up her arms and over her shoulders, covering her breasts.

He moved away, turning his back while he hastily pulled on his trousers and fastened them over his arousal with a wince.

She pulled her skirts down over her legs. Before she could jump down from the table, he turned back and helped her, holding her up when her legs threatened to buckle.

Never had she felt so languid, so wonderfully relaxed…or so inadequate.

He brushed her hair back from her face and peered into her eyes. 'Satisfied?' he asked in a mocking voice.

'Yes,' she admitted, but wishing she'd been enough of a woman to bring him to completion.

For breathless minutes, she had felt like a siren. Now she knew her husband had spoken the truth. As a woman, she really was a failure.

In silence, he finished dressing, picked up his coat and walked out into the night, leaving her to shiver in a blast of cold air.

What on earth had just happened? Clearly she was not the woman he wanted. He'd found her inadequate. Undesirable.

Why would she feel surprised? Or hurt? Deeply hurt. No man, not even her husband, wanted her in that way. She just wasn't the kind of woman men found appealing and she'd pushed him into doing something he hadn't wanted.

And now he was gone. Out into the night. Leaving her feeling sickened by shame.

She stared at the door.

Her heart stopped still in her chest. What if he never came back?

No. She wouldn't believe he would abandon her out here in the wilderness. He'd been angry. He'd gone to cool off. To settle his temper. To take care of his needs. Mortification washed through her that she wasn't enough.

He would come back.

He had to.

The hours of waiting passed interminably slowly, and while she had lain down beside the fire and huddled under her cloak, she didn't sleep. It was fear making the time crawl.

Finally, she gave up pretending and rose and folded the blankets. She put more peat on the fire, coaxing it into a blaze. Lit the candle, wishing there were windows that would spill light out into the night and welcome him back.

Inside she trembled.

What if he didn't come back?

He had looked so disgusted. So appalled. Even in the little light given off by the fire, and the single candle, she had seen his revulsion. As if what had happened was her fault.

She should have fought him the moment he touched her. Fought him? That was a lie. She should have fought herself. While she could still not believe the strength of her climax, something she would never forget, her heart ached for the loss of their growing friendship. He'd laughed with her. And she'd spoiled it all by throwing herself at him like some frustrated spinster.

No wonder he'd walked out with that look of disgust on his face.

She let go a shuddering breath and paced around the small room. Walking to keep warm and to dispel the fear inside her, the burgeoning panic. And as she walked she could not help looking at that door. Waiting for him to return.

But he didn't.

And when she couldn't bear it anymore, she peeked out. The sky had lightened. It was morning. And he hadn't returned. Had he taken his horse?

The idea robbed her of breath.

If he had ridden away, did that mean he wouldn't return? Her heart pounded hard in her chest. She picked up her cloak and pulled it around her.

His horse would be there. He would not have taken it unless he planned to go far away. He wouldn't do that. He had promised to see her safe to the duke. Swallowing the dryness in her throat, she opened the door wide and peered outside. The wind tugged at her cloak, trying to rip it from her clutching hand as she took in the view.

The clouds still lowered over the hills, obscuring their tops. And it had snowed again during the night. There were no tracks.

She walked around to the back of the bothy. Her horse raised its head and pawed at the ground. Drew's mount was nowhere to be seen.

If his horse was gone, then he had left. And she was now on her own. Alone in the Highlands and no idea where to go for safety. Her knees weakened. Threatened to give way.

She forced herself to stand straight, took a deep breath and glanced around at the white landscape. If only she had looked at the map before they left. She had left it all to him. Trusted him to see her there safely. There was nothing to tell her which way to go.

Should she go and risk getting hopelessly lost? Or stay and freeze once the peat for the fire ran out?

Quite the conundrum. The sort of problem she sometimes set for her pupils as an exercise in logic for their young minds. In the warm comfort of their schoolroom it hadn't seemed quite so terrifying.

But whereas she might want to be mastered in

her fantasies, in real life she needed to be strong. She'd sooner die trying to rescue herself than simply wait for the end. And that meant she'd have to gather up her belongings and try to find her way to a village. Or back to McRae's inn.

The inn would be closest, if she could only remember the way.

Downhill. She would head downhill away from the bothy. She strode back inside. The heat inside the little house felt blissful on her chilled face. She went to the fire and stood over it, revelling in the warmth percolating through her clothes. It would be hard to leave such lovely heat and head out into the unknown with only hope and a vague sense of direction as her guide. She looked at the pile of peat against the wall. It might last another day. Perhaps she should wait. Trust he would come back.

And set out if he did not.

Her stomach growled.

If she was hungry now, she would be worse later. She crouched down and ransacked his saddlebag. There was the handful of oats, the bread roll, a tinder box, a handkerchief and a pouch of coins. In the bottom she found the little bag of tea leaves. And beneath that she felt a small book. Not her business.

She frowned as the thought occurred that he'd taken nothing with him. He must have meant to come back.

Perhaps something had happened to him? Her stomach roiled. Could he have run into the smugglers and come to some harm? Were they even now on their way here? If so, she'd be a fool to remain.

Whatever those men wanted, they had meant nothing good.

She looked at the tiny hoard of victuals spread out on the blanket, wishing she had also thought to bring food. She broke a piece of the crust and chewed it slowly. And then another piece. And then half of it was gone and her stomach ached for more, urging her to finish it all. She forced herself to put it back in the saddlebag, stuffing everything back inside. She might need the rest of it later. Although a few tea leaves in hot water would help with her hunger. And warm her, too.

She would make tea, and then she would leave. The door opened. Cold air filled the cabin.

Surprised, she sat down on her rump with a bump and stared at the tall figure in the doorway.

Drew. He'd come back. He stared at the saddle-bag and then up to her face.

Relief flooded through her, chasing away the fear. Followed swiftly by anger. 'Where have you been?'

He dropped a bundle of fur on the floor. Rabbits. 'I went hunting.'

'How dare you leave without a word?'

Anger blazed in his eyes, like the rage of a cornered beast.

She'd said too much. She turned away, her hands clenched together, searching for words that wouldn't have him disappearing again. 'I thought you'd left for good.'

There was a long silence. And then the door opened. She swung around, heart in her throat.

He paused in the doorway, looking back. 'I'm going to clean these wee beasties so we can cook them.' His voice was harsh and raw. He went out with a slam of the door.

She closed her eyes. He had come back.

Outside, behind the bothy, Drew skinned and eviscerated the rabbits. Even that act of violence wasn't enough for the rage deep inside him. He wanted to hit something.

He was rock hard. Again. He'd thought he'd dealt with that problem. He'd walked away to distance himself. To get himself back under control. Then he'd come back and done exactly what he said he would never do again.

Let himself be seduced by a woman. Her frightened face had left him wanting to hold her. And to use her again.

Guilt swirled in his gut. He'd used her as if he was some sort of animal. He could see from the pain in her face that he'd hurt her. He'd shamed her. Forced her to submit to his disgusting fantasy. As if she was *her.*

And she wasn't. She was a strong, brave woman who deserved so much better.

At least she wouldn't trouble him anymore with her sweet smiles and soft eyes and the temptations of her sweet body. It would not happen again.

He quartered the rabbits, then sliced the meat thin. It was little enough, but it would fill their stomachs before they set out. He walked a little distance off from the bothy and hid the remains under a few rocks. Foxes or other scavengers would no doubt find it, but it wouldn't be obvious to any casual observer that it was human killed. He'd retraced their flight from the previous evening for a good long way and, as far as he could tell, the smugglers had not followed them, which didn't mean they wouldn't, but it did mean they had time to eat before they set out.

Steeling himself for more of her anger, he went back inside to discover that she had put water in the pot and it was already beginning to steam.

'Good thinking,' he said gruffly.

He was not surprised that her smile was small and painful, as though it hurt. She gestured to the bit of bread he had brought from the inn. 'I ate my half while you were gone.'

He heard the guilt in her voice and looked into her smoke-grey eyes.

'I really thought you weren't coming back,' she added softly.

He wanted to say she should have known he would. But how would she? He'd behaved like the worst cur imaginable. He shrugged. 'It took longer than I expected.'

She took a deep breath. 'Did you see anything of them? Those men?'

'No.' Her face said she didn't believe him. She was too clever for such an offhand assurance.

'Not that I'm thinking we've seen the last of them,' he continued. 'But they'd be here by now if they'd followed us last night, and I saw no sign of them on the track. And if they've waited for morning's light, as I believe they have, then it will be a while before they make their way here. By then we'll be gone.' He pulled a thin, flat rock from his pocket and set it on top of the fire. As a skillet, it wasn't much, but it would serve a turn.

Soon the little stone room was filled with the aroma of roasting meat and they were taking turns at sipping from the mug containing the last of his tea. He broke the remains of the roll in half and offered her one.

She shook her head. 'You need it more than I.'

He raised a brow.

'There's more of you,' she said, her smile tentative.

A soft feeling invaded his chest at the kindness of her words. He'd forgotten that women could be kind. *She* had always eaten first and thrown him whatever scraps were left. And if he had angered her, she'd given him nothing but punishment. It still shamed him that he'd let her treat him that way. Let her use him, at first out of gratitude and then out of weakness.

But he couldn't let Rowena's kindness sway him into being soft. It would make it too difficult to keep his distance. He grunted. 'Your choice.' He turned the meat on the stone. It looked ready. He cut into a piece with his knife to ensure it was cooked through.

'How did you catch them?' she asked.

Surprised by her interest, he looked up. 'With a snare.' He pulled a piece of looped string from his pocket. 'I learned a great deal from the Indians. They are clever hunters.'

He skewered one of the strips and held it out to her.

She pulled out her handkerchief and took it from him, blowing on it to cool it, then took a small hesitant bite. A smile spread across her stern face, making her look younger and almost pretty, more like the woman he'd pleasured in the night. He hardened. The devil confound him, why would his mind keep going back to that?

'Oh, my,' she said. 'That's delicious.'

Warm pleasure at her compliment spread through him. Warmth he should not be feeling. 'Because you're hungry,' he said curtly.

She flinched. And he ground his teeth at the look of hurt in her eyes. He preferred her anger.

He divided the strips between them and they tucked in. He ate his with the bread. It didn't take very long and he wished there was more, but he was used to an empty belly. She wasn't. He could see it in her face.

'Let us be on the road, then,' he said. 'If we are lucky we will reach our journey's end in time for supper.'

The look of longing on her face filled him with guilt. He couldn't even feed her properly. He was supposed to be protecting her, not putting her in danger. She'd come to him for comfort and he'd treated her like some low class of woman. But it was too late to put the beast back in the cage. All he could do was go forward so she would not have to suffer his presence for very much longer. Soon she would not be his responsibility.

The thought caused him to suffer a pang in his chest. Bloody indigestion, that was all.

He rose and began tidying up. 'We'll leave it just as we found it. For the next traveller.'

In silence, they began packing up.

Chapter Eight

After an hour or so of slow riding through the drifts, the sun came out. The glistening snow made it hard to see, but despite the cool wind, Rowena felt the warmth of the sun on her shoulders. She watched with interest at the way Drew had looked up at the sky, then adjusted their course.

'Do you know where we are?' she asked during one of their stops to rest the horses.

'Roughly.' He pointed ahead. 'That way is north-west. The map I saw showed that mountain due north of where we are headed.' He pointed at a distant jagged peak.

'How do you know that is the mountain you saw on the map?'

'I've been here before.'

'You have?'

'A long time ago. I was on my way to London.'

He urged his horse into motion and she followed suit, catching him up.

'You've been to London?'

'For my sins.'

She had the feeling he didn't want to say any more about it, but she could not hold back her questions. 'Is it as large as they say? As grand?'

'It is much bigger than Edinburgh, certainly. And crowded and dirty. Except for the small area occupied by the very rich. Mayfair and St James's. That is grand enough, I suppose.'

She digested this in silence. 'You don't sound very impressed. Why did you go?'

'Family business.'

And that was all he was going to say on the matter, she realised from the finality in his voice. A stab of hurt twisted in her chest. She forced herself to ignore it. Men did not like women poking their noses into their business, private or personal. She meant nothing to him. She couldn't even bring him the most basic of pleasures.

Heat rippled across her skin at the memory of the pleasure she had found in his arms. And the disgust she had seen on his face. Perhaps if she could make him understand that she had been true to her husband until that very moment, he wouldn't think her quite so wanton. And perhaps if he understood she planned never to marry again, he wouldn't fear he'd be trapped. She was a widow and she could do as she pleased, provided she was discreet, if that was what had bothered him so.

Clearly what had happened had been a mistake. For both of them. It would not happen again. Because he didn't want it to. The hollowness inside her grew.

They mounted up again and as the path narrowed she let her horse fall back, content to follow, and only glanced back over her shoulder occasionally, when she heard the sound of a bird or some other small noise.

Just in case it was those horrible men.

When they arrived, late that afternoon, the house was nothing like Drew expected. It was a mean and ill-appointed stone two-storey dwelling, lying ten miles from the duke's residence and five from the nearest village. It stood at the edge of a small forest of pines with a burn wandering through an overgrown patch of snow-covered

garden. Why send her to a place so far from anywhere? As if he didn't want her talking to anyone.

It wasn't as bad as the bothy they'd so recently
left, but not far off.

Rowena looked about her calmly, though also
clearly disappointed. He could not help but admire her calm manner when dealing with adversity.

She had not been so calm when she thought
he had abandoned her, he acknowledged wryly,
but who could blame her? He had walked out
on her without a word, shamed by knowing he
should have stopped what had happened. He
still could not believe he had treated a lady so
roughly. He'd expected recriminations. When
they hadn't come, he'd felt worse, realising she
feared he would abandon her to her fate.

But there was little he could say to explain.

He leaped from his horse. 'The place looks deserted.' He helped her down.

'It does,' she said, glancing up at a chimney
absent of smoke.

He tied the horses to a fence post and tossed
the saddlebags over his shoulder. 'Let us take a
look inside.'

She handed him the key the Pockles had passed on from Jones the morning they had left. The front door opened with a painful shriek of rusted metal. He wanted to curse the duke. Instead, he stepped over the threshold. Inside it smelled musty and dusty and damp. He grimaced at the smell. 'I think you might have to take rooms at an inn until the place has been aired out.'

She stepped around him and peered into the first room leading off the hallway. A parlour, of sorts, furnished with a sofa and a chair and table for eating. The room at the end of the hallway was a small kitchen with a door out to the garden, the path leading to a shed at the end, which might be assumed to serve as a stable. There were holes in its thatch and boards missing from the walls.

'You can't stay here,' he said as she turned back.

The glance she gave him caused him to close his mouth with a snap.

He followed her up the stairs. Two bedrooms. The one at the front a decent size. He trailed her into the one at the back. It overlooked the untidy garden.

'Is there an attic?' she asked. 'For servants?'

He went out to the landing to check. 'Not that I can see.'

'You'll stay in this room, then.'

He shook his head. 'I'll stay with the horses.' He didn't trust himself to sleep so close to her. 'We have enough explaining to do.'

Was that disappointment he saw in her face as she turned away to look out of the window? Surely not?

'You can't sleep out there,' she said.

He huffed out a breath. 'Well, I canna sleep in the house. There is no excuse for it. And Mrs Pockle will need the room when she arrives.'

'What if the smugglers come after us?'

'They willna'.' He huffed out a breath. 'But if they do, I'll hear them long before they get close. Dinna fash about that.' He gave her a mischievous grin to take the force out of his words. 'And Pockle will ha' to sleep out there, too, since there's no separate quarters for servants.' It wasn't right for married servants to cohabit with a single mistress. What could Jones have been thinking?

'Poor Mr Pockle.' Her eyes were large and sad, her smile tight. 'As you wish.'

Dammit, it was nothing to do with what he

wished. It was what was right. 'It won't take me long to repair the worst of the holes and we'll be as snug as bugs for a night or two. Then you will send a message to the duke and tell him that this really won't do.'

'I can't afford to stay at the inn.'

'But the duke—'

'Mr Jones was very clear. This is all the duke is prepared to give until my claims are settled. I am to stay here and await his pleasure.'

'It isna' right.'

She turned to face him. 'I know. And that is what makes me think there is something underhanded going on. I intend to get to the bottom of it.'

The determination on her face made him want to smile. 'I can't argue with your sense of unease. I have it, too.'

She frowned. 'I am to wait here until the duke sees fit to receive me. In the meantime, I have only sufficient funds either to hire a maid or to buy food.'

'I have what is left of your husband's money,' he said.

'But he gave that to you.'

'He gave it to me to see you safe home to his relatives.' He winced. 'There isna' verra much left.'

She sighed. 'Samuel was not blessed with the ability to hang on to his coin.'

'Or yours.'

Her smile was brief and pained. 'And what about you? Do you not need the money to continue your journey? It seems once you have answered the duke's questions you will have more than met your obligation. Indeed, the money is yours by right. You must keep it as payment for your service.'

He stiffened. 'I didna' do it for pay.' It was guilt that drove him. But that was something she did not need to know and so he lied. 'The money is yours.' He pulled the pouch from his pocket and held it out to her.

She looked at it for a long moment. 'My honour tells me I should refuse. My need tells me I do not have the luxury of honour.'

The bitterness in her voice struck a painful chord deep in his chest. He knew that feeling only too well. 'You can pay me back, then. When things are settled.'

'I will.' Determination filled her voice. She turned away, but not before he saw her cheeks flush with embarrassment. At being in debt to him, no doubt.

'I'll light a fire in the kitchen and take care of the horses, then see if I can snare some fresh meat,' he said, as if he had not noticed. 'The Pockles are sure to be here in the morning with our luggage.'

She turned away from the window with a sigh. 'I had hoped they might have arrived before us. I do hope they are not lost.'

Or attacked by the smugglers. He tried to look confident. 'Pockle's travelled the route many times before, winter and summer, he told me so.'

'Let us hope he was telling the truth. The duke might not be pleased if we have somehow mislaid his cousin.'

Drew narrowed his eyes at the thought. Hell, it might even give the duke the excuse he needed to refuse to acknowledge her at all. It seemed nothing about this affair was straightforward. 'If that time comes, I will see to it that he is found.'

'It seems I do nothing but accept your help, Mr Gilvry.' She pressed her lips together for a moment, then released a breath. 'Would you leave if I told you to go?'

'No.'

'Then it seems I have no choice but to accept your assistance. Thank you.'

Feeling very much like an intruder, he turned and clattered down the stairs. 'I'll be back with something for supper.'

What was she going to do? Rowena turned in a circle at the bottom of the stairs, looking at the little house in which she was supposed to live. A house that was hers, yet belonged to the duke. In the middle of nowhere.

She loved the Scottish countryside. The grandeur. The wildness. From a distance. She'd been raised in Edinburgh and lived there all her life. A city full of culture and education. How could she live in a place like this?

She could not. Not for very long, at least. Somehow she would have to find a way to see this reclusive duke and either convince him to honour the settlement left by her husband, if any, or seek another position.

Having come to a decision of how to proceed,

she set about dealing with her circumstances. When the Pockles arrived, she would have a change of clothes. In the meantime, if Drew was going to hunt, she was at least going to make the place habitable.

She turned up her sleeves and went into the kitchen, the only warm room in the house, and gazed in disgust at the dust and the dirt. First things first. Water.

She trudged through the snow in the garden to fetch water from the little stream to fill the kettle. Hands on hips, she surveyed the shed, now containing the horses. It was worse close up than it had been from a distance. It was barely good enough for a horse, let alone a man. And so she would tell him. Her heart sank. Perhaps he preferred to be out here, rather than inside with her. Perhaps he feared she would attack him while he slept.

She wouldn't. She wasn't that bold. Not now that she knew he found her unattractive. An antidote. Bad enough to make a husband run off to America.

She sighed. No, he wouldn't stay in the house,

even if she begged him. She struggled back to the house.

Very well. She was on her own. An independent woman. Not even the duke could take that away. And if there was some money owed to her from Samuel's will, perhaps she could start her own little school. For girls. Teach them to think for themselves. She blinked. Could she?

A sound at the front door sent her heart leaping in her throat. She ran to the window in the parlour that overlooked the front door.

A short middle-aged man stood on the step, knocking the snow off his boots and looking perfectly respectable. And behind him, at the gate, stood a cart. The man knocked.

Smugglers wouldn't knock. But still her heart raced painfully. The man knocked again and stepped back, looking up at the second storey as if he thought she might be still abed. He must know someone was here given the smoke no doubt issuing from the chimney.

Taking a deep breath, she left the room and hurried to the front door. She pulled it open and stepped back warily. Whoever he was, he might think she had no right to be here.

'Yes?' she said.

The man doffed his hat. His gaze took in the kerchief on her head and the rag in her left hand. 'I am here to see Mrs MacDonald.'

Startled by the use of her name, she stared at him. 'Who are you?'

'Jeffrey Weir. Duke of Mere's steward. To see your mistress, if you please.' She took the card he handed over. The duke's steward. Just the man she wanted to see. And since it seemed unlikely he posed a threat, she gestured for him to enter. 'Come in.'

She led him into the parlour.

He sat down. She followed suit. He frowned as if puzzled.

'I am Mrs MacDonald,' she said.

He popped up from his seat, looking thoroughly discomposed. 'I beg your pardon, madam.'

She raised a brow. 'Who else did you expect to answer the door?'

He swallowed and tugged at his neckcloth. 'Your servant?'

With a theatrical sigh, she glanced around. 'This house hasn't seen a servant in months, if ever. As the duke's steward, you must be aware of that fact.' She really shouldn't be so cruel to the poor man, whose face was now as red as a carnation, but she could not help it. If he was the duke's steward, then it was his responsibility to ensure the house was habitable, surely?

'A couple by the name of Pockle,' he managed to gasp. 'They were to accompany you, I understand.'

'Ah, yes, the Pockles,' she said with a lift of one brow. 'Unfortunately, they became separated from me on the road, where I was subsequently attacked by smugglers and forced to flee in the middle of the night. By the good offices of Mr Gilvry did I escape with my life. Only to arrive at a derelict house.'

'I beg your pardon, ma'am. I had intended to be here several days ago. The duke sent me with supplies, but with the snowstorm…' He gestured vaguely at the window. 'The Pockles…'

'At this moment, I have no clue what has happened to the Pockles.'

He swallowed. 'Mr Samuel—'

'His remains are with them.'

'Yes,' he said hurriedly. 'Yes, of course. But the duke is most anxious to see his cousin appropriately interred, you understand. Most anxious.' He gave her a look askance. 'If it is his cousin.'

She stared at him and narrowed her eyes in a sudden suspicion. Was this what they planned? To find a way to deny that Samuel was really dead? 'Of course it is.'

'The body must be properly identified. To the duke's satisfaction.' He pulled a handkerchief from his pocket and wiped his brow. The man was sweating despite the room being as cold as charity. 'And the date of death properly established.'

The date? Aha. Now they were back to the date. 'Then the sooner I and Mr Gilvry, who knows the date, meet with the duke, the better.'

Sounds emanated from the kitchen. Loud sounds. Drew returning. The steward sent her a questioning look.

Rowena smiled calmly, folding her hands in her lap.

The next moment Drew appeared in the doorway, glowering at her guest. 'Who is this, then?'

'This is the duke's steward, Mr Weir,' she said, 'sent to see if I am pleased with my new accommodations.'

Weir, who had been staring at Drew's face with a kind of fascinated horror, rose to his feet and held out his hand. 'You must be Gilvry.'

Drew looked him up and down with a dismissive expression. 'I hope you have apologised to Mrs MacDonald for the dreadful state of this property. Not a stick of wood or a bite of food in the place. Not to mention the dirt.'

'I…I have indeed begged her pardon,' Weir said in a choking voice. 'I have brought supplies.'

'How long will it take to get to Mere from here?' Drew asked.

'It is a day's journey, on a good day, the roads being what they are. I set out yesterday, but was delayed by the storm.'

'As were we,' Gilvry said in a voice as dry as dust. 'Come on, then, man, let us see what you have. You can give me a hand to unload.'

The steward stiffened. 'I…'

Drew glared at him. Only by dint of will did Rowena stop herself from grinning when the little man seemed to deflate as Drew ushered him out.

Chapter Nine

Something was wrong. Drew could feel it deep in his bones. And in the bitter taste on his tongue.

He stomped out of the front door and made his way to the back of the cart. When he'd heard about the house set aside for her on the ducal estate, he'd assumed it meant a dower house in the grounds, near the duke's abode, not some cottage in the middle of nowhere.

It was almost as if the duke had decided to isolate her from the world. As if she was some sort of dirty secret.

He threw back the tarpaulin. A cage full of chickens fluttered and squawked in panic. His gut fell away as he stared at the rest of the contents. Flour. Salt beef. Ham. A barrel of apples. Winter supplies. And those were the things he could make out at a glance.

He swung around to face Weir, grabbing the man's lapels, bringing him close to his face with a snarl. 'What the hell is going on?'

The steward leaned back, ineffectually batting at Drew's hands. 'How dare you, sir? Release me at once.'

Drew shoved him away. 'Well? Answer my question.'

'I do not take your meaning, Gilvry.'

'I mean,' he said, holding on to his anger, just barely, 'she is the widow of the duke's cousin, damn it. Why is she being treated like some sort of pariah?'

The little man's moustache's bristled. He tugged his coat straight. 'She was Mr MacDonald's responsibility. Not the duke's. She has no official status in the family. He is being more than generous.' He gestured to the house and the cart.

Drew's fingers trembled with the strain of not closing around the other man's throat and squeezing. Hard. 'She's a lady. Is she supposed to raise chickens? Keep a cow? Cook and clean?'

Weir retreated a step. 'The Pockles were hired—'

He snorted his disgust. 'The Pockles. A lazy

good-for-naught and his slatternly wife and no-where to house them decently. I demand that Mrs MacDonald be taken to the duke immediately, as is fitting.'

The little man stiffened. 'Demand, sir? Demand? You are in no position to demand anything. Were you not the man who was present at Mr MacDonald's death? And now the man who sticks like a burr to his widow?' His lip curled. 'And the pair of you giving the Pockles the slip? How many nights is it since the lady had any sort of chaperon?'

Drew's hands curled into fists. Every muscle in his body tensed. 'Are you accusing me of some sort of dishonourable conduct with respect to the lady?'

Weir hesitated, his beady eyes clearly calculating the odds of his escaping with his life. He must have realised they were not good. 'No. Of course not,' he muttered. 'But you must see this from the duke's perspective. A woman who the duke has never heard of arrives, announcing his cousin's demise with the man who said he witnessed the death, and demanding settlement of her affairs. The duke is bound to be cautious. As are his advisors.'

Drew forced his hands to relax. 'The duke owes her the courtesy of speaking to her in person.'

'Perhaps if you and the lady could provide a little more definitive information.' His smile was ingratiating.

'Will her husband's body be definitive enough?'

'Once it is identified it will go part way to easing the duke's concerns.'

Drew smiled, or at least bared his teeth in what might be interpreted as a smile, but clearly was not by Weir, who backed up hard against the cartwheel. 'It can be identified. I ha' made sure of it, if the damned Pockles have not lost the body along the way. Perhaps the duke should be sending out a search party. Does he know there are smugglers using his land for convenient passage?'

'Smugglers?'

'Oh, aye, you know, all right. I can see it in your face. They set upon us at McRae's inn last evening, which is why we have now arrived without the damned Pockles.' A thought occurred to him. His gut clenched. 'We can only hope the Pockles did not encounter them on the road.'

'I doubt smugglers would have any reason to bother a coffin,' the man said a little stiffly.

'Unless that coffin is also a cask full of the best brandy to be found in North Carolina.'

Mr Weir turned green.

Drew glared at him. 'Well, let us get this cart unloaded. We can continue our conversation while we work.'

Rowena watched as Drew piled two sacks onto the steward's outstretched arms. The little man's knees buckled, but he bravely staggered around the back of the house with his burden.

She stared open-mouthed at the crate of chickens Drew pulled off next. Live chickens? Was she supposed to keep them, or eat them? Her only experience of chickens was with a roast or a fricassee presented on a plate on the table. Or paying the butcher's bill.

But without any servants, or money to pay them, she had the horrid feeling she might be learning a whole new way of dealing with them. She glanced down the lane in front of the house, hoping to see the Pockles riding to the rescue.

No. She couldn't rely on anyone else to help her

out of this peculiar situation. She must attack the problem head-on. Take on the duke. She ran upstairs and dug around in her saddlebag. Yes, here it was. The tattered remains of her journal and a pencil Samuel had purchased for her as a bride gift. He had one just like it, only his was bound in blue morocco leather, while hers was red.

What had happened to his journal? It might have shed some light on just what her husband had been doing out there in the wilds. It was completely out of character for a man like Samuel, who liked his comforts, to stray from the pleasures offered in town.

She ripped a blank page from the back and looked at the tip of her pencil. A bit blunt, but not completely useless. She sat at the dresser and began to write.

Your Grace,
While we have as yet to meet, I find myself compelled to introduce myself. I am, as you are aware, your cousin by marriage to Samuel MacDonald. It is most important that you grant me an interview at your earliest convenience, to discuss matters that I believe we

will find of mutual benefit. I look forward to hearing from you as to when such a meeting will be convenient. If you have not come to see me before the week is out, I shall call on you at your residence.

Respectfully yours...

Once more she raked through the saddlebag and this time located a stub of sealing wax and Samuel's ring.

She took her letter downstairs, heated the wax over the fire until she managed to get a few drops to fall on the fold then pressed the ring into it.

She spun around as Mr Weir entered the kitchen with an arm full of logs, followed by a glowering Drew.

'That's everything,' he said.

'Are there candles?' she asked.

'Aye. I put them in the dresser,' Drew said.

'Excellent.' She turned to Weir. 'I have a letter for you to take back to the duke, if you would be so good.'

The man glanced at Drew and shifted from foot to foot. 'It would be my pleasure, ma'am.'

'If I do not hear back from the duke within a

week, do tell him to expect my call,' she said sweetly. 'I am sure Mr Gilvry would be happy to accompany me to the castle.'

A look of panic crossed Weir's face.

She frowned. 'Would that be a problem?'

But the man had already pulled himself together and his face was once more without expression. 'I will give his Grace your message.'

He turned, then realised Drew was standing right behind him. He tried to dodge, but both men stepped in the same direction. Once, twice and a third time. Drew finally took pity on him and stepped aside to let him pass.

'One week, mind,' he said as the man scurried out of the kitchen door.

When she was sure he was out of the house and turning his cart around in the lane, she took a deep breath. 'I don't care what the duke answers. I will not stay here for more than one week.' She paced across the floor to gaze out of the window. Weir and his cart had disappeared. She spun around. 'He queried Sam's date of death.'

'What? Why?'

'It was a passing mention. It is very strange. If

only there was something to prove your recollection.'

A shadow passed across his face. 'I'm sorry,' he said.

Her stomach dipped. His expression was wooden. He had thought of something, but it did not suit him to tell her.

He must have seen the doubt in her face because he grimaced, the movement pulling at the scar on his cheek and making his lip curl more than usual. 'Perhaps the duke will take a man's word without cavilling.'

'I don't think they mean to impugn your honour,' she said. 'It seems to be more a matter of legalities.'

'It is some sort of bureaucratic nonsense, if you want my opinion.' His fingers flexed, then he let out a short breath. 'I know for certain he died on September fifteenth and so I will swear before God and the courts.'

'Then we have to hope it will suffice.'

'Aye.'

Such a wealth of meaning in that one word. Distrust. Regret. Anger. Drew Gilvry was a complex man who had secrets. And he wasn't going to part with them for a mere duke. Or for her. Not unless it suited him. But if he did have some sort of proof of the date, what possible reason could he have for keeping such a thing a secret?

No, her suspicions were groundless. It was wishful thinking that something good could come from all this. She sighed. 'In the meantime, I suppose we must kick our heels until we hear back from the duke.'

'Indeed.'

'Then it is a good thing I gave him an ultimatum.'

'Aye. I suppose it is.' He sounded amused.

She shot him a hard stare. 'Then let us see if we can turn some of those supplies into a decent meal.'

'Oh, I think that can be done, Mrs MacDonald.'

The next afternoon, the Pockles arrived.

Sans the barrel.

'Where is it?' Drew barked at Pockle, looking into the back of the cart.

'That is what I would like to know,' Rowena said, marching down the path. 'I am glad to see you have not lost my luggage, but what have you done with my husband?'

Pockle touched a finger to his forelock. 'We broke a wheel when we were setting out from McRae's. We were only hours behind you, but had to stay until it was repaired.'

She looked down her haughty nose, like a queen observing the lowest of her subjects, and Pockle seemed to shrivel. Drew held his tongue. She didn't need any help from him. Pockle was most definitely cowed.

Mrs Pockle gave her a look of dislike. 'One of the duke's men met us on the road. Mr Weir. He took charge of his Grace's cousin. And glad of it I am.' She shuddered.

Rowena's eyes widened. She glanced at Drew, worry clouding her gaze.

'Why did he do that?' Drew asked.

'He said the duke was anxious to see his cousin's remains decently cared for.'

And if the duke saw fit not to identify them as his cousin? He could see the same thought flickering over Rowena's face.

'I think we should not wait for his Grace to agree to a meeting,' Drew said.

Pockle stared at him. 'What? No. You are to stay here until the duke sends for you. Weir said so.'

'I don't answer to Mr Weir,' Rowena said. 'Or the duke, actually.'

'Och, now, listen here,' Pockle said. 'His Grace is to send his lawyer to visit you. In a day or so.'

Weir had said nothing about sending the lawyer. It was something Weir must have made up on his way to meet the Pockles. Now, why would he do that?

'You mean Mr Jones, I assume,' Rowena said sweetly.

Pockle scratched at his shoulder. 'That's it. That's the name he gave.'

'I already met Mr Jones. The person I have not yet met is his Grace.'

'We will set out first thing in the morning,' Drew said.

Mrs Pockle gave a sort of a wail. 'But we only just got here.'

'You don't have to come with us,' Rowena said.

Pockle glowered. Drew tried to hide a smile as she lifted her chin and the man seemed to crumble.

'There is one thing I wanted to ask you,' Drew said. 'Did you run into a gang of smugglers at McRae's?'

'No,' Pockle said. 'But I heard they attacked the inn. You were lucky you escaped with your lives.'

'Attacked the inn, did they?' Drew said his voice dry. He could imagine McRae covering his own arse in case he or Rowena went to the duke, demanding justice.

'And the one I shot?' Drew asked.

'Dead.'

Drew swallowed a curse, not wanting to worry Rowena, but he had the feeling that he wouldn't have heard the last of the smugglers if he'd killed one of their number. Something else to lay at his brother's door.

'Did McRae say anything else?' he asked. Such as he'd slept in Rowena's chamber?

'He said he was sorry it happened under his roof,' Pockle said, his eyes innocent of any slyness. 'He asked me to apologise. To say he would not have had the lady so inconvenienced for the world and so he would tell the duke if need be.'

And if Rowena didn't blame him for what happened, no doubt he would say nothing about their pretence to be a married couple.

He noticed Rowena eyeing her bag with eagerness. He could imagine why. The poor lass hadn't had a change of clothes in days. He lifted it down and carried it into the house.

'Don't bother carrying it upstairs,' she said, following him in, 'since we will be carrying it out again tomorrow.'

'It is no trouble, madam,' he said, and marched upstairs.

'And where do I sleep?' he could hear Mrs Pockle asking Rowena.

'There is another bedroom at the back,' she replied. 'Pockle will join Mr Gilvry in the stables until we can make a better arrangement. It is something I mean to take up with the duke.'

He grinned at the sound of Pockle's groan of displeasure. But it made a point: that he had not been sleeping in the same house as a woman on her own. Whether the Pockles would believe it was another matter, but since he had made his bed out there last night and the evidence was quite plain to be seen, there was no reason for them not to believe it.

And having Pockle for company, much as he despised the man, would keep him from succumbing to the temptation he'd barely resisted the previous night. Not that he expected Rowena would welcome his company.

He dropped the bag on the floor and could not help from glancing at the bed, the covers neatly straightened as if no one had slept there.

All last night he had kept envisaging the way she had surrendered to his uncouth demands. How she had submitted to his rampant lust. His blood ran hot. And then he remembered the shame on her face. The embarrassment. His blood chilled as if he had stepped neck deep into the stream in the garden.

Thank goodness they were leaving tomorrow. Once under the duke's roof there would be no further opportunities for temptation.

If he felt disappointment at the thought, it was because his inner beast had no conscience. But he did. And the weight of it was a heavy burden. He made his way downstairs.

Rowena, with a grumpy-looking Mrs Pockle, met him at the bottom. He gave the servant a hard look. 'Mrs MacDonald will be needing hot water to bathe and a change of clothes.'

He bowed to Rowena. 'If it is all right with you, I will go and see if my traps have resulted in fresh meat. Hopefully, Mrs Pockle can make stew for dinner. Or perhaps a nice rabbit pie.'

'That would be wonderful,' Rowena said.

Mrs Pockle looked as if she wanted to hit Drew over the head. He made good his escape before she found a rolling pin.

Pockle drained his tankard of small beer and leaned back in his chair, folding his hands over his belly. 'Very nice, Mrs Pockle,' he said.

Drew's traps had yielded up some game and, with the supplies Weir had dropped off and the surprisingly excellent cooking skills of Mrs Pockle, he had to admit dinner was excellent.

Rowena was dining in solitary state in the parlour, while he and the Pockles ate in the warm, if somewhat overcrowded, kitchen.

'Yes,' Drew said. 'Excellent meal. My compliments, Mrs Pockle.' He drained his own tankard and pushed his chair back.

'A moment afore you go, Mr Gilvry,' Pockle said.

'Yes?'

'You and Mrs MacDonald seem to have a pretty good understanding.'

Drew stiffened. 'What do you imply?'

Pockle blinked. 'Why, naught but to say that she seems to take your advice. Can I suggest that you advise her to wait here at the duke's pleasure? It is not a good thing to go upsetting a duke, ye ken.'

It was definitely a warning. Likely something cooked up between the Pockles while he was out in the woods, no doubt. 'You think he will turn her away from his door?'

Pockle leaned forward. 'He's a duke. Who knows what he will do? But Mr Weir's instructions were very clear. It won't do her any good to set his Grace against her, now will it?'

'Do you know why he would not want to receive a visit from Mrs MacDonald?'

Pockle rolled his eyes. 'Dukes don't confide in the likes of me.' He picked up his tankard and looked into the bottom of it, clearly hoping it wasn't empty. He put it down again with a sigh when he was wrong. 'All I'm sayin' is that Mr Weir made his orders very clear.'

'And you want me to speak to Mrs MacDonald about it.'

Mrs Pockle nodded her head vigorously. 'She won't listen to us, but she might listen to you.'

'Not if her mind is made up.' Still, it would be an opportunity to talk over their strategy for the morrow in private. 'Verra well. I'll talk to her.'

'You do that, lad,' Pockle said.

Ignoring the urge to shove the word *lad* down the other man's throat, Drew got up from the table. He closed the kitchen door behind him and strode into the parlour.

Rowena had made little of the meal he saw and was now seated beside the hearth.

'You should eat more,' he said.

When she looked up, her gaze was bleak. 'I'm worried about tomorrow.'

And there wasn't much he could say to ease her concern. 'Do you think we should wait? You did give the duke a week to respond.'

'Is that your advice?'

He shook his head. 'There is something havey-cavey going on.' He raised a hand. 'I know. I am not being completely helpful. Still, it seems odd to me that Weir did not inform you that Jones was to pay you a visit. It was almost as if he thought it up on the way to find Pockle.'

Some of the worry left her face. 'You thought that, too?'

'I did.' He went to the door and looked down the hallway. The kitchen door remained closed. 'I think attack is the best form of defence. And surprise will give you an advantage.'

'Then it's settled.' She rose to her feet. She was wearing the same gown she'd been wearing the first time he saw her. She'd looked so calm that evening. So controlled. So much in command. It was hard to put that side of her together with the woman who had subjugated herself to his dark desires.

He wanted to apologise. Beg forgiveness. To do so would be a lie. Because if he had the chance, he would do it all over again.

Chapter Ten

Castle was a complete misnomer, Rowena thought as the cart rocked its way up the long drive. Yes, off to the right there were some ruins that might have been a castle once, long ago. The ducal residence was in fact a grand mansion built some time in the late seventeenth century that had somehow survived the wars between England and Scotland.

Its walls were grim and grey, as was the statuary decorating the corners and niches across its face. It had a slightly shabby look about it. Imposing, yes, but here and there brickwork showed through the stuccoed facade. And some of the statues were missing an arm or a bit of their drapery.

A place like this would be enormously expensive to keep up.

'Have you been here before?' she asked Mrs Pockle seated beside her on the cart. Drew and Pockle rode either side of them, like an honour guard.

The woman nodded. 'My family lived on the estate. So did Pockle's, but ne'er did I expect to go inside the house.'

She might not enter upon this occasion either, if the duke turned them away at the door. Rowena glanced down at her clothing. She'd worn her second-best gown and spencer. Fortunately, a governess wore subdued practical colours and dark grey was very nearly appropriate for mourning. They halted outside the front door. Drew helped her down from the cart. She eyed the imposing entrance askance. No sense in hesitating. She squared her shoulders and walked towards the front door.

Drew kept pace. As usual he wore Samuel's coats and linen as well as snug-fitting doeskin breeches, and his boots were polished to a high shine that did not hide that they were neither new nor in the first stare of fashion.

But for all that the greatcoat was too tight across his shoulders and chest, he looked remarkably handsome. And to his surprise, she had told him so before they left.

He'd touched his cheek and she'd shaken her head. 'I hardly notice it, you know,' she had said. An odd look had softened his usually harsh expression, but he had turned away before she could interpret it.

Now he strode at her side, looking grimly purposeful, as if preparing to fight a dragon on her behalf. How could she not feel safe with such a strong, commanding man at her side? Yet it would not do to rely on him too much. He had made it quite clear he intended to hand off his responsibility for her at the earliest opportunity.

He rapped on the monstrous wooden door.

It creaked open, loudly proclaiming it needed oil. Something a good housekeeper would never allow.

An elderly footman looked at them with enquiry.

'Mrs MacDonald to see the duke,' Drew proclaimed and handed him her calling card. Or rather the card she had created from a flyleaf at the back of her woebegone journal.

With a muttered, 'Wait here,' the man shut the door in their faces.

Rowena raised a brow and looked at Drew.

He shrugged. 'He didna' say go away.'

So they waited. After five minutes, Rowena wondered if she should ask Drew to knock again.

She opened her mouth to do so, but the door once more protested on its hinges and swung inwards. This time, a butler stood at attention, wearing a black frock coat and a severe expression.

'You are to come in,' he said, and gestured for her to enter.

Relief slid down her spine in a whisper. It seemed the duke was not as unreasonable as his minions seemed to indicate. She stepped over the threshold and Drew followed her in. The butler, a man well into his sixties, with a few grey hairs pasted to his bald pate, took their coats. He looked at Drew and then at her. 'Who else shall I say is calling, madam?'

'This is Mr Gilvry, my man of business. Mr Jones is acquainted with him.'

'Will you send someone to see to the horses?'

Drew requested. 'And Mrs MacDonald's driver and maid.'

The butler bowed. 'Yes, sir.' He walked to one of the doors leading off the great hall and opened it. 'If you would wait here? I will inform her ladyship.'

'Are you speaking of the duchess?' Rowena asked.

'Lady Cragg, madam.'

'We wish to see the duke,' Drew said.

'The duke is indisposed.' He whisked away before they could ask more questions.

'I have no idea who Lady Cragg might be,' she said to Drew.

'Nor I. It is not a name I have heard on anyone's lips before now.'

'It seems odd that the duke would send someone who is not a family member to receive me.'

'She could be a cousin. Or a companion to the duchess.'

Rowena frowned. 'Is there a duchess? I wish I had been able to look him up in *Debrett's*. Indeed, I should have thought to do so before we left Dundee. It just didn't occur to me.'

The sound of quick, sharp footsteps on marble echoed in the great hall on the other side of the door. 'I suspect all is about to be revealed,' Drew said.

'Dear Mrs MacDonald, it is my pleasure to welcome to you to Mere, despite the sadness of the times.'

The woman who entered, holding out her hands and offering a gentle smile to Rowena, was in her sixties, with crimped grey hair beneath a black lace cap. She was wearing deep mourning. For the recently departed duke? She was followed in by Jones, the lawyer. He must have set out for Mere at the same time they had. Why had he lied about going to Edinburgh?

'Thank you,' Rowena said, clearly taken aback by the effusive welcome as she let the woman take both her hands in hers, but her frowning gaze had fixed upon Mr Jones, who bowed and smirked.

'I am Lady Cragg,' the other woman said. 'Also a distant relation to your poor husband. You know Mr Jones, of course. Please, do sit down.'

Rowena sank into the offered chair. The woman looked pointedly at Drew and then recoiled as she took in his face. He should have worn his scarf. Her gaze wandered over his too-small coats and shabby boots, and her lip curled in a sneer. He met her gaze with a glower. 'Andrew Gilvry, my lady. At your service.' He bowed.

'Please, do be seated, Mr Gilvry.'

This was a woman very much used to obedience and a woman very much in command of the situation. A strange prickle ran across the back of his neck.

Drew sat to the right and a little behind Rowena, offering his support, but making it clear she was in charge. After pulling the bell rope, Mr Jones sat on a gilt chair a few feet from Drew.

'I wish to speak to his Grace,' Rowena said, gathering herself once more.

'Sadly, he is indisposed,' Lady Cragg said calmly. 'He was laid low by the death of the late duke, and I, as his only living relative, am charged with looking after his affairs until his doctor indicates he is well enough to face the world.'

Rowena frowned. 'I understood that there was no direct heir to the dukedom. That there were some doubts—'

'All doubts have been resolved,' Mr Jones said. 'Even now the late duke's will is in probate.'

'That is the reason I wish to see the duke. I understand that my husband, Mr Samuel Mac-Donald, left the duke as executor to his will. So far, Mr Jones has been able to give me very little information about my husband's financial affairs. While the duke is kind to provide me with a house, I really prefer my independence. So I have come to sort out my affairs.'

Nothing like attacking a problem head-on, Drew thought with admiration.

'I understand your anxiety, Mrs MacDonald. Indeed I do. You must understand there have been many petitioners coming forward seeking financial redress of the duke. A most distressing time for all. Clearly as family, you have more claim than most, hence the offer of a house until matters could be resolved. Am I to understand that you are rejecting the duke's largesse?'

Drew looked to see how Rowena would receive what was obviously a reprimand. Her face was pale and her expression worried. His anger pushed to the fore. 'Mrs MacDonald has no wish to discommode anyone, Lady Cragg,' he said.

'But the house is most unsuitable for a widow of her standing. Not only is it in the middle of nowhere, but it is practically in ruins.'

It was pushing it a bit, but he could not sit by and see her bullied.

Lady Cragg turned her gaze on Drew. While her smile was pleasant enough the brown eyes were shrewd and calculating. 'Ah, yes. I understand from Mr Jones that you are the man who brought Mr Samuel back to Scotland and that you are acting as Mrs MacDonald's man of affairs.'

She made it sound sordid. Had the Pockles said something to Weir about them spending a night together alone after all? He glared at her. 'I am. And it seems to me, that as a member of Mere's family—'

'Your defence of your client is commendable, Mr Gilvry,' Lady Cragg said. 'And I wholeheartedly agree with your sentiments. I don't know what Mr Weir was thinking when he suggested that cottage. Likely it was the only vacant property available. I was appalled at Weir's description when he returned yesterday. You must understand that our lives have been at sixes and sevens here at Mere for some weeks now.' She bowed her head slightly. 'I apologise for his mistake.' Her smile was tight and a little forced. 'Please, Mrs MacDonald, do forgive us, and may I welcome you to reside at Mere Castle until the duke is able to meet with you. You may be sure that appropriate arrangements will be made for your future. The duke is not one to avoid his obligations.'

That took the wind out of their sails to be sure and the worry out of Rowena's face. 'You are very kind,' she said.

It was just too easy. 'What sort of arrangements?' Drew asked.

The gimlet eyes returned to his face and she visibly repressed a shudder of distaste. 'I do not believe Mrs MacDonald will require your services any longer, Mr Gilvry. The remains have been identified as Mr Samuel MacDonald's. Mr Jones is undertaking the probate of his will along with that of the duke's…' She frowned. 'You are not a lawyer, I understand?'

'No, I am no' a lawyer,' he said. 'I stand as a friend and an advisor—'

'I am sure Mrs MacDonald will be more than happy to leave legal matters in Mr Jones's capable hands?' She looked at Rowena, who in turn looked at Drew.

'What about the matter of the date of Mr Mac-Donald's death? There has been some importance placed on this issue in our conversation with Mr Jones. And with Mr Weir.'

Lady Cragg waved a dismissive hand. 'Mr Jones was following my instructions, I am afraid. Our concern was the interment, the carving of the stone. A date is required.'

He glanced at Rowena, who was looking at her open-mouthed. 'I gave Mr Jones the date. He said he needed proof.'

Lady Cragg raised her iron-grey brows at Mr Jones, who gave a little cough behind his hand. 'A misunderstanding, I'm afraid. I was confusing the date with that of the duke. A most unfortunate lapse. I do apologise. Your word is not being questioned.'

He gaped at the smarmy young man, who shrugged.

'May I have a moment alone with Mrs Mac-Donald?' Drew asked.

'Certainly,' Lady Cragg said. 'I will arrange for tea to be served in the parlour, Mrs MacDonald.

Ring for a footman to show you the way when you are done here. Mr Gilvry, you have been of great service to our family. You will attend Mr Jones in his office when you are ready to leave and you will be recompensed as is only right.'

She got up and swept out.

Jones bowed to Rowena. He looked at Drew. 'I will wait outside in the hall.' He also withdrew.

Drew frowned. 'They seem very...accommodating.'

Rowena rose to her feet and paced around the room. 'Almost a complete about-face.' She looked at him. 'Do you think I should trust them? Lady Cragg seems very nice. Very open. The date is no longer an issue and they are my husband's family...'

Did being family make Lady Cragg worthy of trust? He wouldn't trust his own family. Not anymore. But his responsibility ended here. He had done what he set out to do and they were accepting his verbal account. 'If you feel comfortable, then it seems my presence is no longer required.'

She took a deep breath and gave him a smile that was gentle and quite endearing. 'I do thank you for your help. And your patience.' She col-

oured and looked away. 'Perhaps, once this is
settled and I have returned to Edinburgh, you
might wish to call.'

Stunned, he stared at her. He had not expected
her to wish to continue their acquaintance, not
after the way he had treated her. His heart gave
an odd little lurch. A pang of longing. Desire
heated his blood.

But when he left here, he was going to seek out
Ian. And once he found him, he wouldn't have a
future. 'I don't think—'

'No. No, of course not. You have your own affairs to consider. It was foolish of me to ask.'

Now, why the hell did she sound so embarrassed? And even a little distraught.

She held out her hand. 'Then I must wish you
goodbye, Mr Gilvry. And thank you for all your
help.'

He bowed over her hand. 'My pleasure, Mrs
MacDonald.'

An empty space filled his chest and, with a
sense that he was leaving something very pre-
cious, he strode out quickly, in case he did what
he really wanted to and disgraced her before her

family by taking her lovely mouth in a punishing kiss.

Feeling strangely hollow, he found Jones waiting in the corridor outside the drawing room, too far away for him to have been listening to the conversation inside the room, yet he looked relieved when Drew appeared, as if he had not been sure of the outcome of his discussions with Rowena.

Was there some meaning to that worry?

'This way,' Jones said. 'We'll go to my office in the east wing.'

He followed the lawyer along a series of passages and down a flight of stairs. The office he entered was small, with a window overlooking the stables. Its shelves were lined with law books and ledgers.

Jones pulled out a metal box from the bottom drawer of a plain wooden desk and unlocked it with a key from the chain attached to his fob. He drew out of it a leather pouch that landed on the table with a heavy thump. 'For your trouble. There's enough gold here to carry you far from here. Back to America if you wish.'

Drew's jaw dropped. 'What the devil is this for?'

'Your reward for bringing Mr Samuel home.'

Guilt was a sour taste in his mouth. 'I need no payment for doing my duty.'

'Then take it as payment for your discretion.'

If Drew had been uneasy before, something in his head was sending messages of alarm. 'Mrs MacDonald—'

'She is no longer your concern. You can hardly expect Mere's relative to acknowledge any sort of connection with the Gilvrys of Dunross.' Jones gave him a narrow-eyed stare. 'Any sort of connection.'

A warning. That Rowena was above his touch. Weir or Pockle must have given voice to suspicions. Jones was buying him off. 'Stuff it,' he said crudely.

Jones looked startled, then shrugged. 'As you wish.' He swept up the pouch and locked it away again. 'I'll have a footman see you out.' He reached out and pulled at the bell on the wall behind him. The liveried footman had clearly been waiting nearby, since he appeared almost immediately. 'Good day, Mr Gilvry. Jeremiah, please escort Mr Gilvry to the stables.' He gave Drew a look that contained an element of triumph. 'You will find your horse ready and waiting.'

He walked out.

Outside in the corridor, another footman was also waiting. He fell in behind Drew as he followed Jeremiah out of the house and across the stable yard. They weren't taking any chances. What, did they think he would steal the silver?

Not that a couple of pampered footman could stop him if he decided he wanted the silver. But he didn't. He just wanted to be on his way. To be rid of the sickening emptiness in his gut that accompanied the understanding he would never see Rowena again. He recognised the feeling. Loss.

He'd had the same one when he'd said goodbye to his family six years before. And again when he'd realised just how permanent Ian had intended that parting to be. Well, Ian was in for a shock. And it would give Drew a good deal of satisfaction to see it in his brother's face when he met his end.

He mounted up and his escort saw him out of the gate.

He focused his mind on the form that shock would take and not on the distance he was putting between himself and Mere Castle.

* * *

The suite of rooms assigned to Rowena were at the far end of the west wing. They were sumptuous indeed. A sitting room adjoined the bedchamber to which was also attached a dressing room with a truckle bed for her maid.

Luxury, indeed. She had not lived in such fine surroundings since she'd left her father's house after his death.

'I hope you have found Pockle to your satisfaction,' Lady Cragg enquired after showing her around her apartments. 'She is the only maid I have available at the moment. We keep minimal staff here at Mere.'

'I can't say I have had much of an opportunity to judge,' Rowena replied. 'We were separated from the Pockles after the first night of our journey.'

'Separated?' Lady Cragg's voice rose in shock. 'You were left alone?'

'No. Mr Gilvry was with me.' She blushed at the sight of the other woman's horrified countenance.

'Oh, my dear.' Lady Cragg's voice faded. 'Think

of your reputation. Of Mere's good name. Never speak of it again.'

'Very well,' Rowena said. 'But—'

Lady Cragg raised a hand. 'Pockle tells me you do not have attire suitable for mourning. It must be attended to at once. We should not wish to show any lack of respect, either for your husband, or the duke, should we?'

'Certainly not,' Rowena said, as expected.

'In the meantime, you will keep to your rooms if you do not mind. We have guests at Mere who would be shocked if… Well, you do understand, do you not?'

The question was purely rhetorical.

Lady Cragg smiled. 'In the meantime, do, my dear Mrs MacDonald, make yourself comfortable. I am sure you need to rest after your journey. I will have supper sent up to you later.'

'When will I meet the duke?'

The woman paused, her expression altering into lines of sorrow. 'The duke is much affected by all the bad news. Prostrate upon his bed. Perhaps when you are appropriately gowned? Believe me, you will see him at the earliest opportunity.'

She bustled out.

Rowena sat down in the armchair beside the window that looked out over the formal grounds. To her surprise, a small boy of about five, bundled against the chilly air, was skipping along one of the walkways trailed by what she could only assume was a nurse. The duke's child? Or perhaps he belonged to one of the visitors. The nurse caught him and swung him around before carrying him out of sight.

Rowena stared at the long drive leading out to the gate. No sign of Drew. He would be long gone by now. She would have liked to have discussed in more detail his impressions of Lady Cragg and the duke's household. For example, why was Lady Cragg so evasive? So set on her having gowns made before she saw the duke? Still, it was no secret that the grandest families set a great deal of store by the proprieties and she certainly didn't want to do anything that would set up the duke's back. Not before she had a chance to air her concerns.

But she was going to miss Drew. Both his company and, if she was honest, the unbelievable pleasure she had experienced only once.

She closed her eyes to ward off the pain she felt around her heart. Because it was nonsense.

Someone was watching him. He could feel their gaze like a knife piercing a layer of skin between his shoulder blades.

It wasn't the first time he had been hunted.

And his discomfort had nothing to do with the regret he'd felt at leaving Rowena; that was a hollow ache in his chest. It would fade. Eventually. And besides, he wouldn't have to suffer it long, once he carried out his intent.

But this other sensation was annoying. The sensation of being watched by a predator. And since there were neither bears nor wolves nor large cats in Scotland, there was only one other alternative. Men.

He rose up in his saddle and looked about. Hills and rocks, scattered pine trees, clumps of gorse rising from the snow. All could serve to hide a man who did not wish to be seen. Footpads? One look at his nag and mean dress and no self-respecting thief would be interested in such poor pickings.

Though there were a great many in poorer

case than he was. He'd seen that in the streets of Dundee. But his size and obvious strength should act as a deterrent. And if it did not, he had his pistol.

Something rustled in the gorse off to his right.

He brought his horse's head around to face the danger as his right hand went for the pistol in the holster on his saddle. His heart hammered a warning in his chest. His gaze narrowed, inspecting the gorse for signs of movement, then wandered up the hillside to the line of trees not far distant. Holding the horse steady with his knees, he slowly undid his coat buttons for ease of access to his knife.

Nothing.

He turned to continue down the road. A man stood in the road five yards ahead, a rifle levelled.

A man he recognised. One of McRae's smuggler friends, the one he had thought of as their leader, Morris.

The rifle barrel jerked. 'Get off the horse,' the smuggler called out.

Drew weighed the odds of riding away without taking a bullet. Not good. Not with a rifle, if the man knew how to use it. He swung down out of the saddle and put his hands up.

More men rose up from behind the gorse and heather on each side of him, their pistols cocked and levelled. It seemed he'd made the right choice.

Drew cursed as the men closed in on him.

Morris wagged the rifle and grinned. 'Now, there's blasphemy for you.'

'I've verra little coin,' Drew said. 'And only the clothes on my back and the horse. It's no' a verra good horse, but you are welcome to it.'

'It's not what you have that McKenzie cares about. It's what you Gilvrys already cost him.'

Drew gave him a level stare. 'You've got the wrong man.'

'Edinburgh. O'Banyon,' the man said, as if those two words held all the information he needed.

Ian. It had to be some underhanded dealing his brother was involved in. 'I've not been in Edinburgh in six years. I have never heard of O'Banyon.' He started lowering his hands.

'Hands up,' the man said. 'Take his pistol,' he ordered.

One of the other men sidled up to him and took

his gun. Drew dropped his hands and let them hang loose at his sides, aware of the knife nestled against his spine beneath his shirt.

'There's also the matter of Geordie.'

At Drew's blank look, he grinned, revealing two missing teeth. 'The man you killed at McRae's.'

'You don't blame a man for defending his lady, surely?'

'Your lady, is she? Then, where is she now?'

He gritted his teeth. Of course, Rowena wasn't his in the sense the smuggler meant. 'She employed me to see her safe to her destination. And I have.'

'Sandy, take charge of that there sad-looking beastie. You—' he grinned at Drew '—start walking. That way.' He pointed up the steep valley side. 'It seems there's more than McKenzie who wants a slice of your hide. And is willing to pay handsomely for it, too.'

'More than one? Who would the other be, then?'

The man shook his head. 'Not your business, my lad. On ye go.'

Could Ian have heard about his return? It was

possible. Did that mean his brother intended to finish the job he had started six years ago?

The next morning the skies over Mere were clear. Having nothing to do while she waited for her new clothes, and needing some fresh air, Rowena slipped down the servants' stairs and out into the gardens. As long as she avoided any guests, who were unlikely to be abroad at so early an hour, she couldn't see how a walk in the grounds could cause any problem. Since her cloak was black, she wouldn't be offending any-one's sensibilities even if she was to encounter someone.

And if she just happened to run into the duke, that would not be such a bad thing. If only she knew what he looked like.

According to Pockle, the park stretched for miles, but since it was covered in snow, Rowena confined herself to the formal gardens she had seen from her window.

She toured the rose garden, laid out with fine gravel walks between the beds. Not that there were any flowers or leaves to be seen. It was simply a matter of stretching her legs and getting some fresh air into her lungs. It was something she always insisted on for her pupils, winter and summer.

As she turned a corner of the leafless hedges that formed a maze, she saw two men deep in discussion in the parterre. Mr Jones and someone she did not recognise. The duke? If she could be sure it was he, then she might consider approaching him, but if it was not the duke, it would be highly embarrassing. And Mr Jones would have no hesitation in reporting her to Lady Cragg.

The men were deep in conversation and had not noticed her. It would be rude to interrupt, so she slipped into the maze where she found a stone bench. She would sit here until they were gone and then return to her room.

The sound of footsteps crunching on the gravel on the other side of the hedge brought her to her feet.

'He seemed a decent enough man,' Mr Jones's voice said.

She should not be listening. It was extremely rude. She started to move deeper into the maze, away from the men.

'A pity about the scar, though.'

They were talking about Drew. She couldn't help it; she stopped to listen.

'His face won't matter where he's going,' another voice said. A deep voice with a strong Highland burr. 'You are sure McKenzie's men have him?'

'They do, my lord,' Jones said. 'I spoke to their leader this morning.'

'They know they are to take him to Edinburgh and put him on the convict ship leaving for Botany Bay next week? He survived my efforts to be rid of him once. He won't do so again. They are to let McKenzie know he's to leave the rest of them to me.'

Who did he mean by the rest of them?

'And Mrs MacDonald?' Mr Jones asked.

Rowena stifled a gasp with her gloved hand. She tiptoed closer to the hedge, which despite its lack of leaves was tangled and woven and so wide she could not see either man with any clarity.

'I've already advised Lady Cragg on the matter. Get her married off to a relative of Mere's and furnish him with a nice competence. I'll provide the land in America. There can be no possible objection to such generosity.'

Really? No objection?

The sound of gloved hands rubbing together filtered through the hedge. 'With all legal concerns put to rest, I'll expect those who owe allegiance to Mere to support me against Gordon, when he speaks in the House in the new year.'

'Have no fear of that, my lord.'

What legal concerns was he talking about? What possible harm could she do to a duke? The footsteps crunched away. Rowena sat down to wait until she was sure they had gone.

Marry her off? Send her to America? Why on earth would they think they needed to do that? All she was asking for was what was rightfully hers, so she could go about her business. Indeed, she wasn't even sure there was anything left from her husband's estate. Who was this other man who had spoken with such authority, dishing out orders as if he was in charge? At first she'd thought he must be the duke. But Mr Jones had called him my lord, not your Grace.

But she could not worry about that now, not when she knew the smugglers had captured Drew. She had to find him before they put him on board a ship bound for Australia.

Chapter Eleven

When she got upstairs to her room there was no sign of Pockle. Just as well given her plan for immediate departure. She picked up her reticule with its few coins and changed into a pair of sturdy shoes. She looked regretfully at her valise. Anyone seeing her with that would guess at what she was doing and she had the feeling that letting them know she was leaving might be a bad idea.

Reluctantly, she removed her cloak and hoped she'd be warm enough in her riding habit. When she opened the door a footman was standing outside.

'Can I help you?' he asked.

Shocked, she stared at him. 'I…er… Yes, do you think you could direct me to the library?'

'Certainly, madam.'

She ignored his unspoken question. It was none of his business if she was bored and wanted a book to read. 'Please, lead the way.'

He set off down the hallway and she followed along. They went down one flight of stairs, which brought them to the first-floor landing. He opened a set of double doors. 'The library, madam.'

She stepped inside. 'Thank you. That will be all.'

'I'll have Arthur let Mrs Pockle know where you are, shall I, madam? She was in a bit of a taking when she discovered you were not in your room. Luckily one of the gardeners saw you taking the air and was able to set her mind at rest.'

So that was why they had posted a footman outside her door. 'Thank you. Have him tell her I will expect at least one of the gowns to be ready by noon.' Hopefully that would keep her plying her needle instead of checking up on Rowena's whereabouts.

The footman went out and she heard him conversing with one of his fellows in the hallway. Was it normal for ducal footmen to follow guests around? Or was it something they were doing especially for her? It would make slipping away far more difficult, but then she supposed that was their purpose.

She went to the door and, as she suspected, her footman was standing just outside. 'Can I help you, madam?' he asked politely.

'Oh, no, thank you. I am just going to close the door to keep out the draught.' She swung the door shut and eyed the key. Should she lock it? He would hear her do so and that might make him suspicious.

She hurried over to the window and looked out. The library overlooked the back of the house. Beyond the balcony and down a set of stone steps was a large expanse of lawn. Off to the right she could make out the gardens where she had walked earlier. And to the left the stables.

There was no one in sight.

She ran to the shelves and pulled a book at random. If anyone came in she wanted to be ready with her excuse. Then she went to one of the French windows leading out to the balcony. After a bit of a struggle with the latch, she managed to get it open. She shivered in the cold blast of air.

She waited to see if the footman noticed anything and decided to take a look.

Nothing.

Drawing a deep breath, she stepped outside on the balcony, and, preferring not to know if anyone was watching from the windows, she walked briskly to the stables as if she had every right. With each step, she expected to hear a cry of alarm, until finally she entered the building.

The smell of sweet hay, manure and warm horse filled the air. Now to find the beast she brought with her. To her surprise, there was a horse saddled and waiting. Not her horse, though. A big chestnut gelding. The groom must have readied it for one of the guests and then gone off on another errand.

Hanging on a peg nearby was a rather ratty-looking frieze coat and an old battered hat. Belonging to one of the grooms, she supposed. Just what she needed to keep her warm. She slipped the coat on and after a moment's hesitation put the hat on, too.

'Caleb,' a rough voice shouted down the length of the stables, 'get a move on. Her ladyship won't be best pleased if she's ready to go riding and that horse be misbehavin' for want of a run.'

Lady Cragg's horse, then. She touched a hand to her hat, hopped up on the mounting block and climbed aboard. Would the groom giving the orders notice her skirt? She glanced his way, but he had already disappeared back into one of the stalls.

Praying her luck would hold, she rode out of the stables and headed for the gates at a canter. She didn't dare look back to see if she was pursued, but she couldn't help straining her ears for a shout. It wouldn't be long before Caleb returned and discovered the horse missing.

Wind whipping her cheeks, her breath rising in front of her face, she dashed through the gates and out into the road, where she turned the horse in a circle. Which way?

Well, she'd come from Dundee and it lay to the right. Ergo, Edinburgh lay in the opposite direction.

She put her heels to the horse and set off.

As a lad, Drew had spent many nights outdoors in the Highlands and thought nothing of it. But it wasn't the cold that had his nerves stretched to their limit. It was his anger at being hog-tied for the second night in a row.

Last night their leader had left him in a small cave in the hillside while he went off to confer with someone he called the chief. He'd come back and announced they were headed for Edinburgh. Away from Dunross. Completely the wrong direction as far as Drew was concerned. But he'd said not a word. All day, as they'd walked parallel to the road, he'd done his best to allay any fear they might have that he'd run, and they'd still tied him hand and foot.

One of the men got up from the fire and kicked him in the ribs.

Drew grunted at the pain and cursed him foully.

The man grinned, his teeth gleaming red in the light of a fire too far away for Drew to feel much of its warmth.

'Tha's for the merry chase you led us in Edinburgh.'

'I told you. You've got the wrong man. I haven't been to Edinburgh in six years.'

'I'd know that face anywhere. It cost us a lot of money, even if it did get all scarred up.'

'The scar is old, you fool. The man you met was my brother Logan.'

'Brother, is it? Well, one Gilvry is just as good as another.' He drew his foot back.

Morris, the leader of the ruffians looked up. 'Leave him be, Sandy. Break his ribs and you'll be carrying him tomorrow.'

'Why don't we just kill him and leave him here?' his tormentor asked.

'Because that's not what we are being paid to do,' the leader said, getting up from the fire and pulling a brand from the flames.

He sauntered the few feet to where Drew was lying on a blanket on top of hard-packed snow. He held the brand high. The warmth of it on Drew's face was welcome even if it destroyed his vision for the moment.

'It's not the same Gilvry,' he pronounced. 'He's older. Darker skinned. And the scar has been there a very long time. Now get back to the fire, Sandy, and leave him be.'

Sandy stomped off.

Morris crouched down. 'So what is your name, Gilvry?'

Surprised, Drew looked at his unshaven face

and dark eyes and saw pity. He forced himself not to react. 'Andrew. They call me Drew.'

'Never heard mention of you. I thought there was only three Gilvry brothers.'

A pang twisted in his chest. Dead and forgotten, then. His rage against Ian sparked to life. But that was no one's business but his own. 'I've had naught to do with any of them of six years. I've no love for my brothers and mean no harm to you or McKenzie.'

'I suppose you think I should let you go?'

'There is no reason you should not.'

'Sorry, laddie. That's not what I've been told. But even though you shot one of my men back at the inn, I've no quarrel with you. We both did what we were paid to do.' He bent down and cut the rope around Drew's ankles. 'Come closer to the fire. There's no sense in having you frozen by morning.' He untied his hands from behind him and tied them loosely in front.

'You mean you want to ride the horse, rather than have it carry my lifeless body,' Drew said.

The man chuckled. 'Smart lad.' He helped Drew to his feet, picked up the blanket and rolled it, before setting it down near the fire. 'Sit there and Sandy will give you some bread and cheese to fill your belly and a mug of tea to warm you.'

'Thank you,' Drew said. He'd have preferred to hit him over the head, but that wasn't going to get him anywhere. Having his bonds a little less tight did, however, give him a huge advantage for when it was time to leave.

The tin mug warmed his palms and he let the heat steep into his skin before putting it down to eat the bread and cheese that Sandy had tossed into his lap. It had been a long day of walking, but he was used to rough going. He picked up the mug to take a drink and Morris leaned forward and splashed a drop of whisky into it from a flask. 'That'll help keep you warm.'

'Thanks,' Drew said and meant it. 'I'm sorry about what happened to your friend.'

'He was an idiot. He could have killed you or the woman, and that was against our orders.'

They'd been lying in wait for them? Drew tried not to show his shock. Or his fear for Rowena. 'Whose orders?'

Morris chuckled wryly. 'Everyone's.'

'My, I am a popular fellow.'

Damn it all. He thought he'd left Rowena safe

with her family. This didn't sound good. He and this group of ruffians would have to part company, and soon. Thank goodness for the knife he had hidden away in his boot when they were sleeping.

The other man jerked his chin. 'How did you come by such a nasty scar, lad? Properly put paid to those good looks of yours.' Drew felt an echo of the old pain he'd felt when he first saw the results of the near miss. It hadn't been a physical pain, but something much deeper and more permanent. And it had been nowhere near as bad as it was now. Just to torment him, *she*'d made it much, much worse.

'A woman,' he said.

'Cheated on her, did you?'

He'd refused to cooperate. To be *her* idea of a good slave. To his shame he'd given in when he realised she meant to have his eye on the point of her knife if he gave her any more trouble. His gut roiled at the recollection of the nights of service he'd given in exchange for his sight. 'She thought so,' he said.

Ian was going to pay for that, too. He swigged

his tea and welcomed the heat of the whisky sliding into his belly. He wiped his mouth on his sleeve. 'What do you hear of my oldest brother, Ian?'

'The Laird of Dunross, is it?'

'Aye.'

Morris grimaced. 'Got himself a rich wife and a castle in the bargain, I'm hearing.'

Drew stiffened. 'What rich wife?'

Morris shrugged. 'Albritten?' He shook his head. 'Something like that.'

'Albright?'

'Aye, that's it.'

The image of a tiny blonde girl sitting beside Ian on the sand in Balnaen Cove flashed into his mind. 'Lady Selina,' he breathed.

'Aye, that's her. Got a babe, too, they say.'

The slow-burning anger inside Drew quickened, flaring hot. His fists clenched. 'The bloody hypocrite.'

Morris looked at him curiously. 'Not to your liking, then?'

'Not much.' Ian had apparently married the daughter of his family's enemy. And Alice's friend. It was she who had betrayed him to Ian before he could carry out his plan. And Ian had married her, curse him.

His body shook with the effort of containing the blistering rage consuming his thoughts. 'Is it a son? The child?'

'I dinna ken, man. Does it matter?'

'No.' Son or daughter, it would soon lack a father. Great heavens, if it was a son, a half-*Sassenach* Albright brat would be the heir to the Gilvry name. But that didn't mean the clan would choose the child as laird. They wouldn't. Drew would make sure of it. His father and grandfather would never rest in their graves if such a thing came to pass. He couldn't believe that Niall and Logan had gone along with such a travesty.

'Do you hear aught of my brother Niall?'

'The lawyer? Doing well for himself. Got an office in Old Town and a house in New Town. Got himself a title.' Morris offered him the flask. 'More whisky? I've plenty more where that came from.'

Stunned, he reached for the flask. Heaven help him, he needed it after such news. But not too much. He needed his wits sharp and ready.

* * *

Frozen to the bone, Rowena looked longingly at the flicker of the fire farther up the hillside. She'd ridden hard all day, terrified of pursuit, worried that she wouldn't find Drew on the road. But if she didn't, she knew where they intended he should end up. She stroked the gelding's sweating neck. 'Do you think that is them?'

She glanced up at the sky, at the twinkle of stars that disappeared behind the occasional scudding cloud. She'd been lucky with her departure from Mere Castle; the gelding was fast and full of spirit, and she'd been lucky with the weather. But could she really have been lucky enough to catch up to Drew? Or rather, Drew and a dangerous gang of smugglers. She winced.

But she couldn't afford to wait. At any moment, Mere's men might arrive. She climbed down from the horse and led it clear of the road. She patted its rump. 'If we come out of this safely, I promise you'll have the best bucket of oats money can buy,' she whispered. The horse started cropping at the bushes.

As quietly as possible, feeling her way over the rough terrain, she approached the fire. She could see shadowy figures, but was one of them Drew? Something deep in her bones told her he was there. A feeling she'd never had before. Dare she trust it? Heart thundering in her ears, terrified of tripping and attracting attention, she crept closer. Starlight did little more than make some shadows stand out more than others. She could only hope she wouldn't fall over a smuggler standing guard.

She inched forward at a crouch. After what felt like a very long time, she ducked behind a clump of gorse. She was close enough to see not only that there were four men seated around the fire, but that one of them was blonde.

A horse whickered from somewhere nearby. Drew's horse. Had it somehow recognised her?

Drew straightened, looking in the direction of the sound, and then out into the darkness. Could he see her? She froze.

He said something to the man sitting beside him. The men chuckled and the man closest slapped him on the back. Drew rose and walked directly to her gorse bush.

'Who's there?' he whispered so quietly she could barely hear him. He opened his coat and undid his falls, turning half away from her. Then came the sound of a man answering the call of nature.

'Me. Rowena,' she whispered.

The sound stopped and then started again. 'Good God,' he murmured. He glanced over his shoulder, then adjusted his falls. 'Wait here.'

He turned and walked back to the fire and sat down with the men. He accepted a metal container from the man beside him. It glinted as it caught the light of the fire.

One of the others was sipping at a steaming brew. Hot tea? She would give her soul for a cup of something hot. She huffed on her freezing fingers and hunched closer to the gorse bush, curling in on herself for warmth.

Fortunately, while the old coat she'd grabbed in the stable was coarse to the touch, it was surprisingly warm. She stuffed her hands into its pockets.

A hand on Rowena's shoulder and another clamped over her mouth to silence her cry of alarm brought her awake.

She stared at the shadow looming over her.

'It's me,' Drew said.

She collapsed in relief. He took her hand and led her away from the camp. While she struggled not to trip, he seemed to walk as if it was daylight. Finally he stopped and pulled her around to face him.

'Gracious, lass. What are you doing here?'

'I thought you were in some sort of trouble. Have you taken up with the smugglers, then?'

A breath hissed through his teeth. Anger? Worry? She wasn't sure.

'I thought I left you safe in the bosom of your family.'

Anger, then. 'I decided I would prefer to go to Edinburgh.'

'The devil you did.'

'Besides, I heard someone say you were going to be transported to Australia. I thought you might not like the idea.'

'What?'

'I overheard someone speaking to Mr Jones.'

'What someone?'

'I don't know his name. I wasn't introduced.'

She could hear him breathing hard.

'How did you manage to get free of them?' she asked.

'I waited until they fell asleep and cut the rope,' he said almost mechanically. 'Your horse?'

'Near the road.'

'Good.' He gave a soft whistle. His horse loomed up out of the dark with a small whuffling sound.

'How—?'

'Shh. It is no' important right now. Come on, we'll need to be far from here before they wake.'

'Where are we going?'

'Where they will least expect us to go.'

'And where is that?' she said as he helped her to walk down the hillside.

'Edinburgh.'

When they reached her horse, he threw her up. 'You'd already planned to escape from them, hadn't you?' she asked.

'Yes.'

Of course he had. He hadn't needed her help at all.

After two nights and two days on the road, Drew was glad to see the lights of Edinburgh gleaming in the distance. It had taken longer than it would have by road and they'd slept rough, sharing body heat since they hadn't dared risk a fire.

The beast inside him had wanted to do more than sleep beside her, but he wasn't prepared to risk letting it out of its cage. She was just too tempting and he had no illusion that he could keep things normal.

He'd pushed hard, through snow and wind, and kept them both too exhausted for anything but sleep. Which didn't mean he'd slept o'er much.

But here they were, at their destination. He pushed on until they reached the entrance to Old Town. It looked pretty much the way it had before he left. The castle crouched on the mountain, the palace at its foot and the tenements of Old Town sprawled between the two.

Their horses walked wearily up High Street. 'What now?' Rowena asked.

'We can do nothing tonight but find lodgings. In the morning we will get ourselves a lawyer and find out what the hell is going on.'

She frowned. 'I have very little money, I'm afraid.'

'That's more than I have.' He'd left a fortune on Jones's table back at Mere Castle, but even if he had accepted it, it would not have done him any good. Morris would have taken the lot, just as he had taken the few coins in his purse. 'But I may have a contact who might be able to offer some help.'

Niall. Would he be willing to come to their aid? Niall had always been the most reasonable of his brothers. Had always listened to all sides of a story before deciding whose side to take. He could only hope he hadn't changed. Hadn't been influenced too much by Ian.

'We could try the Whitehorse Inn, near Holyrood Palace,' Rowena said doubtfully. 'I might just have enough to pay for one room.'

'With no luggage, and us as dirty as a couple of gypsies?' He shook his head. 'One look and they'll turn us away.' They also needed somewhere safe. Somewhere no one would could possibly find them.

'I don't think my cousin would take us in,' she said. There was pain in her voice. 'Do you think your family—?'

'No.'

Her shoulders slumped.

If he'd been by himself, he'd have gone to a tavern and nursed a drink all night, or slept on the floor in a stable. But he wasn't alone. The only other place he could think of was little better. But it was better. And Belle could be relied on to keep a still tongue in her head.

'I have a friend. She's not exactly respectable, but if she can, she'll give us a room.'

Rowena perked up. 'Then let's go there.'

And he'd tell her just what Belle was, when they knew whether or not she could put them up for the night. No sense in causing a fuss before it was necessary.

He turned into one of the narrow wynds behind the grass market and dismounted outside the back door of a six-storey-high tenement. He helped Rowena down and knocked on the door.

It was opened by a burly individual with a much-broken nose and a cauliflower ear. 'We're closed.' He started to shut the door.

Drew thrust his foot in the back. 'Bobbie. Dinna ye ken me, man?'

The man peered at his face, blinked and opened

the door wide. 'Gilvry. It's a long time since we saw you here. What happened to your face?'

'I ran into a knife.'

'Careless of you, man.'

'Aye. Is Belle in?'

Bobbie gazed over his shoulder at Rowena. 'She's no looking for any lasses just now.'

'Full house, is it? She must be doing well.'

'Well enough since the king came to visit.'

'The king came here?'

'To Edinburgh. Where have you been?'

'Abroad.'

'Och, aye.'

'I need to see Belle, Bobbie.'

The man looked up and down the alley and then seemed to make up his mind. 'Always had a soft spot for you. You'd best come in, then.'

He stood back and Drew ushered a very puzzled-looking Rowena in. She had set her face in stern lines and her back was straight. She looked very disapproving, but knowing her as he did, he could tell she was scared. 'It's all right. I have friends here.'

'Wait here,' Bobbie said. 'I'll fetch Madam Belle.'

'What is this place?' she whispered.

'You ken verra well what it is,' he said.

She gazed at the lurid red walls and the badly done *trompe l'oeil* images of cupids. 'A brothel.'

He nodded. 'Leave the talking to me.'

A few seconds later the rustle of skirts announced the arrival of the establishment's owner.

'Drew,' Belle said, her faded fair face beaming with pleasure.

She stopped with a gasp. 'Oh, your poor face.'

Drew touched the scar with his fingertips. 'I thought it made me a touch out of the common.'

'Oh, Drew,' she said softly. 'Still not one to let down your guard. Welcome back. Some of the lasses you know are still here and will be glad to see you.'

He'd always paid well for what he needed. The lasses had liked that part of it, at least.

She turned to Rowena with a guarded expression. 'And who is this, then?'

Rowena drew herself up to her full height and looked down her nose.

Belle recoiled.

'Belle, this is my wife, Rowena.'

Belle swung back to him with a horrified look

on her face. 'Your wife! What are you doing, man, bringing her here?'

'I need your help,' he said simply. 'Or I wouldn't have come. Will you turn me away?'

She stared at him for a moment, then reached her palm to his face. He flinched.

Rowena quickly stepped forward and forestalled the touch. She smiled and her face transformed from stern to young and vulnerable.

'We would be very grateful if you would permit us to stay the night. We find ourselves at a standstill, you see. No one must know we are in town.'

Belle narrowed her pale blue eyes, finally smiling back. 'Then step this way. You can wait in my private parlour while I have the maid prepare a room. My stock in trade is discretion, so you need not fear loose tongues here.'

'Thank you,' Rowena said with genuine warmth.

'This way,' Belle said. 'I'll have a bite of supper sent up while you are waiting. And a dram of whisky.'

'Tea for me, please,' Rowena said. 'If you don't mind?'

'Not at all. It will be a pleasure.' She looked at Drew. 'You are a fortunate man. I didn't think you'd find one.'

She left them in a small parlour at the back of the house and bustled away.

'What did she mean?' Rowena asked.

Drew knew. She was talking about his preferences. Not something he wished to discuss. It was bad enough that she'd endured a small part of what he liked. 'I suppose she never thought I'd be married.'

Rowena nodded, shrugged out of her disreputable-looking coat and went to the fire blazing in the hearth to warm her hands while she looked around the room.

'It could be anyone's parlour,' she said.

'Aye. They're just lasses, you know.'

Her face softened. 'Yes, I suppose they are.'

Belle returned with a smile. 'Your room will soon be ready.' She looked at Rowena. 'Eva will be glad to help with your dressing and such. She does it for all the girls.'

'You are very kind,' Rowena said.

Bobbie entered with a tray. Tea for Rowena and whisky for Belle and Drew. Rowena poured her tea, while Drew did the honours for him and Belle.

'I havena' seen Niall or Ian for ages. Both married well. I was sorry to lose their business.' She trilled a knowing laugh. 'But glad to see them happily settled.'

They weren't going to be so happy when they realised he was back and why. 'What about Logan? He must be up-and-coming.'

Belle shook her head in mock sorrow. 'He never came here. Nor anywhere else as far as I know and him as beautiful as you were in the old days.'

Drew raised a brow. Not about his brother's good looks, but about what Belle's words implied. 'Too bad,' he said non-committally.

'He's married.'

He swallowed his surprise and adjusted his thoughts. 'Logan? He's still wet behind the ears.'

'Married a widow, I hear. I have never seen her. They are rarely in town. Well, if you are ready I should be able to show you up to your room.' She looked at Rowena. 'Drew will have to play ladies' maid tonight, I'm afraid. Eva will be busy getting the girls ready for this evening.'

Drew clamped his mouth shut on the urge to

say it would be a pleasure. It would be. But that didn't make it right.

Rowena blushed. 'I'm sure I can manage.'

They followed Belle past a downstairs drawing room where some of the girls were gathered waiting for their customers, up the stairs and along a corridor on the third floor. She stopped by a door at the end. 'It's probably not what you are used to, Mrs Gilvry,' she said, 'but I hope it will do. You'll find it clean and tidy. The young lady who used to be here found herself a protector a month ago and I have been waiting to see if she would come back or no'.' She flung open the door to reveal blood-red walls, curtains and bedcovers. 'A bath is waiting.'

He ushered Rowena inside. 'I'll owe you a debt for this, Belle,' he said, turning back to her.

She shook her head. 'You were always good to my girls, Drew. I am glad to return the favour.'

She turned and headed back down the hallway. Drew closed the door. The perfume of roses filled the air, clearly coming from the hip bath in the corner.

Rowena was standing in the middle of the room, looking about her with an odd sort of expression. One he couldn't interpret. He winced. 'I'm sorry.'

She shook her head and gave him a hesitant smile. 'I find it…interesting.' She coloured.

She was embarrassed. He looked at the bath. Of course she was embarrassed, if she thought he would stay.

'I'll leave you to bathe in peace,' he said. 'There are public baths nearby for me.'

'Oh,' she said. Was that disappointment he heard in her voice, or simply wishful thinking? More likely the latter. But then she turned her back before he could be sure.

'Would you unlace my stays before you go, since the maid is busy?'

'Aye,' he said hoarsely. He put down his hat and undid the strings of her gown and then the tapes of her stays. The temptation to kiss the silky skin of her shoulders tingled on his lips, but when he glanced up he realised she was watching him in one of several mirrors strategically placed around the room. He bit back a curse and stepped away. 'I'll be back. Lock the door behind me.'

He paused outside the door until he heard the key turn.

Chapter Twelve

Erotic. It was the only word Rowena could think of to described the chamber as she soaked in the tub, with the scent of roses filling the air and the warm water making her feel sleepy.

She hadn't been at all surprised when Drew had declined to play lady's maid. She'd seen his expression of distaste when he undid her gown and stays. She wasn't the sort of woman a man liked to look at. Too tall. Too angular. Not enough meat on her bones, Samuel had said. It wouldn't surprise her one little bit if he decided to spend the night with one of the buxom creatures she'd spotted below.

The thought sent a piercing pain through her chest. Tears blurred her vision. She squeezed her eyes shut. Forced the hot moisture back where it belonged. Unacknowledged.

What had happened in that cold little bothy had been the result of the terrible events of that night. They'd sought comfort from each other. It meant nothing. Not to him, certainly, since he'd found no relief in her body. Or to her. Not really. She'd revelled in the shattering bliss he'd given her and the brief sense that she could let him shoulder her worries. But in the cold light of day, she didn't want a man ruling her life. She certainly wasn't going to give another one the opportunity to break her heart.

Not that Samuel had, she acknowledged. With him it was more her pride that had been hurt. But with Drew it would be different. If she gave him her heart and he threw it away, she would want to die.

No, what she had was the memory of his touch. The way he made her feel. Dreamily she stroked her feminine flesh, recalling the way his fingers had felt. And his tongue.

Languorous pleasure blossomed low in her belly. Good. But nowhere near as delicious as his touch had been, or as arousing as his harsh commands. A flush travelled over her skin at the memory.

A knock sounded at the door. Hot with arousal and embarrassment, she jerked upright in the tub, water sloshing on to the floor.

'Who is it?'

'Eva, *madame*. Belle sent me up to ask if you are done with the tub and to send up a bit to eat to tide you over until dinner.'

'Thank you. Wait a moment and I'll open the door.'

'No need, ma'am. I'll leave the tray outside. Bobbie'll be up in a minute or two to take the tub and bring your clothes down to be washed.'

'But I have nothing else to wear.'

'You'll find a robe in the cupboard,' the girl said cheerfully. 'Help yourself.'

Afraid Bobbie might arrive at any moment, Rowena stepped out of the bath and dried herself off. The porter, she suspected, wouldn't raise an eyebrow at finding her unclothed, given the place he worked, but she wouldn't feel at all comfortable. The offered robe she discovered was a little diaphanous for her taste, but beggars could not be choosers. She opened the door and carried the tray in and set it on the table.

A bite to eat consisted of a round of cheese and a heel of bread, with a pat of fresh butter, cake and a pot of tea.

Whatever one might think about her profession, Madam Belle was clearly a very kind woman.

A few minutes later, Bobbie and a young lad came for the tub. Rowena wrapped herself in the red quilt before she let them in and watched with interest as, working together, they lifted the tub and tipped the water out of the window after a shout of 'Gardy loo!' to anyone unfortunate enough to be walking in the alley below.

'Will there be anything else, ma'am?' Bobbie asked, his gaze fixed at a point above her head.

'No, thank you.'

He and his lad trundled out with the tub and she locked the door behind them. She went to the bed, intending to rest until Drew returned. Her foot hit something beneath the bed. Thinking it might be a book, she bent to take a peek. Beside the chamber pot was a wooden box. Intrigued, she picked it up and set it on the bed.

She opened the lid.

And her eyes nearly popped out of her head.

* * *

Drew nodded to Bobbie when he let him in the back door.

'The missus is finished with her bath,' the bruiser said with a wink.

An image of Rowena naked flashed through his mind, doing away with all the good effects of the cold plunge. His shaft gave a happy little twitch. He gave Bobbie a hard-eyed glare and headed upstairs, rubbing his close-shaven chin with his thumb and wondering if she might welcome him in her bed a second time. If he kept things on an even keel.

Behaved like a gentleman.

As if. And nor did he want her to. He still couldn't believe her courage. She'd actually risked her own safety to rescue him from McKenzie's men. He owed her more than he could ever repay. He was not going to take advantage of the kind gentle woman who hid behind the facade of stern reserve. Samuel MacDonald had been a fool not to realise the treasure he had in his wife.

He tapped on the door.

'Who is it?' Her voice was husky, almost breathless.

Had something happened? 'Drew. Let me in.'

There was a scuffling sound, then the door opened. Her face was bright pink. He took in the see-through robe she was wearing. It clung to every swell and hollow, revealing more than it hid: the small, high bosom, the curve of her waist and swell of her hips. He jerked his gaze up to her face. Far from trying to avoid his gaze, she seemed to be trying to block his view of the bed.

A sharp blade of something ugly twisted in his chest. 'What's going on?'

'Nothing.'

Guilt filled her voice. He stepped around her. His gaze swept the four-poster bed and… His stomach lurched. Cold as ice, he turned to face her. 'Where did that come from?'

She gave an awkward laugh and unsuccessfully tried to look severe. 'I found it under the bed.'

Had Belle brought it up, thinking he would want it? His mouth dried. His heart pounded hard. His shaft hardened to rock.

He brought his gaze up to her face and saw excitement in the flush of her skin and the sparkle in her silvery eyes.

He had to be imagining it. If she had opened it, she would be horrified.

Her gaze slid away. She gestured to the table. 'Belle sent up tea for me and whisky for you, if you would care for some. Supper will be sent up later, I understand.'

Whisky might dull the terrible ache in his groin. He strode to the table against the wall and with a shaking hand poured some into the glass. He swallowed the liquid in one swallow. Felt it burn all the way to his belly and poured another glass, glad to see his hand had steadied.

He nodded at the bed. 'It must have been left by the previous occupant.' He looked into his glass. 'This whisky is excellent.' Much better than the gut-rot he'd shared with McKenzie's men.

'Eva said it comes from Dunross. The…er… mistress of the house orders it for her special clients, though Eva says she never tells them where it comes from.'

He rolled another sip around in his mouth and she was right—it tasted of home. A wave of longing surged through him. He ruthlessly crushed it. 'I thought it tasted familiar. Did Eva say why they keep it a secret?'

She gave a little shrug. The filmy fabric skimmed over her nipples, making them pearl. His breath caught in his throat.

'Something about McKenzie not liking the competition,' she said. 'Apparently, it's all right to tell me because I'm a Gilvry. I didn't disabuse her of the notion.'

He finished his drink and turned to pour another, then put the glass down. Too much whisky and he'd lose what little control he had.

Again his gaze strayed to the bed. Rowena moved away from it with a look of embarrassment. As she would, given that they were alone in a room in which the bed was the focus. She wasn't an innocent. She would know what went on in a bawdy house, if not in detail, then in general terms at least.

He just wished she hadn't found that box. Its contents were all too familiar. Too damned tempting and she was too good for him and his needs.

How awkward that Eva had not delivered her clothes before Drew arrived. More awkward yet, he had returned before she'd had a chance to put the box and its strange contents back under the bed. Just looking at what it contained had sent her blood pounding through her veins, which in turn had made her feel hot all over. The slide of the silky robe on her sensitised skin had only made the strange feelings grow worse.

Her imagination had run riot as she'd picked each item out of the box. Her body had tingled and burned. She'd wanted to stroke her breasts, touch her— She blocked out the wicked thoughts. Only Drew's arrival had stopped her from behaving in the most shameful way.

And now he was looking at the box with a dark expression. Not anger. It held too much sensuality for that, but not interest either. A kind of dread.

'I stubbed my toe on the box,' she said, her voice sounding a little breathless. As if she'd been running. Was it her imagination or had the chamber become warm and close? She swallowed and looked away from the piercing look he shot her from under his brows. 'It's...um...things. For use by the girls who work here, I assume.'

'Are you saying you looked inside?' he asked, his voice low and gruff and incredulous.

She gave a small laugh that sounded forced. 'I was curious.'

He turned away, staring down at the decanter, his face rigid. He must think she was dreadful. Wanton.

But she couldn't seem to stop herself from asking the question that had been on her mind since she opened the box. 'Do you think they use all those things?'

'Things?'

A shiver rolled down her back. 'Chains. Ropes. Blindfolds. A schoolmaster's leather strap.' Her inner muscles tightened with a pleasurable little pulse and she swallowed a gasp.

He made a sound of disgust. 'I'll have them come and fetch it away.'

'Yes.' She looked down her nose at the polished wood. 'Of course. But Eva told me she would be busy downstairs for the next little while.'

When she looked back at him, he was watching her with hooded eyes, but even so she could feel the heat of his gaze on her skin.

Oh, how she wished she had never opened that

box. She moved to the chair by the fireplace and looked up at him. 'Were the baths to your satisfaction?' she asked as a mean of distraction.

'Aye. Yours?'

'Oh, yes. Eva took my clothes to be washed. You might want to give her your shirt if we are to visit your brother tomorrow.'

He moved to the window and looked down into the street. 'I'll take it down later.'

With the box. *Stop thinking about it.* She clasped her hands together in her lap. 'I expect you are looking forward to meeting him.' Oh, heaven help her, she was babbling.

'Yes.'

His monosyllabic answers were unravelling her nerves, but she couldn't seem to stop asking questions. 'Do you know where to find him?'

He turned back from the window, his face expressionless. 'The attendant at the bathhouse gave me the address. I went round to take a look at the building. He's in a wynd just off Princes Street. The office opens at half past nine in the morning.'

'Oh,' she said, mollified by the fullness of his answer. 'So we know where we are to go.'

'Aye.'

'He will be surprised to see you after all this time.'

'Surprised, aye.'

'And pleased,' she hazarded.

He shook his head. 'Doubtful. But he's not one to turn his back on his own.' His jaw flickered. 'Not the Niall I knew anyway. Things may have changed since…' He let his voice trail away. He seemed to be looking into the past. He shook his head. 'There's no sense in guessing.' His hands opened and closed.

He was worried. And not only his tension gave him away. She could see concern in the shadows darkening his eyes from their usual emerald to the colour of pine forests.

'I saved you a piece of cake,' she said, pointing to the tea tray. 'To tide you over until dinner. Unless you ate while you were out?'

'No. I didna' realise dinner would be late, so I didna' give it a thought.' He picked up the slice of cake and it disappeared in one bite.

'I should have saved more of it.'

'I'll be fine. I'm more used to an empty belly than you are.'

She wasn't so sure of that. Governesses did get fed, but they often had to wait until after their charges were looked after.

'I should write to my employer again,' she said with a sigh. 'Tell her where to send my wages.'

She frowned. 'And if in the end there is no money set aside, I fear it will be difficult to find another position without a letter of reference.'

His face looked grimmer than ever.

'Please, Drew, don't blame yourself. I should have known better than to think Samuel would have done anything so sensible as provide for me.' She tidied up the tray. 'Eva said to put this outside the door. One of the footman will pass by and pick it up.' She glanced at the bed. 'We could leave that outside, too, if you wish.'

He gave the box a look of dislike. 'Aye. It would be best.'

She hurried to the bed and picked up the chest. For some unaccountable reason her hands were shaking. The heavy weight slipped through fingers that seemed to have lost all of their strength and it crashed to the floor, scattering its contents across the carpet.

Drew let out a curse. In one long stride he had

reached the site of the disaster and crouched at her feet.

She dropped to her knees beside him as he righted the box. She picked up a pair of manacles. They were heavy and lined with velvet. She glanced up and found his gaze fixed on her hands. She rubbed at the velvet with her fingers, her breasts tightening. His gaze drifted from her hands up her body to her nipples, which she was sure he must be able to see through the fabric of the robe, and then continued up to her face.

His breathing sounded harsh in the silence as their gazes met.

She licked her lips and swallowed the dryness in her throat. Her heart was rattling in her chest, making it hard to form words. 'Have you ever…?' she whispered. 'I mean, do you know…?'

'What?' he said his voice harsh. 'Do I know what?'

'How they are used?'

He stilled. Something changed in his expression; it lightened, and though he frowned, the glint in his eyes was curiosity, not anger. And yes—at least, she was almost sure—hope.

'Do you like the idea of being shackled?' His

voice deepened and became silky and dark and mesmerising as his eyes seemed to look right into her soul. 'Of being held in chains. Helpless to defend your honour against a man who will do with you just as he will.'

Her insides melted. She gasped, helpless against the deliciously wicked sensations rippling through her body. Afraid to breathe. Afraid to speak. Afraid of what she might reveal. Fearing he would turn away in disgust. Then she nodded and waited for his revulsion.

'And would you submit to such a man, obey his every dark demand?'

Her eyes fluttered closed on a little moan of helpless pleasure.

'Rowena,' he said, his voice a rough whisper. 'Look at me.'

She opened her eyes. His mouth was so close to hers. His breath warm on her lips.

'Rowena,' he murmured, 'would you submit like that to me? Let me do as I willed? Give way to my every wish?' He drew in a harsh breath. 'If I promise I wouldna' hurt you? Not really?'

All her life she had longed for a man who would want her badly enough to take command of her body and soul. Could she humble herself enough to ask for what she wanted? 'I have dreamed of a man who…' He would find her disgusting.

'Of a man who what?' he asked hoarsely. 'Who what, Rowena? Answer me.'

'Who would be my master and I his slave.' She blushed and bowed her head in shame. 'It is a foolish fancy.'

She started to rise.

He put a heavy hand on her shoulder. 'Do not move.' He picked up the box and set it on the table beside the bed.

She looked up at his face, the face of half devil, half angel. 'I—'

'You do not have my permission to speak.'

She shuddered with pleasure.

Drew stared down at her bowed head. Had he understood? He thought he had. Or had he simply wished to hear what he wanted? Or had she agreed because she was afraid?

'Look at me, Rowena.'

She raised her gaze to meet his and he saw excitement and breathless anticipation in her expression.

'You don't have to do this,' he said. 'Not if you don't want to.'

'I do,' she said. 'If you think you would like it.'

Like it? He had a feeling it would kill him if she changed her mind. 'If anything I do, we do, makes you afraid, you can always stop me. Cry "uncle" and I'll stop at once. I swear it. Do you understand?'

'Uncle,' she said, nodding.

'So you want to stop?'

'No. Not now. Not yet.'

He looked down at her, saw the courage in her eyes and the melting softness. Had he actually found a woman who liked this game as much as he did? She always seemed so strong, so self-contained. But as she knelt before him, he could see that this was something she wanted and he let the beast inside him out of its cage. Not loose—never did he let it go entirely free—but he would let it play a while. Just for a moment or two.

'Stand up, girl, and face me.'

She did as he bid. He could see she was trembling, the sheer fabric of her robe shivering at the hem.

'Do you know who I am?'

She shook her head.

'I have captured the ship on which you travelled and will sell you in the slave markets of Algeria if you do not please me.'

Her soft mouth parted on a gasp and her breathing quickened. His blood pounded in answer to that betraying little sign of pleasure.

'Let your hair down. I want to see it free around your shoulders.'

She pulled the pins free and it tumbled down. It reminded him of the way he'd seen it at McRae's. It was long and straight and a pretty shade of chestnut brown.

'Untie your belt, girl. Quickly now.'

Her lovely long fingers hastened to do as he bid and the robe fell open.

Just as he recalled from the night in the bothy, her breasts were small and high and beautifully firm. The curls at the juncture of her thighs were a lovely dark chestnut, darker than the hair on her head.

A desperate urge to touch her with hands and mouth almost overwhelmed him, but she was not yet ready. 'Let the robe fall.'

'Must I?' she asked, raising her gaze to his.

Ah, a little bit of defiance. He let his mouth curl in a mocking smile. 'You must if you don't want me to hand you over to my men.'

A shiver racked her body. She let the robe fall from her shoulders and slide to pool at her feet.

'Up on the bed with you.'

She glanced over her shoulder and then shook her head. 'Sir, would you steal my innocence?'

His shaft hardened inside his trousers at the words and the sound of her breathy voice. 'Everything belongs to me now.' He selected the whip from the box, a light riding crop, and ran it through his palm suggestively.

She licked her lips, staring at the whip, then looked into his face.

She would tell him no. He knew she would. Rowena wasn't that kind of woman. His kind of woman.

She turned, walked to the bed and climbed up.

He let a breath go and stalked after her, standing at the side of the bed as she watched him approach, her arms and hands covering her body.

'None of that now,' he said with a scowl, tapping her fingers with the tip of the whip. 'I want to see my prize. Lie back and put your hands at your sides.'

After a moment's hesitation she lay back on the pillows and placed her hands flat on the bed, her grey eyes fixed on his face, her breasts rising and falling with little breaths. Slowly her milk-white skin flushed and the air filled with the scent of arousal. Hers. And his.

Damn, she was lovely. And she wanted him. Like this.

Slowly, lightly he ran the whip down her body, over her breasts, watched the peaks tighten to hard rosy little nubs and heard a little whimper from deep in her throat.

Not fear.

She was too brave to be afraid. Too courageous.

He couldn't believe how aroused he was. It was a long time since he had played his little games with a woman. And he didn't remember one who had entered into it with such abandon. He stroked the leather across the flat plane of her belly. Lord, but she was slender. Almost thin, as if she'd not been well fed.

A surge of anger at her husband rippled through him. And guilt that he hadn't noticed. He circled her navel with the tip of the crop and her flesh quivered beneath the touch. He traced the jut of her hip bones and the sensitive hollow.

She flinched. Just as he knew she would.

He shook his head. 'Lie still, I said. Now you must be punished. Roll over.'

She hesitated.

'Now,' he said harshly, giving her the tiniest flick with the crop. Not enough to leave a mark. Not enough to cause anything but a lick of pleasure-pain. And she moaned and rolled over, burying her face in the pillows, her hands on each side of her head.

Her back was long and lovely, every bone of her spine visible through the skin. Her bottom was beautiful. Womanly. Round, high and firm, with its dark shadow below her tail bone. It really was the most delectable sight he had viewed in a long time.

He hardened to rock and revelled in the agony of denial. For only when he was sure she was satisfied could he take what he wanted.

He stripped out of his breeches and shirt, knowing she could hear what he was doing, and, seeing her hands curl into the sheet, he knew she wanted to look at him the way he was looking at her. Somehow she knew better than to take a peek.

'It's too late to be good,' he said. 'You deserve all you get.'

Her buttocks tightened in anticipation. He bit back a groan at the sight of that little twitch. He wanted to bite each cheek until she cried for mercy.

He knelt on the bed beside her and raised his hand. He slapped that lovely, sumptuous flesh, not hard enough to hurt—to hurt her would kill him—just enough to cause it to tingle and warm.

She gave a little squeak of surprise.

'That earns you five more,' he said. And waited.

She tensed.

So he waited.

Slowly she relaxed and he slapped her again, carefully, just enough to feel the weight of his hand, his strength. And he counted out loud until he reached five.

Her bottom was a delicious pink, and warm beneath his hand.

He swept her pretty brown hair aside and leaned over to breath in her ear, to flick his tongue around the tender little curls, then kissed the leaping pulse below her ear. 'Will you disobey again?'

She made no sound and his heart tumbled over. 'You may answer.'

'No,' she said. 'I'll not disobey again.' The laugher in her voice said she probably would. And something warm and very tender filled his chest, soothing the ugliness inside him.

'Turn over and face me.'

She flipped on to her back. Her gaze raked his body, her eyelids drooped sensually, a smile curved her wide mouth, making her look beautiful and lascivious as she took in his rampant arousal.

'So,' he said, jerking his chin, 'you like what you see.'

She raised her gaze to his face. 'I like it very much.'

'Speaking again, unbidden?'

She bit her lip.

'Another punishment is in order.'

She eyed the whip warily.

He set it down alongside her and rummaged in

the box. 'Ah,' he said, like a gloating pirate who had just found buried treasure. 'Close your eyes.'

When he turned back to her, her eyes were squeezed shut. He quickly tied the blindfold around her head. Now the real fun would begin.

Darkness. Not a scrap of light penetrated the silk binding her eyes. All she could hear was the thunder of her heart and her rapid breathing. And all she seemed to feel was the slight sting of her buttocks. It seemed so much more intense now she couldn't see.

Panic surged. The word *uncle* forced its way up into her throat.

A firm warm hand gave her shoulder a gentle squeeze. 'Give me your hands, little one,' his dark voice murmured.

Little one? She choked back a laugh, more hysterical than amused. No one had ever called her little. Not since she was a child. But this was Drew. Humouring her with the game she'd wanted to play. Not some terrible stranger wanting to do her harm.

Her fears dissipated. Her body relaxed and she lifted her hands.

He caught them in his and she heard the clink of metal and felt the grip of something solid around her wrists. Solid, but soft. The manacles lined with velvet. She remembered how she'd held them in her hands. They snicked closed.

Slowly, infinitely carefully, her hands were drawn upwards and another click above her head made her test the bonds that held her fast.

'You'll not be escaping from there,' he said gruffly.

But she could. She just had to say the word and he would let her go. But she didn't want him to, not yet. The shivers of fear had turned to trembling excitement. What would he do next?

Something stroked across her breasts. She gasped at the way her skin tightened at the unexpected touch.

What was it? Not the riding crop. It had been nowhere near as light a sensation. It swirled around first one nipple, then the other. Her breasts seemed to become heavy and full. Her nipples hardened. She could feel them puckering and pulling tight. It felt wickedly delicious. Unbearable.

She almost cried out when it stopped. Almost

begged for more. And then it touched her lips, a delicate whisper of touch. The feather. It had to be the feather. Who would ever have thought such a soft delicate thing could create such torment?

She moaned.

'Ah, my little beauty,' he said. 'If you think this is bad, just wait.'

The feather, for she was certain that was what it was, trailed a path across her cheek and swirled in her ear. She shivered and twitched.

'Be still,' he ordered, without a smidgeon of mercy for her predicament.

She was trying, but it was hard in the face of such delicate torture. She gulped in a breath of air and tried to control her body's reactions.

He chuckled softly as she lay still.

'Oh, my brave beauty,' he said softly.

The touch of the feather left her. Silence surrounded her. Every nerve in her body awaited what he would do next.

The feather ticked her inner thigh.

She gasped. Shocked. Surprised.

'Open,' he said in a rough command.

A shudder of pleasure hit her hard. She complied instantly.

He continued his torment, stroking each inner thigh in turn, then gently brushing her woman's flesh, which sprang to life, hot and wanting.

Did he want her, too?

She didn't know, couldn't tell in her dark world, though she could hear his harsh breathing somewhere beside her. Above her. All around her. Her fingers twitched in their bindings with the longing to touch him, to feel the hard mass of his arms and the deep chest she had glimpsed so briefly.

But she couldn't. He had her held fast. His captive.

Her insides seemed to melt. Her body flushed with the heat of desire.

The feather returned to her breasts, stroking all the places that loved to be touched: behind her knee, the rise of her breasts and the hollow of her throat.

And tormenting all the places that jumped and flickered: the hollow of her hip, the soles of her feet, the place below her ear.

And never did she know where he would touch her next. She was panting and breathless and almost out of her mind with longing and pleasure and exquisite pain from her sensitised skin. Almost ready to cry *uncle*.

The bed dipped. Him, shifting his weight. Then the warmth of him beside her hip. A knee pressed between her legs. 'Wider,' he said.

And then he was between her thighs, the rough hair on his legs just as tormenting as the feather.

Then she felt his fingers at her entrance, parting her folds, and the blunt tip of his shaft pressing against her.

'You will take me,' he said. 'All of me.'

And he drove home to the hilt and she dissolved into bliss.

And he continued to drive into her, bringing her to the peak and beyond twice more, before he withdrew and spilled his seed on her belly.

He collapsed beside her, his hands reaching up to untie the blindfold.

She blinked at the sudden light as she regained her vision. He was up on one elbow, working the lock of the manacles. She was rewarded by seeing a look of sensual bliss and contentment on his face. He looked younger. Less careworn.

He freed her wrists and looked down at her

face. She couldn't stop herself. She stretched up and kissed his mouth.

He gazed at her with what was clearly astonishment. 'Are you all right?' he murmured softly.

'Oh, yes,' she whispered, smiling. 'Thank you.'

If anything his expression of astonishment grew more intense. He shook his head. 'Rowena, rest now.'

He must think her exceedingly strange, but there was a slight smile on his lips as he lay down beside her and pulled her into the crook of his arm, positioning her so her head rested against his shoulder. Gently, he stroked her hair where it fell over her breast.

'Little one,' he said. His eyelids drooped and his breathing deepened.

'Mr Gilvry.'

Rapping. On a door. And a weight on his shoulder. Drew jerked awake. The warmth at his side was a woman. Rowena. The knocking on the door?

Careful not to wake his sleeping companion, he slid out of bed to another round of knocks.

'Who is it?'

'Eva, with your supper.'

Right. No food since earlier in the day. No wonder his belly felt empty. He glanced over at Rowena. She pulled the sheet up over her head with a mutter about the racket.

He scooped his shirt from the floor, pulled it over his head and unlocked the door.

Eva trotted in. She glanced at the tangled sheets on the bed with a knowing grin. 'Madam Belle thought as how you might be in need of a bit of sustenance.' She set a tray on the table.

'Thank her for me.'

The girl gave him a saucy smile. 'She's lucky, your lady is, having such a well set-up fellow as you, even with that face. You should see some of the flawns and dodderers the girls have to put up with.'

'I'll take that as a compliment.' Drew fished sixpence from his coat pocket and slipped it into the girl's palm. 'I'll leave the tray outside when we're done. No need to come back until morning.'

'Thank you kindly, sir.' She dipped a little bob and scuttled out.

Drew locked the door behind her.

Rowena threw back the sheet and gazed at him, her expression puzzled and her eyes misty with sleep. 'What is happening?'

'Eva with supper.'

'Oh.' She sat up, careful to keep herself wrapped in the sheet. As if he hadn't seen her a few minutes before in nothing but her skin. And a beautiful skin it was. Very responsive. And silky soft.

His blood thickened and his thoughts must have shown on his face, because hers turned red.

Dammit. He hadn't wanted to make her embarrassed. Not after she'd given him the most pleasurable interlude in his life.

He still couldn't quite believe that he had found a woman who had participated in his deepest, darkest fantasies. Had her enjoyment been real or out of gratitude?

Even as the thought flittered through his mind, he knew it wasn't true. The blush on her face was not embarrassment. It was desire. For some unfathomable reason, the fates had sent him a woman who liked the opposite of what he liked.

He hardened. And inwardly cursed the thrum of hot blood in his veins. Even if it had been a long time since he'd been able to indulge in his particular vices and even if she was willing, he'd tormented her enough for one night.

They had important matters to see to tomorrow and they would both need their wits about them. 'Come, sweetling. You need to eat.'

She blinked and then smiled. 'I can't believe how hungry I feel.'

'It's not surprising,' he said, raising a brow. He picked up her robe from the floor and handed it to her, turning his back so she could slip out of bed and put it on.

He didn't do it because he didn't want to see her. He did it because he knew if he caught so much as a glimpse, she would never get as far as the table.

He pulled out a chair and she gave him a smile and sat down. 'What have they sent up?'

It was a cold supper of the sort of plain fare Belle would have available to her customers downstairs. He'd partaken of it often enough in the past. Cold meats and haggis, fruit tart, bread and cheese and a flagon of small beer. They tucked in. He was glad to see that she ate heartily, though nowhere near as much as he, and when she was done she watched him finish his meal.

'Do you really think your brother will help us?' she asked when he, too, sat back with a sigh.

Of all of his brothers, Niall was the most likely not to toss him out on his ear. But if he did? What then? 'Dinna worry. We'll find someone else, if he cannot.' There was something else troubling him. 'I still do not see why Lady Cragg was so set against me.'

Rowena frowned. 'I never heard her say any such thing.'

'Did you no' say that she told Mr Jones she would be glad to see me deported? That was why she had McKenzie's men lying in wait for me when I left.'

'Oh.' Her eyes widened. 'It wasn't Lady Cragg talking to Mr Jones. It was a gentleman.'

'The duke?'

She frowned, as if trying to recall something. 'It could not have been the duke. Mr Jones called him my lord. Not your Grace.'

'It might have been a slip of the tongue.'

'Mr Jones does not seem the sort of man who would make such a mistake.'

'Aye, but if it was no' Lady Cragg or the duke, who the devil was it? What did he look like?'

'I couldn't see him very well, he was the other side of a very thick hedge. I had the sense he was an older gentleman, by his voice.'

'If you heard that voice again, would you ken it?'

'I believe so. The air was clear and their voices carried, farther than they might have guessed, I think.'

'It is too bad I didn't know this when I was a guest of McKenzie's men,' he mused. 'Morris liked to talk. He might have told me.' He frowned. 'He did say something about me giving them the slip once before. I assumed he was talking about Logan.'

It couldn't be Ian. Not if it was an older man. But someone working with Ian? Someone like... Carrick?

Not possible, surely?

But the men who had delivered Ian's message had been Carrick's men. And it was Carrick who had offered him a place in his American business.

'What is it?' Rowena asked. 'You look worried.'

It surprised him that she could make out any

expression at all on his face. It was as if she saw right past the ruined flesh and only saw the man behind it.

His heart gave an odd little lurch.

Now she was looking worried and he did not want her bothered by his musings, which had nothing to do with her problems. 'No, not worried. Just thinking. Don't be concerned about Niall. We'll know very quickly if he will help us or no'. We have a great deal to do in the morning, I think it is time you went to bed.'

She looked down her nose at him. 'I'll decide for myself when I'm ready for bed.'

He let his glance slide to the chest standing on the table.

Her breath gave a little hitch. 'Oh.'

He shook his head. 'Much as I'd like to play some more, I need my sleep, even if you don't.'

She went bright pink. 'Oh, I'm sorry. I didn't wish to be disobliging, I just didn't want you to think you could order me around.' Her colour went brighter. 'As a general rule, I mean. In the daytime.'

Heavens, she really was an absolute treasure. It

was a shame he didn't deserve her. 'I understand,' he said. 'You take the bed. I'll take the floor.'

'Oh, no. I wouldn't hear of it. We will share.'

'So you intend to boss me around, do you?' he said with a teasing note in his voice.

'Certainly not. I am just being sensible.'

'Sensible. Aye. Then I'll accept your kind offer.'

His hands were unsteady as he laced her stays. Eva had returned her clothes along with the water for washing. He was glad Rowena had her back to him right at that moment and could not see his reaction to touching her.

He wanted her again. And she had given him so much already. In his heart he knew he would never get enough of her, and it wasn't right. Not when his future was so unsure.

'Your brother is going to be very surprised to meet us, I think.'

Us.

His fingers stilled. He'd been alone for so long, fighting for his own survival, it came as a shock to think of himself as something more. He pulled at the laces and tied off the bow. 'Aye. He'll be surprised.'

She seemed satisfied with his answer.

He went to the mirror and tied his cravat while she put on her stockings. Such lovely long legs she had. He glanced at the tumbled bedclothes and then at the clock and wondered if there might be time…

A knock sounded at the door. 'Who is it?'

'Eva with your breakfast.'

'I'm ravenous,' Rowena said.

So was he. And not only for food. With a regretful sigh he went to the door and opened it. The young maid bustled in with a tray.

'Madam Belle wants to know if you'll be wanting this room tonight, as well?'

He glanced at Rowena and discovered she was looking towards the bed with what he could only describe as a hopeful expression. His groin tightened at the thought that she was actually looking forward to another night with him. It seemed so improbable that he would meet a woman, who on the outside seemed so self-assured, and yet who craved what gave him pleasure.

How wrong her husband had been to call her cold and reserved. She was a passionate delight who had somehow filled a very empty place in the deepest reaches of his soul.

'Tell Belle, yes, if she can spare us the room.'

The maid whisked off. He seated Rowena and as she lowered herself on to the chair she looked up at him with a pink wash of colour. How could he ever have thought she was plain, seeing that blush over her pale-as-milk skin that covered every inch of her body?

She spread butter and jam on her toast. 'We will go together to your brother's office,' she said in the decided way that she had. She used it to hide her uncertainty, he realised. Her fear of rejection.

Such a small insight into her vulnerability, but it made him feel suddenly protective.

'We will,' he agreed, selecting bread and slicing off a lump of cheese. 'After all, this is your business. Not mine.' His business was with Ian. The urgency to face his brother seemed to have faded. Because it would mean leaving Rowena and likely never seeing her again? He pushed the thought aside, unready to deal with that part of his future.

He had sworn to give her his aid and he would see it through to the end.

Breakfast over, they dressed for the chill of a winter morning in Edinburgh. He wrapped his muffler around his face. 'No sense in setting the dogs to barking,' he joked when he saw her watching him.

She shook her head. 'I hardly notice the scar any longer. It's your expressions I see. Your kindness.'

As he had suspected the previous evening, but to hear her say it made something hard and uncomfortable rise in his throat. He swallowed it down without examining the emotion at its source, though he had a feeling it was gratitude. He was grateful to her for so many things, it seemed. Would it give her some sort of power over him? Make him weak? He pushed the thought aside. 'Let us go.'

They hurried down the back stairs and out the side door. He gestured for her to stay in the shadows while he took a quick look to see who was about on the street. There were the usual hawkers—the baker, the milkmaid, a girl with a basket of turnips—crying their wares. A dustcart rumbled by. No sign of the smugglers. 'Gardy loo!' He dodged back into the alley to avoid a stream of night soil from a front room of the brothel.

'All seems well,' he said, holding out his arm.

She took it. They walked briskly. Rapidly enough to show they had purpose, without looking hurried or anxious. At the corner of the street where Niall's office was located, Drew stopped. 'Let me make sure it is safe.' He'd been both hunter and prey. He knew better than to be caught out in the open.

She nodded. He peered around the corner.

Drew had no trouble identifying the man standing on the opposite side of the street against the apothecary's window. His friend from two nights ago. Morris. Cursing, Drew came back to Rowena.

'What is it?' she asked.

'The smugglers are watching Niall's office.' And they could be watching the nearby streets, too.

He grabbed her hand and they ran, ducking into alleyways and doubling back. He didn't stop moving until he was sure they weren't being pursued.

Out of breath and panting, Rowena leaned against the wall. 'Did they see you?' she gasped.

He shook his head. 'No.' He was almost sure they had not.

'What now?'

'We could try his house...'

'But they might be waiting there, too,' she finished.

'Aye. Likely. If they know of his office, they would easily discover where he is living.'

'And we wouldn't want to put his family in danger.'

How did she know what he was thinking at the same moment he thought it? He grinned at her, then realised that beneath his muffler she wouldn't be able to see his expression. Probably just as well. Right now he was feeling a little too besotted for comfort.

'Do you think we could ask him to visit us at the brothel?' she said. 'Send a note.'

'We will send a note, but we'll not meet him at Belle's. We need to find somewhere we can be sure *he* isna' followed.'

'What about Waterloo Place at Regent Bridge?'

'They finished it, then?' It reminded him just how long he had been away. A painful reminder full of resentment that made his fists clench as he thought about Ian and his treachery.

'There is a clear view in both directions,' she said.

'It sounds ideal.'

'Is something wrong?'

Clearly the bitterness in his heart showed in his voice. 'No. Nothing wrong. Let us go back to Belle's and write the note.'

Despite Drew's assurance that nothing was wrong, he'd left her at Madam Belle's the moment his note to his brother had been dispatched. He had wanted to look at the place they had set for the meeting. And he'd wanted to go alone, leaving Rowena sitting on tenterhooks fearing he'd be caught.

The lad they had sent to his brother's office was to wait for a reply. Given their fear of interception, Drew had kept the note very brief. It had talked about there being no need to climb the bridge to collect the eggs. It would, he had said, let his brother know who was seeking the meeting, but would mean nothing to anyone else.

A rap sounded on the door. 'Who is it?' she asked, having been warned by Drew not to open it to anyone unless she recognised the voice.

'Me, ma'am. Nat.' The errand boy.

She opened the door. The boy grinned and waved a piece of paper.

'You saw him? Lord Aleyne?'

'Not me. His clerk. He'd not be letting the likes of me near his lordship. But he did send a reply.'

Too bad Drew wasn't here to receive it. Heavy footsteps on the stairs made her look up. It was Drew. 'We have a reply,' she said.

He took the note from the boy, gave him a coin and came inside and closed the door, tapping the note against his gloved palm.

'Open it,' she said. 'If he says no, then we will find someone else to help us. My father had a lawyer. Mr Murchison. He might be willing to talk to us.'

Drew set the note on the table, removed his gloves, coat, hat and scarf. She wanted to shout at him, he was so deliberately slow. But she did not blame him. This was his brother from whom he was estranged. She sensed that if the note was a rejection he would take it hard.

He sat down on the bed and patted the place beside him. She joined him on the bed. Breath held, she watched him open the note. He handed it over without a glance at the contents.

'Read it.'

So commanding. Pleasure unfurled low in her belly. She took it from him.

The hand was bold and black and the words brief.

'"Logan, what game are you playing? If you are in trouble with the law or with McKenzie, I will have your head on a plate. Niall."'

She wrinkled her nose and looked at Drew. 'He didn't know it was you.'

The muscles in his jaw flickered. 'Perhaps it is just as well. If he had guessed it was me, he might not have replied.'

'Oh, Drew,' she said, feeling the hurt in his voice as a pang in her chest.

He squared his shoulders. 'But he will come for Logan. So perhaps it is just as well he did not recognise my writing.'

'He mentions McKenzie, too.'

'Aye. God knows what Logan is about. He always was a wild scamp.' He looked at the small clock on the mantel. 'It is but a half hour to the time I set for the meeting. We had best get going.'

The clouds had rolled in over the city, grey and heavy with the threat of snow. People in the streets scurried head down about their business. To Rowena, everyone looked suspicious, but after a circuitous route, Drew stopped for a second.

'No one is following. Unless they are very, very clever.'

She breathed a sigh of relief, trusting him to know and happy to leave such matters in his hands.

Finally, they were in sight of the bridge. Standing right at the centre was a young man in a dark coat and hat, pacing up and down and slapping his arms across his chest.

'That's him,' Drew said, at the place where the bridge began to cross the old Calton Road. 'Niall.'

She took his hand, as much for his comfort as for hers. He tucked it into the crook of his arm and patted it lightly.

Niall stopped his pacing and looked towards them. He was dark, not blonde like Drew. He took a step in their direction and then stopped, frowning, but he wasn't looking at Drew, he was looking at her, and as they came closer his frown deepened.

'What the devil is going on?' he said as they came within earshot. His gaze dropped to where their arms linked. 'Who is this?'

'Is that a proper greeting for a brother you haven't seen in six years?'

There was a careless drawl in his voice. A devil-may-care note she hadn't heard before. His arm beneath her fingers had tensed. It was as rigid as a board. He was ready for his brother to turn away. Steeled against it.

Rowena could only watch as the other man peered into Drew's eyes uncertainly.

Drew pulled down the muffler.

Niall reared back. 'What? Who? My God, Drew!' he whispered. 'Can it really be you?'

Drew nodded stiffly. 'It is.'

Niall lunged forward, clutching his brother to his chest, then leaning back to look at his face. 'We heard you were dead.'

'Not yet,' Drew said drily.

'Hell's teeth,' he said, his eyes taking in the scar. 'What happened? Why didn't you come to the house? Why the strange message? I have been standing here for the past half hour, thinking Logan was in some sort of trouble. Just wait until Ian knows you have returned. And Mother.'

'Mother is… She's well?' His voice sounded strained.

'She'll be all the better for seeing you.'

If Drew noticed the evasion, he didn't mention it. He glanced around. 'To tell you the truth, Niall, I am in a wee spot of trouble. Is there somewhere we can talk? Somewhere we won't be seen?'

Niall stared at him, smiling, seemingly lost in some sort of reverie. 'You have to meet my wife. And Ian's Selina. And—'

'Niall, we don't have time. There are dangerous men—' He looked over his shoulder. 'Damnation.'

Rowena followed the direction of his stare. Her heart sunk. Walking towards them was the man whose narrowed gaze focused only on them.

'You were followed,' Drew said. 'My note said to take care no one followed you.'

'Damn it, Drew. I bloody well did.'

'There's no time for this,' Rowena said. 'We can't risk—'

The smuggler must have realised he had been spotted because he started to run, one hand tucked under his coat. Probably holding a pistol. Drew looked the other way and groaned. Another one was coming from the other direction.

'There's only one thing to do,' Niall said. 'Rush the man coming from the far side of the bridge.'

'Come on, then,' Drew said grimly. He took Rowena's hand and she hoiked up her skirts in the other and they ran straight at the smuggler.

He must have thought they hadn't seen him because he started to grin and unbuttoned his coat. Rowena could see the grip of a pistol sticking up from his waistband.

'He's got a gun,' she gasped.

'I see it,' Drew said.

'He's not the only one,' Niall said. He reached under his coat and pulled out an ornate duelling pistol. He cocked and fired. The smuggler hit the ground with a howl.

And then they were over the bridge and running alongside a building.

Rowena glanced over her shoulder. The man they'd seen first was catching them up and he had drawn his pistol. She tried to run faster.

'Stop them,' the smuggler behind them yelled at passers-by. 'Stop, thief.'

A burly man on the pavement in front of them put his arms out to block them.

Chapter Thirteen

'Let them pass,' Niall shouted at the man standing in their path. To Rowena's surprise he stepped aside.

'Guard the door,' Niall said to him. 'Don't let anyone in.' He dived through the building's nearest door.

Drew thrust Rowena ahead of him, lifting her off her feet in his rush to get her inside.

Niall slammed the door and locked it.

'What the devil?' Drew said, staring at his brother. 'Who was that outside? I thought we were done for.'

'Bodyguard,' Niall said. 'I'll explain in a moment.' He led the way down a narrow corridor that opened out into the great hall of a sumptuous office building. A porter hurried forward to greet him with a bow. 'My lord?'

Drew made a snorting noise through his nose.

Niall ignored him. 'We need a room where we can be private, and brandy.' He glanced at Rowena.

'Tea, please,' she said, still gasping from their wild run. How they had managed to cross the bridge ahead of their pursuer she wasn't quite sure. It seemed that with Drew holding her hand, her feet had barely touched the ground.

The servant opened the door to a small sitting room tucked away behind some columns. 'Will this do, my lord?'

'Excellent,' Niall Gilvry said. No, he was Lord Aleyne, Rowena reminded herself.

She sank down on to the nearest sofa and perched on its edge, watching Drew eye his beaming younger brother warily.

Aleyne stepped towards Drew as if he would offer an embrace, but Drew stiffened and took a half step back. Aleyne shook his head, but his grin remained. 'I can't believe you are here.'

'Believe it.'

'We heard you were killed in a hunting accident.'

'Heard from whom?'

'Carrick. By way of the hunting party.'

'Is that so? Well, whether you like it or no', I am still alive.' His voice was hard and grim.

'Good heavens, Drew! Are you saying you think I would be glad if you were not?'

The muscle in Drew's face flickered as he fought some emotion he did not let show in his eyes. Rowena had the feeling it was pain. But it could just as easily have been anger.

'You've been missed,' Aleyne said. 'By Mother, especially. You were always her favourite after Logan. She refused to accept you were gone. Not without proof. And, by Jove, she was right.'

At that last, Drew turned away and paced to the window.

Aleyne stared at him, a puzzled frown on his face. 'Dammit, Drew, so much has happened since you left, I have no idea where to start. All of us are married. Even Logan, and to the un-likeliest of women. Though she has been good for him. Settled him down no end.' He shook his head. 'And you? What happened to you? Why didn't you let us know you were alive until now?'

'It is a long story,' Drew said. 'And not relevant to our current situation. What is all this I hear about you being a lord? And why the body-guard?'

Aleyne's handsome face hardened. 'Also long stories. But since you ask, my title came through my wife.'

Drew curled his lip. 'Married an heiress, did you? Ian thought it was all right for you, then.'

'Ian had no knowledge of it until it was done. Ours is a love match.' His tone held disapproval.

Drew winced. 'And he married the Albright woman.'

'Lady Selina is a grand lass and has been very good for our Ian.'

'Not to mention good for the family coffers. She brought him Dunross, I understand.' Drew's voice and eyes were as cold as ice. 'Whereas I was banished for trying to save the family fortunes.'

Aleyne shook his head. 'You have no idea how much he regretted… But I should let him tell you himself. He will be here tomorrow to meet with Lord Gordon.'

'I'll be here then, too,' Drew said. To Rowena it sounded like a threat.

'Good. He's bringing Mother, too, to see a specialist for her lungs.'

'Why the bodyguard?' Drew asked abruptly.

'Ian's idea,' Niall said. 'There are some unsavoury elements who have caused us problems recently.'

'Do they work for a man named McKenzie? They mistook me for Logan, at first.'

Now, why was he not telling his brother everything with respect to the smugglers? Didn't he trust him? Were there things about his family Drew hadn't told her?

'He does look like you, Drew,' Niall said. 'His hair is lighter and he doesna'…' He winced.

'His face isna' scarred,' Drew said. 'It was what finally convinced the blackguards I wasna' him. It seems like young Logan has been creating quite a stir.'

'Aye. McKenzie is our competitor. Logan runs rings around him. The man would like nothing better than to see an end to him. You were lucky to escape with your life.'

Drew looked at Rowena. 'I had help.'

That look warmed her through.

Niall looked shocked. 'You want to be careful. They are dangerous.'

'So we discovered,' Drew said.

Rowena expected him to say more. To speak of his capture. He didn't. He looked at her. 'I should introduce you to my companion. Mrs Samuel MacDonald, this is Niall Gilvry, my brother, Lord Aleyne.'

Aleyne stared at her open-mouthed and then looked from her to his brother. 'Hell's teeth! You have the missing MacDonalds?' He turned to Rowena. 'Is your husband with you?'

Rowena gaped at him. 'My husband is dead.'

'What do you mean?' Drew asked at the same moment. 'The missing MacDonalds?'

Niall looked from one to the other. 'Haven't you heard? Mere died some weeks ago, in a boating accident. The lawyers for the estate have been trying to contact surviving family members.'

'I have indeed been in contact with the Duke of Mere's lawyers. The duke was named executor of my husband's will,' Rowena said.

An odd expression crossed Aleyne's face. 'And how do you come to be involved in the case, Drew?'

'Case?' Drew said. 'I was there when Samuel MacDonald met his end. I was tasked with bringing his remains home to his family.'

'I see,' Aleyne said thoughtfully.

Drew narrowed his eyes. 'Just what is it that you see?'

'The matter was in all the papers. The search for the heir. The estate is in a state of limbo until all the relevant relations have been contacted.'

Rowena stared at him. 'No one mentioned any word of this. Indeed, I understood that the new duke was already in place. I never met him when I visited Mere Castle. I was told he was indisposed.'

'It is all verra odd,' Aleyne said. 'To whom did you speak?'

'Mr Jones, the duke's lawyer,' Rowena said.

'Jones? Never heard of him. He certainly wasn't the old duke's lawyer,' Aleyne said. 'Carstairs and Raglin have served the Dukes of Mere for three generations. And I can tell you that there is no lawyer or clerk named Jones in their office. I deal with other clients of theirs on a regular basis.'

'But he met us at Mere,' Rowena said.

Drew nodded in confirmation.

Aleyne looked at her with consternation.

'And then there was Lady Cragg,' Rowena said.

'And who might she be?'

She looked helplessly at Drew. 'I don't know. I thought she must be the duke's hostess. A member of his family. She was in charge of the servants.'

'A distant cousin of the old duke, perhaps,' Aleyne said. 'There is no new duke confirmed as yet. Though there have, as I understand it, been a few claimants to the title.'

'Surely a duke would know the identity of his heir,' Rowena protested.

'You would think so,' Aleyne said. 'But though we are calling him the old duke, he was younger than I am by a good bit and he was about to be married. I doubt he expected to cut his stick quite yet.'

'Are you saying that you think that perhaps my husband might have been his heir?' Rowena finally said. She'd kept trying not to think that this was what all this meant, but logically what else could it be?

'Only someone from Carstairs and Raglan could say for certain. But he was one of those mentioned in the papers as being sought. Another is a small lad barely out of petticoats.'

'I saw a small boy,' Rowena said. 'At Mere. He was playing in the gardens.'

'Why didn't they tell Rowena all of this?' Drew asked.

Rowena stiffened as Lord Aleyne's sharp gaze went to her face at Drew's use of her first name. She looked down her nose at Drew's brother. 'That is a question I would like answered,' she said tersely. 'Lady Cragg did mention the need for legal matters to be ironed out.'

Lord Aleyne went to the hearth and leaned an elbow on the mantel, looking at them both with a frown. 'I will speak to Will Carstairs. He's a friend of mine. Of course, he won't give away any confidences, but there are things he might be able to tell me. I will need the answer to a few questions before I see him.'

'What would you like to know?' Rowena asked.

'First, is there proof of your husband's death?' Aleyne said.

'There is,' Drew replied. 'We delivered his remains to Mere Castle on our way to Edinburgh.'

Aleyne's frown deepened.

'There is something else I should mention,' Drew said, leaning back. 'This man Jones, who said he was the duke's lawyer, seemed very insistent on establishing the exact date of Mr Mac-Donald's death. Or at least, he was for a while. When I told him I didn't have proof, he suddenly didn't seem to care.'

'Do you know the date of death?' Aleyne asked in a strange tone of voice.

Drew shot him a hard look. 'Tell me why it is so important.'

'The date, Drew,' Aleyne said.

'September fifteenth,' Drew growled.

'By all that's holy,' Aleyne whispered. 'Are you sure?'

Drew bristled. 'I wouldna' say it if I wasna'. I suppose now you will be asking me for proof.'

Aleyne turned his gaze on Rowena. 'If you have it, you are a very wealthy woman, your Grace.'

Drew felt the same as he had below decks on the ship. As if he was suffocating. Rowena stared open-mouthed at his brother.

'What are you talking about?' she asked.

'If your husband died on the fifteenth of September, he died as the duke,' Niall pronounced.

'It doesn't make him any less dead,' she said.

'But it makes you the dowager duchess.'

Rowena's eyes widened. 'An empty title, Lord Aleyne.'

Drew had a strange sense about where this was leading. He kept his face impassive and waited to see what his brother would say.

'And there will be settlements and privileges that attain.'

Drew felt his chest squeeze. 'It all hinges on the date of MacDonald's death, then.'

'Do you have proof?' Niall asked.

An image of the page from MacDonald's journal leaped to his mind. 'Is my word not good enough for you either?'

Niall cocked his head to one side. 'Not when large sums of money are concerned. You would have to be proved a witness without any interest in the outcome.'

'I have none,' Drew said.

'You are travelling together,' Niall mused. 'Which might not be a problem. I assume you have not—' he hesitated and gave a grimace of distaste '—been indiscreet? Your past reputation for dalliance...'

'That was years ago.'

'A clever lawyer would not hesitate to use it if it suited him.'

Drew bit back a curse at all lawyers.

Niall looked at Rowena. 'I assume you are travelling with a companion? Or a maid?'

Rowena blushed fiery red and Drew wanted to hit Niall for making her look so embarrassed. 'Mrs MacDonald's private life is no one else's business.'

Rowena gave him a smile of gratitude, then shook her head. 'Lord Aleyne is right. Innocent or guilty, facts will be twisted by others who have an axe to grind.' She looked down her long nose at Drew. 'We have spent more than one night alone together.' Her blush deepened. She was, of course, embarrassed by what they had done.

'It will be an expensive fight, Mrs MacDonald,' Niall said regretfully. 'And a difficult one without any proof.'

She bowed her head. 'It is your advice that we not make the attempt and I accept whatever they feel inclined to offer, then?'

Niall sighed. 'It might be. Let me consult with Carstairs before we come to a decision.'

Bile rose in Drew's throat. He didn't want to deprive Rowena of what should be hers by right. A dowager duchess! Who would ever have guessed such an outcome?

But if Drew offered the proof he had of the date, circumstantial evidence at best, and it was not accepted, the shameful revelations in the journal would have been made for nothing.

No. They must take his word. The journal was a last resort. 'We will hear what these friends of yours have to say before proceeding further.' He looked at Rowena. She nodded.

Niall bowed his head. 'That is also my advice. Where are you staying?'

Drew tensed. He didn't want anyone to know where they were staying. He took a deep breath. This was Niall. Not a stranger. Not a renegade. Or a smuggler. 'At Madam Belle's.'

Niall's jaw dropped. He swallowed. 'Interesting choice.'

Rowena's expression became remote. Drew glowered. 'It's where no one would think to look for us.'

'McKenzie's men,' Niall said. 'I'd almost forgotten. What the deuce is going on?'

'Something to do with Logan.'

'But they must know you are not Logan.'

Rowena leaned forward. 'Someone else means Drew harm. A man visiting Mere Castle. I heard him talking.'

'Let it go, Mrs MacDonald. It's not important,' Drew said. It was something he would solve on his own.

'Someone else?' Niall's eyes narrowed. 'Who?'

'I have no idea.' He couldn't keep the bitterness from his voice as he kept his suspicions firmly behind his teeth. Niall would never hear a word against Ian without proof, and that he didn't have. Yet. 'How long will it take for you to get the information from Carstairs?'

'I should have something by noon. Come home with me and wait. I know Jenna would be thrilled to meet you. She's heard so much about you. Us. Our antics as boys.'

Had she heard about how he was banished from the family and why? 'These men are trouble. You don't need them at your house.'

Niall nodded. 'As I know only too well.'

There was something in his face Drew didn't quite understand, but he thought better of asking. He didn't want to get too close to his brother. Not given what the future held.

'I don't want them showing up at Belle's either,' he said.

'Where shall we meet, then?' Niall asked.

'In a private parlour at the Whitehorse Inn.' It was public enough and had entrances and exits to make it a place of safety.

Niall nodded. 'When Logan arrives tonight, I'll ask him if he has any idea of what McKenzie is about.'

'He'll be in the city, too?'

'He and Charity are visiting for a few days. Ian called a meeting.'

His gut lurched at the sound of his older brother's name. He forced himself to remain impassive. 'I suppose there's no harm in asking Logan about McKenzie. What I need right now is a back door out of here.'

'That I can do.'

Drew brought Rowena to her feet and escorted her to the door. He opened it. Niall caught his arm as she passed through the door. 'Drew,' he

said in a low voice. 'Man, we've missed you.'
Drew shook off his hand.

'What's wrong?' Niall said. 'Aren't you glad
to be home?'

A lump of something hot seemed to stick in
the back of his throat. 'It's complicated,' he said
and was horrified at the thick sound in his voice.

Drew paced back and forth across the private
parlour in the Whitehorse Inn like a caged animal. And every time Rowena opened her mouth
she closed it again, because she sensed that whatever was going on in his head, he would not welcome an interruption.

Finally, he stopped and stared out of the window into the courtyard below, his body stiff and
rigid.

Unable to bear the tension in the room any longer, she took a deep breath. 'Were we followed
here, do you think?'

He shook his head slowly and turned back to
face her. There was resolution in his expression.
'No.'

'Then what is wrong, Drew?' she said softly,
treading warily.

He reached inside his coat and pulled out a small book bound in blue leather. 'Your husband's journal.'

'Oh,' she said and frowned, a cold sensation rippling through her stomach. 'It must contain some pretty damning things if you have kept it hidden all this time.' Her husband must have said the same vile things about her in there as he had said to her face. How like Drew to want to protect her from Sam's wicked tongue.

His eyes widened. His mouth twisted in a wry grimace. 'Damning. Aye.' He held it out to her.

'I don't want to see it.'

He hesitated, then thrust it towards her as if it was hot and he wanted to be rid of it. 'You need it,' he said. 'It proves he was still alive two days after the duke died.'

For a moment she couldn't assimilate the words. 'Proves?' She rose to her feet and took the book. 'You have had this all along and you said nothing?' She shook her head, staring at the book he held out to her. 'Of course. You had not yet read it. When did you discover...? Why say nothing to Lord Aleyne?' She raised her gaze to his face and was shocked by the pain in his eyes and the cruel twist to his mouth. 'Drew?' she said.

'I've known it all along,' he ground out through a jaw clenched hard.

'But—'

'It didn't suit me to hand it over.'

An odd sensation ran down her spine. Her scalp prickled and tightened. What was he not telling her?

Again he thrust it towards her and this time she took it, running her palm over butter-soft leather, still warm with the heat of his body. She started to open the cover.

'Wait,' he commanded. The usual shiver ran down her spine, but this was not the game they played at night. He was not in charge of what she did or did not do.

She lifted the cover and moved to the window for more light.

'Please, Rowena,' he said.

The agony in his voice halted her, made her look at him. She'd been wrong—he wasn't angry, he was suffering from some sort of dread.

'What is it?' she asked.

'There are some things I must tell you. Before

you read what is there. Before you learn them from others.'

She'd always known he was a man with secrets. That he would want to share them with her made her feel warm inside. She glanced down at the book, and then nodded. 'Very well.'

'It might be better if you sat down.' The wry humour was back in his voice. 'If you would.' And he wasn't telling her, he was asking. She returned to her seat by the hearth, the book clasped in both hands.

He looked as if he wanted to continue his pacing, but instead he took the chair opposite and leaned forward, hands clasped between his knees, his gaze fixed on them. 'I told you that I left Scotland in disgrace.'

'Yes.'

'I didn't tell you why I left Scotland. My brother Ian banished me from these shores.'

'Does it matter? Your younger brother seemed delighted—'

He cut her off with a quick shake of his head. 'Likely Niall doesn't know the full story.' He raised his gaze to meet hers and there was sorrow and regret in the shadows of his eyes. 'I seduced a woman and ruined her in the eyes of London society.'

Shock stole her breath and she gasped. 'Why?'

His laugh was short and bitter. 'She was an heiress. We needed money at Dunross. It was the quickest way to fill our coffers.'

Her heart stilled. 'Are you married, then?'

'No. I picked her because she seemed such a practical wee lass. Not one to engage in flights of fancy. Or want to live in my pocket. I was wrong. It turned out she fell head over ears in love and then discovered I was just marrying her for her money.'

'Oh.' Just like Samuel. A pain seemed to grow around her heart.

'Aye, oh. But it was too late by then. Everyone knew she'd been in my bed.'

Shocked, she stared at him. 'And you didn't marry her?'

'She wouldna' have me. Not even to save her reputation. Ian got to learn of what I'd done. He was verra angry. Said he was ashamed of me. I'd dishonoured the family name. You would never have known he was only a year older than me, he gave me such a bear-garden jaw. He said it was best if I left the country and arranged with our clan chief for work in America.'

She waited, terrified of what he might say next.

He huffed out a breath. 'Ian arranged that I would never come back.'

She blinked. 'He said you could never come home again?'

'He arranged to have me killed. And I should have been, if I hadna' stumbled right at the moment his henchman made his shot.' He touched his cheek. 'He was aiming for my heart. Not my head. My head is a lot harder.'

'Oh, Drew.' She reached out a hand.

He shook his head, refusing her sympathy. 'The thing is, I have come back. And Ian is going to pay for what he did.'

'What do you mean, pay?'

'With his life.'

The words were spoken flatly. The sound of it made her heart stand still. Then race. 'Drew, no. You can't mean that. I understand your anger, but he's your brother. How can you be sure of his intentions?'

'His man told me, right before he took his shot.'

She felt sick. 'But what does this have to do with the journal?'

'It has the proof of the date of Samuel's death. I've always known it.'

'And you never said.'

'No. I never said.'

'But why?' She looked down at the little book.

'You'll know, when you read it.'

Her stomach fell away. Her heart began to ache as she realised what he was telling her. 'You knew he was the duke's heir? You seduced me to...to...' Wealth? Position? Was that his motive?

He was staring at her. For a moment, she thought he would deny the charge. He got up and took a short, jerky pace away from her. Then turned back. 'Aye. He told me. He told me he never expected to inherit, though. But I guessed the family would pay handsomely to know what had happened to him. And then there was you. A woman I guessed was about to become a very wealthy widow.'

Anger bubbled hot through her veins. 'You guessed? And never said a word? What, did you think I would marry you?'

'Would you no'? Had I asked you?'

Oh, heavens above. She would have. She had fallen for him, hard. Made the same mistake again.

He smiled cruelly, yet she could almost imagine his eyes told a different story. One of regret.

'Aye, you would have,' he said in harsh tones. 'Any fool would grasp that it would serve my purpose, do you see? With that much money in my pocket, I'd be well able to deal with my brother and no one the wiser.'

'Then why are you telling me this now? Why not just carry on with your foul scheme of ruining another woman's reputation and forcing her to wed you?' The bitterness in her words shocked her, but the hurt in her heart was far worse. She felt as if a knife had pierced right to her soul and she wanted to hurt him, too.

He flinched, then straightened his shoulders and looked down at the journal. 'Because they will no' accept my word about the date. And I find I canna rightfully deprive you of what should be yours.' He gave a bitter laugh. 'And once they see the journal, they will know what sort of man I am. Rowena, if I thought an apology would make a difference, I would make one.

You'll be fine, lass. The journal will prove your claim. You'll be set up for the rest of your life.'

He headed towards the door.

'Where are you going?' she demanded.

'To hell.' He opened the door, then turned to look back at her, his face a mask of beauty and destruction. 'I'm going to do what I set out to do when I boarded that ship with your husband's body. I'm going to see justice done.' There was a wealth of agony in his voice.

He walked out.

He was going to kill his brother. And if he did, there was no doubt Niall would seek his own justice. Through the mighty arm of the law.

The pain in her heart at the way he had used her for his own ends was nothing to her fear for him. He might not have fallen for her, the way she had fallen for him, but that didn't mean she wanted to see him die on the gallows. She had to stop him.

And the only way she could do that was to tell his brother Niall of his plan. She glanced down at the journal and opened it at the length of silk between its pages.

Chapter Fourteen

Yellow Dog melted into the shadows. Watching. Waiting. Patient, the way only a predator could be. Unfeeling as stone.

Yet he wasn't unfeeling. There was a cursed pain behind his ribs like the ache of a festering sore. A wound that would never heal. It was the recollection of the way she had looked at him. Her. Rowena. Of the devastation in her expression. The realisation of betrayal.

Betrayal hurt.

Yellow Dog snarled at the fates that had made him cause that look on her face. Made him say the lie about caring only for the money, for her sake. So afterwards she could live with herself. And forget him. But he would never forget her. Not if he lived to be a hundred. Which he wouldn't. He would be lucky if he lasted the night.

He didn't care. He had nothing left. Except his revenge.

A pedestrian strolled along the street, sauntering with no idea death lurked in the shadows of New Town.

Yellow Dog became one with the darkness as the Indians had shown him.

No. Not Yellow Dog. Damn it. Where the hell had that come from after all these months? He was Drew Gilvry. And he was standing opposite his brother Niall's house for a just purpose. He was waiting for Ian. He was waiting with his loaded pistol and the knife in his boot, because they would not let him in the house with his pistol.

She would have told Niall his intentions.

He had no reservations or doubts on that score. Once the hurt had worn off, anger would have set in. And she would have betrayed him, just as he had betrayed her. And he could not but feel glad of it. For her sake. Tonight, they would both have their justice. And he would love her for it.

Love. Hell. He had never believed in love. Not for him. Not for the way he was. And yet he'd found the one woman who did not revile his disgusting needs and habits. She almost made them seem…acceptable. Despite that his first woman had told him that his proclivities were unnatural. Perverted. Only when need drove him hard had he let them get the better of him.

Until Rowena.

With Rowena, it was like being transported to a different world. He'd felt clean. And he had thought he never would again, after what *she* had forced him to do.

They would all know the truth of it now. Know what he'd been called. And how he'd been used. The slavery. The obedience. It was all in MacDonald's journal. Not quite all. The worst of it, even MacDonald hadn't known. But enough that they would guess.

And so tonight Ian would finally have his way. Drew would die. But so would Ian. And they'd both go to hell.

It didn't matter to him. He'd been in a living hell for the past two years. Death would be a welcome relief.

If it wasn't for Rowena.

Perhaps she wouldn't be there.

He'd seen Logan arrive. So tall. And broad

shouldered. He knew him by his yellow hair, which had caught in the lamplight as he removed his hat to enter the house. His wife had been bundled in fur and he'd seen nothing of her but her height. She was tall for a woman. For a moment, he'd thought it might be Rowena, but he'd known it was not.

The north wind tugged at his cloak, but he didn't feel its bite. He was dressed warmer than he ever had been with the Indians. He'd been lucky they'd given him anything to wear at all.

A carriage rolled down the street.

He let his breath go and remained perfectly still. Not a puff of misty air through the muffling scarf would betray his presence to his prey, because instinct told him this was Ian.

A large man stepped down swiftly and waved off the footman who, instead of letting down the steps, hurried up to the front door to knock. A carriage and a footman. It appeared Ian's fortunes had improved considerably. Anger rose in his throat. He unclenched his fists. Time enough for anger when he faced the man with his crime.

Ian bent to let down the steps. Drew could see him, a moving shadow on the other side of the coach, which was lit by a street lamp. Not one, but two others alighted. Two ladies.

His heart lurched. One was short and the other tall. Rowena. Without doubt. How the hell? This he had not expected.

Niall must have somehow got word to Ian earlier in the day. After his meeting with Rowena, when she would have revealed all. It didn't matter. He'd expected her to be there. To be at Niall's house, awaiting his arrival. He'd assumed Niall would smuggle her in through a back door from the mews behind the house. Ian was taking the threat pretty calmly, then, if he was strolling in through the front door.

Drew eyed the distance between him and his target. And then saw through Ian's plan. If Drew tried to kill him on the doorstep, he might miss and hurt one of the women. He put his hand on the pistol in his pocket. He could make the shot. Rowena was ahead of Ian, her head rising above him as she mounted the steps. In the lamplight, he easily recognised her bonnet. But as he knew only too well, even a clear shot could go awry. He touched his cheek, reminding himself why he was here. Why he could not make any mistake.

A man didn't take kindly to being shot at. A near miss would only prolong matters.

The door was already open when Rowena reached the top step. She stepped inside. The others followed.

Drew couldn't help but feel a spark of admiration for his older brother. Not once did he look around him. Nowhere in his bearing did he show any worry. Yet he must know Drew was out here. Watching. Waiting.

The door closed.

Now to enter the house.

The tension in the drawing room was palpable. Rowena had been introduced to the Gilvry men and their wives, the vivacious little Lady Aleyne sitting beside the hearth, the tall, beautiful and coolly sophisticated Mrs Logan Gilvry on the couch beside Lady Selina, who was as tiny as she was fair. Gorgeous women.

And her. In her shabby governess clothes.

Even dressed as fine as five pence she would have been nowhere near as elegant or lovely as these women. They must wonder at Drew. What he'd seen in her. But of course they didn't. They knew he'd seen money. Nothing else.

The pain of it stabbed her heart anew.

'Are you sure your men will see him if he should arrive?' the Laird of Dunross said, his stern face set in harsh lines as he addressed the golden youngest brother, Logan.

He was what Drew would have been without the scar. Stunningly handsome. His wife had an aura of hardness about her, until she looked at her husband as she did now, with a smile. 'You don't have to worry about Logan's men doing their duty,' she said.

English. Like Lady Selina.

'I have them on all the roofs,' Logan added. 'Not even a wee mouse can creep by without them seeing.'

Ian Gilvry grunted. 'I don't want him hurt, ye ken. Just immobilised and brought in.'

Some of the tension went out of Rowena at the knowledge they wouldn't hurt him. Some. But not enough to make her neck stop aching. 'He's very skilled,' she said and, aware of all the eyes in the room swivelling her way, lifted her chin, giving them her best governess stare. 'He learned from the Indians.'

'One Highlander is better than ten savages, I can assure you, Mrs MacDonald,' Logan asserted with his charming grin. He walked to the window and made as if to part the curtains to look out.

'Logan. Keep back,' the laird ordered.

'If he's out there, he'll ken I'm not you by the hair,' Logan replied, but he let his hand fall.

'Why take the chance?' Niall said. 'If he's been waiting all these years, he'll be ruthless. And desperate to bring it to a close.'

'Then it is a good thing we took your mother and the children to stay with the Carstairs,' Jenna said, her voice a little wobbly.

'He would never harm Ma or the children,' Ian said. 'Not Drew.'

'He's changed,' Niall said. 'I—'

The door swung back slowly. A man in a black greatcoat, head swathed in a scarf, slipped silently into the room and stood with his back against the wall, a pistol in each hand, both cocked, one pointed at Ian's heart.

Someone, perhaps Lady Selina, gave a little scream.

'Your men should be watching the basement windows,' Drew said.

Logan cursed and stepped forward.

'Stay out of it,' Drew said, lining the other pistol up on him. 'I've nae quarrel with you, lad. This is between me and Ian.' He moved the pistol slightly, so it was pointed at Lady Jenna.

Logan halted, looking at Ian, whose face was grim. 'This is nonsense, Drew.'

'Nonsense, is it? That's why you have your men lying in wait for me. No doubt with orders to kill on sight. They failed last time. And they have failed again.'

Ian let out an exasperated sigh. 'They are there to prevent you from doing anything stupid.'

'Why not just admit the truth, Ian?' Drew said, his voice cold and hard. 'Tell them what you did.'

'I did nothing but send you away,' Ian said. He took a step towards Drew, who straightened, his eyes narrowing a fraction.

She couldn't bear it. He was just so damned angry. He wasn't going to listen to reason. Not from his brother. But would he listen to reason from her?

She rose from her chair and stepped between Ian and Drew. 'Don't do this. Please, Drew.'

'Damn you, Rowena. Stay out of this. You have everything you want.'

'Everything except you.'

He flinched. Then shook his head. 'You don't want me. Not now.'

The journal. Her heart ached. Feeling helpless against the barrier he had thrown up, she pressed on. 'Drew, I won't let you do this. It isn't right. He's your brother.'

'A brother who wanted me dead. Well, he'll have his way after tonight. But he'll no' be around to know it.'

Trembling deep inside, she took a step closer. She knew he wouldn't shoot her. But he could so easily sweep her aside. 'He says it isn't true.'

'And you'll take his word over mine.' The hurt in his voice shattered her heart.

'Please, Drew.' She held out a hand. 'I love you.'

His gaze flew to her face. 'No,' he said. 'You're with them.'

The denial pierced her soul. Hot tears welled at the back of her nose. She reached for the pistol. 'Drew—'

'Rowena,' he said, his voice cracking. 'Don't make me choose. You know I need this.'

'No, Drew.'

The pistol wavered. Logan and Niall launched themselves at Drew and threw him to the floor. His hat fell off, his scarf came unravelled as he fought like a wild man to keep his pistols.

Ian stepped in and wrenched one away. Niall took the other and tossed it aside.

In sick horror, Rowena could only watch as he slowly came to the realisation he was out-matched. Niall and Logan heaved him to his feet.

Lady Selina gasped and turned away as she saw his face. Jenna took her hands and said something in a low voice. The other woman, Logan's wife, narrowed her eyes, her mouth set in a straight line.

Logan pulled a rope from his pocket and began binding Drew's hands behind his back. 'So we can talk, aye?'

Drew struggled against the ropes, crashing Logan into the wall, almost breaking free of the two men.

'Stop,' Rowena said. 'Don't...don't tie him. He'll give you his parole.'

Drew lifted his head to look at her and the hurt of betrayal was in his face. 'Will I, now?' he said, his chest rising and falling from the effort. He already had the start of a bruise around his one eye and another on his chin.

'You will,' she said in a voice that had cowed more than one recalcitrant lad.

'Give me your word you'll do nothing until we get to the bottom of what happened,' Ian said.

Drew sneered, 'So you can pull the wool over everyone's eyes, you mean.' His gaze flicked to the Lady Selina. 'You were always very good at that.'

Logan began binding his wrists.

'Drew,' Rowena said.

He glared at her. 'All right. My parole. For now.' He shrugged off the hands that were holding him.

She became aware of Ian staring at him, at the ruined flesh, and of the regret in his face. 'Drew,' he said. 'I am so bloody sorry.'

Drew touched his cheek and turned his face side on, a gesture she hadn't seen from him for a while. It struck a blow to her chest far harder than the mistrust in his eyes. 'I don't care about sorry,' Drew said to his brother harshly. 'I care about justice.'

'Are we all done with the brawling you Highlanders seem to enjoy so much?' a cynical cultured voice said from the doorway.

A tall man with fair hair, handsome in a refined sort of way, sauntered in with an expression of weary distaste.

'Jaimie,' Logan said. 'Any luck?'

The dandy brushed an imaginary speck of lint from his sleeve. 'It is not about luck, dear boy.' He looked up and gave an especially sweet smile to the occupants of the room, his blue eyes twinkling. 'It is about knowing where to look and having the means to do so.' He turned back to the door. 'Bring him in.'

A couple of burly rough-looking men dragged a woebegone figure through the door and pushed down on his shoulders until he sat slumped in a chair. He was conscious, barely.

'Morris,' Drew exclaimed.

'Oh, have you two met already? Allow me to introduce him to the others.'

'I know him,' Logan said. 'Tab Morris. One of McKenzie's bully boys.'

One of the toughs holding him, a man who looked like a bruiser, touched his forelock. 'Ye'll not be having any trouble with him now, milord,' he said in a gravelly voice. He glanced over at Logan's wife and inclined his head. 'Ma'am.'

She smiled at him. 'Growler. Your sister is well?'

'Yes, ma'am. In the pink.'

Both men left the room, leaving their victim behind clutching one of his arms.

Drew was glaring at the man they had called Jaimie. 'Who the hell are you?'

'Lord Sanford,' Ian said. 'Drew Gilvry. Another of my brothers. Mrs MacDonald you met earlier at the Whitehorse Inn.'

Sanford bowed with languid grace, but Drew wasn't watching the lordling, he was looking at her, frowning, guessing that she'd been instrumental in his capture, no doubt.

'He's a friend of my wife's friend, Alice Fulton, now Lady Hawkhurst.' Ian's face hardened to granite. 'You remember Alice, Drew?'

Drew's expression twisted as his gaze went back to his brother. 'How could I forget?'

Lady Selina made a small sound of protest.

'Well, now that the niceties are dealt with,' Lord Sanford said, 'shall we see what this disreputable chap has to say?'

* * *

She'd said she loved him. The force of those words were still battering against his brain even as he tried to make sense of what was going on.

She couldn't have read the journal.

She didna' know yet what he was. What he'd been. Or she had. And she'd decided he was better off out of the way. Because it didn't matter what Ian said, or how many paroles he gave, he was not going to give up. Not as long as he lived.

He forced himself to focus on what the dandified English lordling was saying to Morris.

'Who do you work for?'

'McKenzie,' that man said, wiping a bloody nose on his sleeve.

'There's nothing new in that,' Drew said.

'And what were your orders?'

Morris gave him a resentful look. 'I already told you.'

'Then tell Mr Gilvry…if you wouldn't mind?'

The soft menace in the quiet voice sent a shiver down Drew's back. There was more steel in that pleasant request than in any threat he'd ever heard. Perhaps he was mistaken in thinking him a dandy after all.

'I was to bring yon laddie—' he nodded at Drew '—to Edinburgh and put him in irons on a ship bound for Botany Bay.' He grinned at Drew with an echo of his old defiance. 'It leaves the day after tomorrow. There's still time.'

Drew bared his teeth at him. 'No, thanks.'

Sanford shook his head wearily and Morris hunched his shoulders.

'At whose request?' Sanford asked.

Morris snuffled. 'I wasn't supposed to know that, ye ken, but McKenzie was taking his orders from a lord.' He glowered at Sanford. 'A proper Scottish lord.'

Or did he mean laird? Drew glanced at Ian, who was leaning forward. 'Do you have a name for us?'

'Carrick.'

A collective sigh rippled around the room. His brothers and their wives looked at each other in shock.

'Never,' Drew said. 'That is rubbish. Carrick has no reason to do away wi' me.' He turned back to his brother. 'Do you know what he said? Your man, right before he pulled the trigger? No! Well, you should then. You'd like it, Ian. He said I have a message for you from your brother.'

'It wasna' my message,' Ian said.

'Drew,' Rowena said. 'He swore to me—'

Drew gave Rowena a hard stare. 'And you believed him over me?'

She stiffened against his assault. 'This is the first I have heard about Carrick. But—' she looked at Morris '—was he visiting Mere Castle when we were there?'

Morris nodded. 'It was him who set us on when the laddie left the house.'

'I remember now,' she said, her voice rising as if she was terrified. 'The man I overheard. He said he'd failed to do away with you once, but this time he would personally make sure of it.'

'And it was Carrick who was in deep conversation with Jack O'Banyon before he tried to kill me,' Logan said bitterly, shaking his head, 'just this past summer. Or so Growler thinks.'

'And it was Carrick's steward who tried to kill Selina,' Ian said with deceptive softness.

'It makes no sense,' Drew said, staring at each one in turn. 'He is chief of our clan. He's sworn to protect us.'

'I know,' Ian said. 'I'm having trouble believing it myself.'

'Who shot you, Drew?' Niall asked.

'The men I was travelling with to Boston.'

'Men sent by Carrick, no doubt,' Logan said with a sound of disgust.

Drew frowned. 'I met up with them at the inn near the docks. I had a room there waiting.'

'A room booked by Carrick.'

'Gordon,' Logan said. 'Remember, he said he heard Carrick's men laughing about losing Drew while out hunting? It has to be Carrick.'

'Damn it all,' Niall said. 'He's cousin to my wife. I would never have believed it if I had not heard it with my own ears.'

Drew's head was spinning. He felt sick. He felt the way he had that time he tumbled over the bank and into the river. Dark water closing over his head. The roar of white water. Drowning. He put a hand to his temple and took a deep breath.

'Drew?' Rowena said.

He brushed her concern aside and looked at Ian, tried to hold on to his anger, but found it slipping away. 'Why?' he said hoarsely. Then he knew. 'The land. He wants the land. But it was the Lady Selina's.'

She nodded. 'Yes. And I was to marry one of his kin. Perhaps he was worried you would seduce me next.'

He winced. 'I would ha', if the thought had come to me.'

Ian shifted, his hands balling into fists.

Drew held up a hand. 'A jest.'

Ian relaxed, somewhat. 'A bad one.'

'Aye.' Drew huffed out a breath. 'I was just trying to help, ye ken.' He looked at Rowena's tight expression. 'We were in trouble. I thought an heiress was the answer.'

'Do you think I don't know that, Drew?' Ian said. 'But it was Carrick who advised me to send you off to America. To let the scandal die down. He kindly offered work. I thought it might help the clan down the road if we had someone over there. I feared we might all have to go. It was getting harder and harder to sustain our people.'

He'd known that. He'd wanted to help his brother. And what he'd done to Alice had been inexcusable. He'd seen it as soon as he'd seen the pain he'd caused. He closed his eyes. 'Carrick,' he murmured. He opened his eyes to meet Ian's straightforward gaze. 'I should ha' known you would never—'

'Yes,' Ian said. 'You should have.' He nodded at Morris. 'Take him away.'

Sanford poked his head out of the door and in short order his two henchmen were back for their prisoner.

Morris gave a look of appeal at Drew.

'He's no' such a bad man for a smuggler,' Drew said.

Logan cracked a laugh. 'Want to join the Gilvrys?' he offered.

Morris nodded his head vigorously.

'You can talk about that later,' Sanford said. 'I have need of more information from you, my lad, and if you want to join Logan there, you'll tell me everything.'

Morris groaned and shuffled out with his gaolers, followed by the sauntering Lord Sanford, who departed after making an exquisite bow.

'That's it, then,' Niall said, when the door closed behind Sanford and his odd little crew. He gave Drew a sharp look. 'We are all agreed. Carrick is the man behind all of our troubles.'

Everyone nodded agreement with sombre faces. And Drew found himself nodding, too.

And the anger inside him was gone in the same instant. The rage. The hatred that had sustained him for a great many months dissipated. And he couldn't summon the same measure of feeling against Carrick.

The knowledge left nothing but an empty shell.

He had no purpose. No reason to stay. Not when they all knew how low he had sunk. 'I'll be on my way, then.'

Drew looked Rowena's way, though he did not meet her eyes. He bowed. 'It has been a pleasure, your Grace.'

Rowena's heart sank at his wooden expression. She desperately wanted to ask him to stay, but this was the first time he'd glanced her way in the past fifteen minutes. He probably hated her blatant defiance and for taking sides with his brothers. Even if it was for his sake.

And when she'd told him she loved him, he'd stared at her as if she was mad. Well, telling him had been a bit of a forlorn hope. She hadn't really expected that what was between them was more than bedsport. But she had thought he cared a little.

Apparently not, if he was leaving. When he picked up his scarf and hat and turned towards the door, in her trembling sad little heart, she found just enough courage to risk another rejection. She opened her mouth to speak.

'Wait, Drew,' Niall said. 'Where are you going?'

Drew looked at him. 'It's over. I was wrong. I have no reason to stay.'

'But we haven't yet solved the problem of Mrs MacDonald's claim. You haven't heard what Carstairs told me. If the courts accept your testimony, she'll not only be dowager duchess, she'll be guardian to the new duke. He's six, poor little lad, and in charge of his grandmother, Lady Cragg.' He grimaced. 'A good friend of Carrick's, so I'm told. Carstairs thinks your oath before a judge might well be accepted with the proper character witnesses. Certainly Lady Cragg's involvement in plotting Drew's deportation with Carrick will work against her claim to keep her guardianship.'

Drew frowned. 'What the devil are you talking about? You don't need me to swear to anything. I gave Mrs MacDonald irrefutable proof that her husband was still alive on September fifteenth. Nothing more is needed. You don't need to parade me in front of a judge like some sort of freak.'

Rowena winced at the anger and the lacerated pride in his voice.

She shook her head when he gave her a look askance. 'I didn't give them the....the proof.'

How could she? What Samuel had described was horrible. A man chained naked like a cur and fed from some old woman's hand like a wild pet. Samuel said he only knew the creature was white by his tangled gold-coloured hair and matted beard. And when Sam had looked closer, he'd seen a face horribly scarred.

The Indians had said their yellow dog brought them luck. Even his own guide had warned against noticing, let alone protesting, his treatment, because he feared this particular band would not take kindly to any interference with their prisoner.

Samuel, ever a coward, had decided the prisoner, who had turned his back to them, seemed quite content and had parted company with the

Indians after an exchange of whisky for gold and a description of where it had been found. All Samuel had been thinking of was gold in the hills of North Carolina and convincing the duke to fund another expedition.

The moment she read those few words from September thirteenth, she'd known why Drew had held the journal back. And she didn't blame him. She could only wish he had trusted her enough to tell her. No one would ever see the journal.

'It was very kind of you, *mo cridhe*,' she said softly. 'But I don't care about the money. I care—'

Drew's face had grown more and more thunderous as she spoke, the scarred side of his face becoming more and more devilish looking. 'Give them the journal.'

'You can't possibly want me to,' she pleaded.

In one stride he was standing before her, towering in his anger. 'Will you no' let me have a shred of my pride, then? If I had not escaped and led those savages to your husband, he'd still be alive and you'd be a duchess now. Am I to have not even a morsel of redemption from my guilt?'

'What the deuce are you talking about?' Ian asked. 'What journal?'

Drew kept his gaze fixed on her face. 'Her husband's journal. He wrote in it every day. Including the day he died. Where is it?'

Instinctively, she clutched her reticule tight to her chest. 'You can't have it. You gave it to me. It is my decision.'

He wrenched the reticule from her hands, tore open the strings and pulled it out. 'This shows the last date that Samuel MacDonald wrote in his diary. Two days after Mere inhaled his last breath.' He handed it to Niall. 'There's your damned proof.'

He was so angry, he had lost all vestiges of civility.

'Easy, man,' Ian said.

'Easy? I'm not some dog to be soothed with soft words, damn you.'

Rowena backed away as everyone started shouting at everyone else. She nipped the little book from Niall's hand, the way she had nipped illicit material from more than one pupil in her recent past, and with two quick steps tossed it into the flames.

Not quick enough. Drew had seen what she was about. He lunged for it, pulling it clear of the flames. His sleeve began to smoke. Logan whipped off his coat and swatted at the smouldering cuff. The smell of singeing wool filled the air.

They were all breathing hard.

Ian held up a hand. 'It seems to me that you two need to sort out whatever it is between you.' He took the journal. 'I don't know what is in here, but if it is as bad as Mrs—I mean, her Grace seems to think, then you both must agree, before anyone reads it.'

Drew gave a snort of disgust. 'When did you start putting words before action?'

A small smile softened the laird's hard mouth. 'When I got married. I have the wee book, Drew. I'll keep it safe in my pocket and you'll tell me when you come to a decision. Come on, everyone. Out.'

Another man who liked to dish out orders. But she felt nothing. No shiver. No pleasure. Not even a whisper of a fantasy.

Even so, there was power behind the words, and the room cleared quickly.

Drew stood in the middle of the room, glowering like a fiend. 'There is nothing you can do to change my mind,' he said the moment the door closed and they were left alone.

'I love you,' she said, throwing caution and pride to the wind.

He groaned. 'And I love you too well to saddle you with a man who is little more than an animal. You know now what I was. I would see it in your eyes every day. And I canna bear it.'

She gave a short bitter laugh. 'If you loved me, you'd want to do everything you could to stay. So we could be together.'

He muttered something under his breath.

She raised a schoolteacher brow.

He just stared back at her, immobile, immovable, his eyes full of pain. Pride. It wasn't going to let them be together. And how could she ask him to forgo his pride? It was who he was. It must have been what had kept him alive under the most cruel of conditions. That and his need for revenge. And she'd been the instrument in taking both from him.

There really was nothing more to say. Tears forced their way into her throat and she did her best to swallow them.

'I am such a fool, aren't I?' she said, scrabbling in her reticule for her handkerchief. 'I thought I had actually found a man who would be so much more than my fantasies. A man who would actually understand these strange thoughts in my head.' She tried to laugh, and it sounded pathetic and broken. 'You were just being kind. Pandering to my nonsense. How ridiculous you must have thought me, a dried-up, ageing governess with such dreams.'

'Rowena, no.' He stepped towards her and the heartbreak in his voice gave her leave to hope. A small hope, still lingering. But she was going to have her say, now she had started.

She waved him back with her handkerchief. 'It's kind of you to pretend that you care. I shall always remember your kindness.' She hiccuped. 'Among other things. Please, don't let me keep you from your plans.'

'Dammit, woman. I don't have any plans.'

'Then you must make some, I suppose. But, Drew, I will not have the contents of that journal bandied about. I just won't, and I believe your brothers will agree with me on that score. It would be an unpardonable crime against a man who has suffered as you have. No amount of money in the world would ever change my mind.'

'So you will go back to the drudgery of the schoolroom, no matter what I say,' he said.

'Yes. Now go, before you have me in tears again.' She turned her back. If he was going to leave, she did not want to watch. It would be like stepping on a heart that was already broken.

Warm hands grasped her shoulders. 'Rowena,' he said. 'Beloved. Lord, how I love you. Please, I can't bear to see you cry over me.'

She sniffed. 'I'm not.'

He spun her about to face him, his strength far too much for her to attempt to resist. She gazed up at his face and cupped the ruined flesh of his cheek. 'Oh, Drew, how can I live without you?'

'My dear little love.'

He drew her close and kissed her with ruthlessness and passion. It was just as magical as it had been that very first time. Perhaps more so because they knew each other so much better that they fit together like two halves of a whole.

When they finally came up for breath, he gave her an unsteady smile. 'I see how it is, ma'am. While you may be a gentle modest maid who

will obey my every wish in the bedroom, in daylight you are nothing but a demanding witch of
a woman.'

'Yes,' she said, smiling.

'Oh, saints in heaven preserve me,' he said and
kissed her again.

Epilogue

The family had gathered to welcome Drew and Rowena home from their delayed honeymoon on the Isle of Skye. It had taken weeks to sort things out in the courts without the journal for evidence. It was almost midnight and Drew sat beside Rowena on one side of the hearth, listening to Lady Selina playing the piano.

One of the nurses brought the children for their goodnight courtesies. Ian's daughter and Niall's little boy. Such lovely children. And with them the dark-haired, serious-eyed, six-year-old Duke of Mere, who had been thrilled to leave his grandmama to visit with his new guardians and meet the children of their family.

Mrs Gilvry, Drew's mother, followed them

across the flagstones, leaning heavily on her stick.

Drew leaped to his feet. 'Ma.' He kissed her hands.

His mother patted his arm as if she still couldn't believe he had returned to her. 'I'm awa' to my bed. It's been lovely welcoming you and your bride home, dearest boy.'

Rowena got up and kissed her cheek. 'Can I help you upstairs?'

'No, lass. Enjoy the music. Ian will see me up.'

Rowena had heard how her mother-in-law had blamed Ian for her second son's death. But now that Drew had returned all was forgiven. Frail, but indomitable, she had even forgiven the laird his *Sassenach* wife, as she had much more quickly forgiven Logan for the same transgression. The old lady started down the length of the room. Ian met her before she had taken more than a few steps and with her hand on his strong right arm, he escorted her to the stairs at the end of the vast chamber.

Happy to watch the other couples who were now dancing a waltz, she and Drew returned to their seats.

Drew gazed down at her and she could only marvel at the love in his eyes. Hidden in the folds of her skirts, he threaded his fingers through hers. His brothers were still teasing him about how besotted he was and it was taking him time to become used to their careless jesting.

'Happy, *mo cridhe*?' he asked in a low murmur.

'I have never been so happy in my life.'

'No' too tired? You dinna have to wait up, you ken.'

His concern stemmed from the news the doctor had given her a week ago. She was expecting a happy event at the end of the summer. 'I'm not the least bit tired.' She gave him a haughty look. 'I'm not an invalid.'

He looked at her belly, though there was little to see. 'The doctor said lots of rest.'

'I'll rest when I'm tired.'

He gave her a look that said she'd pay in delicious punishment for that remark and she laughed.

A stir at the door brought his head up.

'Who is it?' she asked. 'Surely we are not expecting more company?'

'A messenger in the Duke of Gordon's livery.'

'Your brother never ceases to surprise me with his friends in high places,' she whispered in his ear.

'It is probably about Carrick,' he said grimly. 'Gordon has insisted he step down as clan chief and retire to the Hebrides where he can cause no more trouble. His oldest son will make a grand chieftain.'

When faced with his crimes, Lord Carrick had confessed the whole to the duke. He had seen the Gilvrys as an impediment to protecting his family and gaining all the land he wanted for his sheep. His first act in his plan had been to rid the family of Drew, who he knew to be Ian's right-hand man. And once he had started down his path of destruction, he'd had no choice but to continue.

But the stir around the door seemed to contain more excitement than such old news would engender. The babble around at that end of the room grew louder.

'Quiet,' Ian said, pushing through into the middle of the room, waving a letter.

Drew helped Rowena to her feet. Not that she wasn't perfectly capable of rising unassisted, but she adored his tender solicitation. Each little thing he did for her made her heart tumble over with a love that grew stronger day by day.

'What is it, man?' Drew said, his voice louder than anyone's. 'Have they put yon Carrick in the Tower?'

Ian's face when he turned to look at his brother held triumph.

'Better than that,' Niall said, striding to stand beside Ian.

'He's done it,' Ian said. 'Gordon has convinced Parliament to pass a new Excise Act. We will soon be a legal business.'

Selina left the pianoforte and came and planted a kiss on his cheek. 'Well done. You have been working very hard to convince the poor man to speak out.'

'Ah,' Ian said. 'It is not entirely for our sakes. I believe he has more than a couple of illegal stills operating on his land.'

'No more smuggling,' Logan said, looking comically dismayed.

Charity wagged a finger. 'You are sure to find some new adventure.'

Ian looked at his brother. 'Dinna worry, I've

plenty for you to be doing.' He looked down at the note in his hand. 'There's a postscript from Sanford. He said Gordon's speech was a work of art and it carried the lords along with him.'

'I expect Sanford wrote the speech,' Logan quipped, to much laughter.

'Well, I for one am glad my family is about to become legal,' Niall said with a saintly expression and a twinkle in his eye. 'I have judicial ambitions, you know.'

His brothers drowned him with jeers and cheers.

Rowena looked up at Drew. He was watching his brothers with an extraordinarily fond expression. He had missed them and was only slowly coming to realise he was with them again.

'So it's over,' she said softly.

He looked down at her with his devilish smile. 'No, my little beauty, it's just the beginning.'

* * * * *